PRAISE FOR DAVID JACKSON

'Horrific, hilarious and often rather moving'
THE TIMES

'Hitchcockian suspense'
FINANCIAL TIMES

'David Jackson is officially the King of One More Chapter'
JOANNA CANNON, AUTHOR OF *THE TROUBLE WITH GOATS AND SHEEP*

'A SERIOUSLY creepy thriller'
MARK BILLINGHAM, AUTHOR OF *IN THE DARK*

'Full of surprises from start to finish. A gasp-out-loud read'
JANICE HALLETT, AUTHOR OF *THE APPEAL*

'The master of razor-sharp one-liners'
MANDASUE HELLER, AUTHOR OF *THE GAME*

'So chillingly addictive you'll forget to breathe . . . Cold and
clever, yet brimming with heart, humour and ingenious twists'
CHRIS WHITAKER, AUTHOR OF *WE BEGIN AT THE END*

'Superb. Creepy, pacy, and oh so witty'
CAZ FREAR, AUTHOR OF *SWEET LITTLE LIES*

'Disturbing, blackly funny and completely compulsive,
David Jackson wrings every bit of possible tension from his
deliciously chilling premise'
ALEX NORTH, AUTHOR OF *THE WHISPER MAN*

D1460156

ONE GOOD DEED

Also by David Jackson and available from Viper

The Resident
The Rule
No Secrets

ONE GOOD DEED

DAVID JACKSON

First published in Great Britain in 2023 by
VIPER, part of Serpent's Tail,
an imprint of Profile Books Ltd
29 Cloth Fair
London
ECIA 7JQ
www.serpentstail.com

Typeset by Crow Books

1 3 5 7 9 10 8 6 4 2

Printed and bound in Great Britain by
CPI Group (UK) Ltd, Croydon, CRO 4YY

A CIP catalogue record for this book is available from the British Library.

ISBN 9781800810242
eISBN 9781782839743

FSC
www.fsc.org
MIX
Paper | Supporting
responsible forestry
FSC® C171272

For Eden

1

This was the third house he had tried today, and his hopes were not high. He expected that this one would lead to just as much disappointment as all the others he had visited in the past week.

The problem was that he didn't have much to go on.

He knew that Rebecca's surname was Covington, and that was his biggest clue to help him find Rebecca's nan. But what if the nan was on her mother's side? In that case, her name wouldn't be Covington and he was wasting his time.

And then there was the area. He didn't even know if he was in the right part of the country.

He knew very little about Rebecca's family. She had once shown him a photo of her parents, but he'd never met them. Which was a pity. He was hoping one day to do things the traditional way and request permission to marry their daughter.

That could still happen, though, once he got her back.

The recollection of the phone call had come to him after weeks of agonising. Popped into his head as if to say, *This what you're looking for?*

He remembered the growing panic on Rebecca's face as she took the call. Remembered her repeating the details she was hearing. In particular, the words 'Wetherley Hospital'.

She had told him afterwards that her nan had fallen over on one of her country walks and had been rushed into hospital, and that she had to go and see her immediately. He had offered to drive Rebecca there, but she had refused.

Later, when it seemed that her nan was recovering nicely, the incident was forgotten.

Until now.

And that's what had brought him to the area around Wetherley, searching for an elderly lady who may or may not be called Mrs Covington. It felt like clutching at straws, but it was all he had.

Rebecca was everything.

He was standing in front of a low rusted gate, staring up the path at a small detached cottage. A cute place, but in need of some attention. He could easily picture an old woman living alone here, and that gave him hope.

The gate squealed as he pushed it open. He stepped along the path to the front door, noting the overgrown ivy, the grimy gnomes, the bird feeders filled with sludge.

Unable to find a doorbell, he rapped on the door and waited.

Nothing at first. Then, as he went to knock again, he heard movement within. A shape appeared through the leaded glass. The door was opened.

She was small and bent, her head tilted to the side to train one dark, beady eye on him, the other eye milky-white. She wore a thick cardigan and a tartan wool skirt. Below, her bare pale legs were marbled with blue veins.

'Hello,' he said cheerily. 'Mrs Covington?'

'Yes?'

'My name's Darren Stringer. I . . . I don't suppose that rings any bells with you?'

'No. Should it?'

His heart sank. Probably another address to cross off his list.

'I'm looking for Rebecca Covington. Is she your grand-daughter?'

'Rebecca? What do you want with Rebecca?'

The question took him aback. This was the first time he'd got a positive response.

Let's not be too hasty . . .

He took out his phone, showed her the photo of Rebecca on his lock screen. 'Is this her?'

The woman took the device from him and brought it close to her good eye.

'Yes,' she said. 'That's my Rebecca. How do you know her?'

He tried to hide his excitement as he took back the phone. 'I'm her boyfriend. She's never mentioned me?'

'No. No, she hasn't. What's your name again?'

'Darren Stringer.'

'No, I'm sorry. She's never mentioned you. What can I do for you?'

There was no softening in her manner. Darren was beginning to fear this would be no easy task.

'I'm looking for her. She's gone missing.'

'Missing? What do you mean, missing?'

'I mean I can't find her. She's not at her house.'

'Which house?'

'The one on Arnold Lane. In Fowerby. She's—'

'She doesn't live there anymore. She's moved out.'

'Well, yes. That's what I meant. She's gone but I don't know where she is, and I was hoping you could—'

'You say you're her boyfriend?'

'Yes. We've been seeing each other for months.'

'And she left without saying a word?'

'Yes.'

'Ever thought there might be a good reason for that?'

He stared at her. A good reason? What was she implying? What good reason could there possibly be for the love of his life simply to disappear, to leave behind everything they had together?

'I don't think there is. She loves me, and I love her. I'm hoping we can get married one day. To be honest—'

The old woman made a noise. Almost a snort of derision. He suddenly hated her.

'What?' he said.

She sighed heavily. 'I'm sorry to disappoint you, dear, but there's only one reason a woman leaves a man without a word of explanation, and that's because she wants to start a new life. Without him in it.'

Darren shook his head. 'No. You're wrong. I think something must have happened to her. Something awful. She probably needs my help.'

The woman pursed her dry, cracked lips. 'Rebecca doesn't

need your help. She's not in any danger. When I last spoke to her, she was—'

'You spoke to her? When?'

He realised how demanding he sounded when her roving pupil suddenly locked on to a spot between his own eyes.

'I spoke to her just yesterday. She's a lovely girl. Tells me everything. If there was something wrong, I would be the first to know.'

He felt his irritation mounting.

'She doesn't tell you everything. She didn't tell you about me, did she?'

'No . . . well . . . Perhaps I should say that she tells me about everything that matters.'

He was convinced he caught a touch of a smile. A hint of satisfaction. He had to force himself not to get mad at her. Tried telling himself it wasn't unusual for old people to be spiteful. But it still hurt.

'Look,' he said, 'I just need to speak to her, find out what's going on. You understand that, don't you?'

'What I understand is that if Rebecca had wanted you to know her business, she would have told you. Goodbye.'

She went to close the door, and Darren knew that, once she did, he would never get her to open it again. He couldn't let that happen.

Which is why he jammed his foot in the doorway.

'What are you doing?' the woman demanded, a note of alarm in her voice. He didn't want to hurt her, not even to frighten her, but he needed to know, he had a *right* to know.

'Just . . . just tell me where she is, okay? I need to talk to her, and she's not answering her phone. If you could just give me—'

She opened the door and then slammed it on his foot, and even though she looked light enough to pick up with one hand, the force of it sent a jolt of pain up his leg.

'Stop that! I'm not here to cause any trouble. I just want—'

She gave his foot another bash. He yelped and then shoved hard against the door, sending the woman reeling backwards into the wall behind her. He saw pain on her face as she rubbed at her hip, and he thought to himself, Got to be careful. Old people bruise easily. They have brittle bones.

He opened his mouth to apologise, but she cut him off with a glare that could stop a clock and then went scurrying down the hallway.

He followed her inside. It was a gloomy, eerie space, with dark wooden floorboards and wall panelling. It had no windows of its own, but relied on the light that trickled through a stained-glass window set high on the turn of the oak staircase.

'Please,' he said. 'I'm asking for your help.'

'Tell that to the police,' she said. She picked up the phone from its cradle on a hall table.

'No,' he said. 'Don't do that.'

He continued towards her, but she began to jab at the phone's buttons with a skeletal digit, and he knew he couldn't allow her to complete the call, so he snatched at the phone. But she refused to let go of it, her strength remarkably out of proportion to her frame. He heard a tinny voice coming from the receiver and realised she had got through to the emergency services, so he wrested the phone from her grasp. But even as he did so, she raked her fingernails down the back of his hand, causing him to gasp and drop the phone to the parquet floor. A panel flew off the back of the device and it spewed out its batteries, terminating the call.

He brought his hand to his mouth and sucked at the bloody scratches, eyeing the old woman as she slowly backed away into the corner of the hallway. He hoped that she was spent now, that they could talk calmly and rationally, that it would become obvious to her how he loved her granddaughter, and that she would do the right thing in bringing the couple together again.

'Get out of my house,' she said.

'I will. Tell me where Rebecca is and I'll go right now.'

'You'll never find her. *Never!*'

She surprised him then. Came towards him, clutching something she'd withdrawn from a cylindrical brass umbrella stand behind her. It was a wooden cane of the type a rambler might use, as twisted and gnarled as she was. She began waving it in front of her.

'Get out of my fucking house!'

The expletive shocked him as much as her attack. For some reason, old people swearing always unsettled him.

He put his hands out. 'This is getting ridiculous. I just want to talk. You don't have to—'

She closed on him then, shrieking as she raised the stick. She whipped it through the air with unexpected velocity, catching him on the wrist with a mighty crack, and he felt excruciating pain.

'Get out!' she demanded. She aimed the next blow at his

head. He blocked it with his forearm, managed to grab hold of the stick.

'Enough!' he said. 'You have to stop!'

She tugged with all her might, her single usable eye burning into him as she formed angry noises in her throat. Darren held on, his mind racing for a way to end this absurd battle.

And then a surge of anger overwhelmed him and he thrust the stick into the woman's chest. She flew backwards, immense surprise on her features.

One of her slippers snagged on the runner, and Darren realised what was happening as if it were in slow motion. He watched her topple, her feet going from under her almost comically, but then he saw where her head would land, and he found himself tensing, his stomach lurching as he wished for it not to happen, willed her to fall slightly to the left to avoid the inevitable collision.

The old woman's skull smacked against the edge of the telephone table with a bang that reverberated throughout the hall. She landed with a thud on the floor, a crumpled bag of bones, trembling and rattling, spittle bubbling onto her parched lips.

He stepped towards her, feeling powerless and at the same time that this must be a dream, this couldn't really be happening. An address – that's all he'd wanted. Not this.

He bent over the convulsing figure. 'Mrs Covington? Are you all right?' But he knew it was a stupid question. Nobody in that state could be all right.

His suspicion was confirmed when she went still, twitched a couple more times, and issued a final sigh. The glint in her good eye faded, rendering it as sightless as its partner.

'Mrs Covington?' he whispered, but he knew the words went unheard. He put his fingers to her neck and wrist in search of the slightest quiver of life. He placed the back of his hand over her nose and mouth, praying for the merest wisp of expelled breath.

But it was all in vain.

She was most definitely dead.

2

Darren straightened up. Tried to get his numbed brain to work properly. How crazy was this?

He didn't know what to do. He'd come to ask a simple, straightforward question, that was all. Nobody was supposed to die, for Christ's sake!

He had to get out as quickly as possible. Nobody need ever know he was here.

He started for the open front door.

And then he paused.

They'll come, he thought. A neighbour. Maybe even Rebecca herself. Then they'll call the police.

But what if I tidied up? Wouldn't they think she just fell and banged her head? She has a history of falls, after all. Why would they even suspect foul play?

Slowly, Darren closed the front door and returned to the body.

And then something else occurred to him.

The phone call. She'd managed to get through to 999 just before she died. They would know that a call had been made from this address.

Shit.

It'll be enough, he thought. They'll get forensics in here. They'll find my fingerprints. I don't know what I've touched and what I haven't. And they can do all kinds of clever stuff these days. They'll find my DNA.

Her nails!

They'll find my skin under her nails! And because Rebecca is her granddaughter, they'll talk to her, and that will lead them to me, and they'll find the marks on my hand, they'll match my fingerprints and my DNA, and then I'm fucked, royally fucked.

Shit!

It seemed so unfair. All he wanted was to get Rebecca back.

Okay, he told himself. Deep breaths. Think logically.

First of all, I may have more time than I thought. Rebecca told me her nan doesn't get many visitors. Also, I don't have a police record. Even when they examine the scene, they won't make an immediate connection to me. In fact, it's possible they may never make a connection to me. Rebecca doesn't know I've been here. She doesn't have any reason to think I know the address. She might not say anything about me to the police – why would she? And when I find her and explain things to her, she'll understand that it was all just a horrible accident and she'll want to protect me.

So, right now, the best thing to do is to buy myself a little more time.

He began to search the house.

Downstairs there was a living room, a dining room and a kitchen. The kitchen wasn't spacious, but adjoining it was a utility room with a stainless-steel sink and the usual appliances.

Including a small chest freezer.

He lifted its lid. Plumes of white vapour billowed over the edges and curled down the sides as he peered into its depths. There was so little food inside it seemed pointless to keep it going twenty-four hours a day.

But that was good news as far as Darren was concerned.

He went back to the hallway and stared down at the crumpled figure. There was nothing to her. With a bit of judicious folding, she might just fit.

Grimacing, he bent down and scooped the body into his arms. He was shocked at how insubstantial she seemed. It was like picking up a sleeping child.

He carried her to the utility room. The freezer lid was still propped open, and already the room felt noticeably chillier.

As reverentially as he could, he began to lower the old lady into her icy tomb, to rest atop her frozen peas.

She didn't fit.

Even though she was now creased up like a concertina, her scrawny legs still protruded above the freezer's edge.

Darren grabbed one of them by the ankle and began to twist and turn it, this way and that. But no matter how much he manipulated the limb, it refused to find a niche. He wanted to scream his frustration at her. It seemed to him that she was being deliberately awkward about this.

Not prepared to let her defeat him, he took hold of the leg

again. Put all of his might into forcing it into the chamber. The icy lining on the inside of the freezer turned pink as its rough surface sloughed away the papery skin from the woman's thigh. As Darren pushed and heaved, he tried to ignore the nerve-jarring sound of ice scraping against flesh, like fingernails being drawn down a blackboard.

When the leg gave way with a sudden audible snap, he almost fell on top of the corpse.

He leapt back, on the verge of spilling his guts onto the tiled floor. It felt as though her whole leg had come away from her body.

It took him a good two minutes of deep breathing before he was able to approach the freezer again. Refusing to look inside, he focused on the other leg. As he started to apply force, he tried to prepare himself for the outcome, but found that it only made the task more unbearable.

When he felt the leg reach the limit of its flexibility, his arms began to quiver, his need to press on perfectly counter-balanced by his reluctance to relive the experience of tearing away the limbs of this woman as though she were a cooked chicken. Only with the release of one final yell was he able to summon up the necessary energy and simultaneously drown out the sickening crack as he drove the leg inside.

Slamming the freezer lid shut, he collapsed on the floor and swallowed back the bile that was rising in his throat. Perspiration poured down his face. Slowly, shakily, he got to his feet and went back to the hall.

He picked up the woman's walking stick and returned it to the umbrella stand. Then he put the phone back together and replaced it on its cradle. As he did so, he noticed a light blinking for attention on the base unit.

A missed call. A message had been left.

Rebecca had told him that as well as getting few visitors, her nan didn't receive many phone calls.

So what if . . .?

He pressed the 'play' button, and his heart stuttered when he heard the voice.

'Hi, Nan! It's Rebecca. Just checking in. Guess what? I've got a new place! It's right by Cardew Park, where you used to live. It's really nice, and there's a gym I can walk to, and— never mind. I'll tell you all about it later. See ya!'

The recording ended. Darren pulled out his own phone and googled Cardew Park. He found one in Ebbington, only about fifteen miles away.

He smiled. This trip had been worth it after all.

3

Elliott Whiston had a cat. He loved that cat. Didn't care much for most other cats, though. That, in a nutshell, seemed to him to be a fairly balanced, sensible attitude to the creatures.

What he couldn't fathom were the people whose views were more extreme. At one end of the spectrum were those who thought nothing of hurting them. If there was one thing guaranteed to provoke his wrath, and therefore his anxiety, since he had never found a quick way of dissipating pent-up anger, it was animal cruelty.

But then, at the opposite end, were people who were utterly obsessed, to the extent that they regarded their cats as their offspring, or, at the very least, more worthy than any human companion.

Mrs Beidecker sat firmly in the latter camp.

She stood in front of the shop counter now, beaming down at Elliott in his office chair. She was wearing a woollen bobble hat that was adorned with a cat's face, including protruding ears and whiskers. Looped several times around her neck was a scarf that had images of cats of all shapes, sizes and colours sewn onto it. Both items, she had informed Elliott last month when the shop had reopened after the Christmas break, had been gifted to her by Wilberforce Merriman. Who also happened to be a cat.

Elliott suspected that even her underwear was covered with cat pictures, but it was a hypothesis he had no inclination to test.

'Helloooo, Elliott,' she said. 'How are you this morning?'

'I'm good, thank you, Mrs Beidecker.'

'And how's my Billy-boy? Keeping all snuggy and warm in this cold weather, I hope?'

Elliott's cat was a British Shorthair whose pedigree name was Meadowlark Bilberry. Elliott usually called him Bill.

'Absolutely. He'll be hugging the radiator as we speak. Either that or he'll be under my duvet.'

'Ah, they do like their creature comforts. I remember when my fluffy little Pom-Pom got too close to the fire once and I thought there was going to be a conflagration. I can't tell you the panic it caused me.'

'No,' Elliott said. 'I can imagine.'

'Anyway, to business. I've brought you some books.' She hefted a weighty plastic bag from the floor and set it on the counter. 'They're all in excellent condition, because I look after my books as all civilised people should, but I'm running out of room and I was going to throw them out, and then one of my darlings – I think it was Augusta – whispered in my ear and mentioned you, and I thought that was such an excellent idea, so here they are.'

Elliott smiled. Mrs Beidecker always brought something on her visits, and it was invariably at the behest of her cats.

'Thank you. I'll put them straight up on the shelves. Books always go quickly.'

'Lovely. And while I'm here, I need to get a little something for my Missy Brighteyes, who's feeling left out because she didn't get a present the last time I came, and you know how jealous she can get.'

'Oh, I do,' Elliott said, even though he had no idea.

'So I'll take a couple of sachets of those cat treats and the toy mouse, if you don't mind.'

'No problem.'

Elliott got up from his chair and fetched the items from the display behind him. He passed them across to Mrs Beidecker, who handed him a twenty-pound note.

'I don't want any change,' she said. 'It's all for the charity. Those poor unfortunates who don't get the same love and care as my little ones. I'd invite them all round to my house if I could.'

'That's very kind of you. I'm sure they'll appreciate the donation.'

As she exited the shop, Elliott was convinced there was a tear in her eye.

For the moment, he was alone again. He didn't mind. There were always jobs to be done whenever there were no customers. Sometimes he had assistance, but that tended to come from unpaid volunteers whose presence in the shop couldn't always be relied upon. Elliott, on the other hand, received a salary, along with the grand title of 'Shop Manager', and that made him important. There were expectations to be fulfilled.

He carried Mrs Beidecker's books over to the shelves and slotted them into the appropriate places according to genre. He was slightly surprised to find that some of her collection sounded pretty racy.

When he had done that, he moved to the clothes section and restored several garments to their rightful hangers. It wasn't a big store, but Elliott liked to think it was clean, neatly organised, and contained some quality goods. While he wasn't paid particularly handsomely, he was amply rewarded by the satisfaction of knowing he was doing a sterling job for the Cat Welfare League.

What he particularly liked about the job was the people he came into contact with. Yes, some were a little eccentric, and some just wanted a bargain, cats or no cats, but many had a heart of gold. They came because they wanted to help, to make the world a slightly better place. They were Elliott's kind of people.

The man who came in an hour later wasn't Elliott's kind of person.

He was tall and broad, with greasy hair and a scruffy beard. He wore an army-style khaki jacket with military insignia all over it. He wandered in, nodded at Elliott, then headed to the rear of the shop.

For the most part, Elliott knew better than to be too hasty in making judgements based on appearance. And yet, although he couldn't put his finger on it, there was something about the man that made him uneasy. While pretending to be absorbed in his magazine behind the counter, he raised his eyes frequently to check on his sole customer.

The man's shoplifting was little short of blatant.

Two or three DVDs were slipped into each of his jacket pockets.

Give him some slack, Elliott thought. Maybe that's just his way. He doesn't like plastic bags because he's an environmentalist, and so that's just the way he carries things around. In a moment, he'll bring them to the counter and pay like everyone else.

The man wasn't like everyone else.

He headed straight for the door.

'Excuse me,' Elliott said, and then, when the man pretended not to hear him, he stood up and repeated it more loudly: '*Excuse me!*'

He expected the man to do a runner at that point. In the couple of shoplifting incidents he'd dealt with so far, that was precisely what had happened. Elliott had decided there was no point in giving chase after desperate criminals who had taken things of little value, especially when they were probably poor and starving, and he had been able to feel satisfied that, in calling after them, he had done his job and the perpetrators were too terrified to face up to someone who was, after all, the Shop Manager.

That's not how it went this time around.

The man halted, turned. Elliott was suddenly convinced the man was a serial killer and that he had made a serious error of judgement in pulling him up.

'You talking to me?' the man said.

'Yes. The, er, the DVDs.' Elliott wiggled his fingers vaguely in the direction of the man's pockets, and realised how pathetic the gesture seemed in comparison to a full-blown finger-point of condemnation.

'What DVDs?'

Oh, crap, Elliott thought, which was about as strong as his language ever got.

'In your . . . in your pockets. I think you may have forgotten to, well, pay for them.' He almost cringed as he said this, and felt suddenly compelled to apologise for being so forthright.

The man smiled, and it was one of the most frightening expressions Elliott had ever had thrown his way. It was like when a baboon bares its teeth before attacking.

'You've made a mistake, pal.' He started to turn towards the door again.

'No,' Elliott said. 'Actually, I don't think I have. You put some DVDs in your pockets. I saw you.' He hated how his voice sounded. Too shrill, and with a discernible quiver.

The man took a couple of steps towards him. Elliott wanted to back up to maintain what seemed to him a safe distance; he was stopped by the wall of cat toys and treats behind him, but his mind was already rehearsing the story that he courageously stood his ground.

'You need your eyes testing. What would I want with your shitty DVDs? Who watches them these days, anyway? In fact, who'd want any of the shite you've got in this shop? You've got clothes that went out of fashion twenty years ago.' He looked Elliott up and down. 'Mind you, I suppose you wouldn't know that.'

Elliott tried to ignore the insult. 'A lot of people want our stuff. And you'd be surprised how many people still watch DVDs. They can't watch them if other people take them.'

There, Elliott thought. That's telling you.

'What's your name?' The man stared at Elliott's name badge. 'Elliott. Ellie for short, right?'

Something hurt deep inside Elliott. 'It's just . . . Elliott.'

'Okay, Ellie. You're a charity shop, right? If I've got your shit, which I haven't, then you could just think of me as a charity case.'

'That's . . . not how charities work. We have to sell stuff to make money, which is used to help cats.'

'Well, there you go, then. I've got a cat. And he likes watching films with me, so everything's cool, right?'

'No . . . Look, if you don't return the items, I'll have to call the police.'

It was as if a switch had been flicked in the man's head. Turning him from somewhat nasty to downright evil.

He closed the gap between them like a snake darting at its prey.

'You're not calling the police. If the coppers come knocking on my door because of you, I'll be back here. And next time I won't be so nice.'

'You . . . you need to put those DVDs back. If you do that, then we can forget all about this.'

The man's hand shot out. He grabbed hold of Elliott's sweater, twisted the material, shoved him hard against the wall. Cat bells jingled and items fell from their hooks.

'Have you got a death wish or something, Ellie? I'm not fucking kidding. Now sit back in your chair like a good little girl, read your knitting magazine and stop being such a prick. All right?'

When Elliott didn't respond immediately, the man thrust

his face forward, bringing his forehead into contact with Elliott's.

'*I said, all right?*'

Spittle landed on Elliott's face. He could smell the man's breath, redolent of stale cigarettes.

He nodded. When he spoke, it was in a strangulated voice, his windpipe almost compressed shut by the tight corkscrew of wool.

'All right.'

The man loosened his grip. Exhibiting his gruesome smile again, he attempted to smooth out the creases in Elliott's top. Elliott wanted to slap his hand away, to swear at him. But he did neither.

'Have a nice day, Ellie,' the man said. And then he left the shop, a swagger in his gait.

Elliott remained where he was for a while, wondering what had just happened. Wondering how he had gone from a light-hearted discussion about Mrs Beidecker's fluffy Pom-Pom to threats of violence from a raging psychopath with kleptomania.

He suddenly realised his legs were shaking so much his knees were almost knocking, and he staggered over to the chair and collapsed on it.

A charity shop! This place was supposed to be about giving. Being kind and doing nice things for others. Not crime or humiliation.

The police, Elliott thought. I should call them. That'll show him. He can't intimidate me. This isn't school. I'm a grown man.

He nodded, then picked up the phone.

And then wondered what he would tell them.

He pictured two burly policemen, men who could take care of themselves, who would laugh in the face of an inconsequential delinquent issuing threats. They would stand here in the shop, jotting down notes at appropriate junctures while looking incredibly bored. And as Elliott recounted his tale, he would notice the exchanges of glances between them. The looks that would clearly tell him what they thought of him, which was that he had acted like a complete wuss.

And, once that ordeal was over, what then? The information he supplied might just be enough for the police to track the man down, but could they prove anything? And, even if they could, what would they do to him for taking a few ancient DVDs? A paltry fine and a slap on the wrist, probably. And then the man would be back here as promised, offering a lot more than slaps in return for his own punishment.

Hating himself more than he had done in a very long time, Elliott put the phone down.

4

Heidi Liu came breezing into the shop at just after three o'clock, all cheery smiles as usual, her ponytail swishing behind her.

'Hey, Elliott,' she said. 'How are you today?'

She beamed perfect gleaming teeth at him. There was nothing wrong with Elliott's own teeth, but he thought that by comparison his gave the impression he smoked forty a day and chewed gravel.

'Good, ta.' Because that's how he always answered, even when he wasn't good, a prime example of such an occasion being this very afternoon.

'Have you eaten? You look . . . pale.'

Heidi liked to look after his welfare. And while he often tried to tell himself he was a grown man who didn't need it, he actually appreciated it. He had spent so many years in a caring role that being on the receiving end was very welcome.

'I'm fine, honestly. I had lunch earlier.'

Which was playing fast and loose with the truth. What he'd

had was one bite of a tuna mayo sandwich before tossing the rest of it in the bin. His appetite was shot for today.

Heidi gestured to the door. 'I can go and get you something else if you like? A burger?'

'No, thanks.'

'Doughnut?'

'No.'

'Pastry?'

'No.'

'Tea, then. I'll go into the back room and make us both a nice cup of tea.'

'Okay, yeah, sure.'

'And biscuits. I think you need some sugar.'

He just gave her a weak smile and watched her skip into the back room. He knew that she had already sussed him out, and that it wouldn't be long before she managed to extract a full confession from him.

Heidi wasn't employed at the shop. She wasn't even on the official list of volunteers. After graduating with a first-class degree in chemistry, she had worked for a huge petrochemical firm for several years. Hating the job, she gave it up and returned to the area to study as a postgraduate student at the university. One day, about a year ago, she had dropped in to Elliott's shop to look at the second-hand clothes. He often smiled at the memory of that first encounter, when she had tried on a coat and invited his honest opinion as to whether she looked like 'a complete bag of shite' or merely 'a woman who valued practicality over style'.

After that, she began visiting the shop regularly. He gradually got a feel for the sort of clothes she liked, and would put them aside for her. He also discovered that she had a love for vinyl records, and again he would keep back those that looked in good condition and that he thought might appeal to her eclectic tastes. For some reason Elliott could never quite fathom, it wasn't only the excitement of new finds that drew her here. Sometimes all she wanted to do was spend time chatting with him. Later, she began to help out, tidying and rearranging things. It turned out that she lived in one of the flats close to Elliott's house, and over time their friendship blossomed to the point where she started seeing him at his home, too. It even reached a stage where he felt he could entrust her with a key so that she could feed Bill while he went up to stay with his sister in Edinburgh.

What he particularly liked about Heidi, and what he was incredibly grateful for, was the way in which she made it so easy for him to open up to her. An hour with her was like a full-on therapy session. She listened and she advised, and she never seemed to want anything in return.

Sometimes, though, he wondered whether he was running the risk of boring her to tears with his problems. Yes, he'd been through some shit, but others had it far worse, and self-pity was tiresome. Envy wasn't much better, but he often looked at Heidi and wished his life could be more like hers. He had so wanted to go to university, to meet people of his age from all over the world, to go to rowdy student parties and get drunk and do stupid things, to travel, to learn and have actual career prospects . . .

But it wasn't to be. Some people had to follow a different roadmap.

He was a little reluctant to enter the confessional this afternoon. Talking to Heidi about misfortune was one thing, but this was different. This was – there was no other word for it – this was *cowardice*. Even someone as sympathetic as Heidi would probably find it difficult not to despise him.

'Digestives,' Heidi announced as she reappeared. 'Not chocolate, I'm afraid, but excellent dunking material.' She put a tray of tea and biscuits down on the desk in front of Elliott. 'Dig in.'

Elliott didn't feel like digging in. Not wanting to upset Heidi, though, he picked up his mug, took a sip and told her how nice it was.

Heidi picked up her own mug before performing a quick scan of the shop. 'And how's Myrtle today?' she asked, moving towards the clothes section. She reached the mannequin, currently bedecked in a long black coat. 'Hmm. A bit drab. Someone could do with cheering up.'

Elliott wasn't sure if she was referring to the mannequin or himself, but he sat back with his tea while Heidi set to work. Myrtle was an established presence in the shop long before Elliott arrived. While he had become quite good at pricing individual items, he fully accepted that the shoplifter had got one thing right when he had cast aspersions on Elliott's fashion sense. It really wasn't his thing. The choice of clothing worn by women was even less his thing. In any case, he always became a little flustered at the odd looks and occasional ribald comments he received when a customer walked in to find him stripping Myrtle naked. For those reasons, he was more than happy to allow Heidi to see to the regular change of Myrtle's clothes.

By the time Heidi had completed her self-appointed task,

Elliott had dealt with two customers, downed his tea and even indulged in a biscuit.

'What do you think?' she asked, coming back to the desk, the shop empty again.

Myrtle was now sporting a jaunty beret and a short jacket with a fur collar. A tiny leather bag was draped over one arm.

'Fab,' he said, although he had no idea how good it was.

'Sold much today?'

'Not bad,' he said. He didn't own up to the fact that one of the shop's visitors had eaten into the profits, but he made a mental note to address that by topping up the cash register out of his own meagre salary. It seemed only fair, given that he didn't intend to report the crime.

'You're very . . . uncommunicative today.'

'Am I? Sorry.'

'Why's that? Has something happened?'

'Happened? No. I've just been . . . thinking.'

'What about?'

'Oh, about me. About what I'm like. And what I'm not like.'

'What are you not like?'

'Chris Hemsworth.'

'The Thor guy? No, you're not like him.'

'Or Tom Cruise. Or Dwayne Johnson. Or Jack Reacher. Or James Bond.'

'Okay, so those last two are fictional characters. But I accept your claims. You're not like any of them. What's your point?'

'Testosterone.'

'What about testosterone?'

'I don't think I have any.'

'Because you don't go around beating people up and saying, "The name's Whiston. Elliott Whiston"? What's led you to this weird conclusion?'

'I don't think I'm . . . manly.'

She stared at him, smiling, and he felt his face begin to glow. This was as embarrassing as being caught in the act of undressing Myrtle.

'Define manly. And not in terms of Hollywood film stars or imaginary people.'

'I mean being, you know . . . butch.'

'Butch?'

'Yes. I'm not exactly an alpha male. I have no muscles, I find it difficult to grow convincing facial hair, and my voice is a whole octave higher than most choirboys can hit.'

Heidi laughed. 'And that's what's bothering you?'

'Yes.' He paused. 'Well, no. Not that exactly. I can't do anything about my excuse for a physique. I tried going to the gym for a month and finished looking weedier than when I started. It's more about how I act.'

'How you act?'

'Yes. With other people. I just want to please everyone.'

'That's hardly a fault, Elliott. If only a lot more people were like that.'

'But some people don't want to be pleased. Some people just want to get angry, and it doesn't matter how nice I am to them, they still want to treat me like crap.'

'Unfortunately, there are a lot of idiots and people with chips on their shoulders. But that's their problem, not yours. You can't let that stop you being nice.'

'I'm not sure I like being thought of as nice. Nice is just another word for boring. Girls aren't interested in nice.'

Heidi flinched slightly, and Elliott wondered why.

'Elliott, has something happened with a girl?'

'Chance would be a fine thing.' Curiously, this appeared to relax her. 'In case you haven't noticed, I am never in the company of a girl.'

'Uh-huh. And what do you class me as?'

'Well, sure, you're a girl, but you're a friend who happens to be a girl, rather than a girlfriend. I don't have girlfriends.'

'Elliott, the reason you don't have a girlfriend has nothing to do with the way you look or speak. Some of us aren't attracted to Neanderthals who walk around with a club looking to bash in the skulls of the tribe in the next village. Some of us prefer guys who are caring and thoughtful.'

He looked into her wide hazel eyes. 'Huh. So what you're saying is . . .'

She moved her face closer to his and raised her eyebrows, urging him on.

'. . . is that you're just as weird as I am, and that's why most of your boyfriends don't last longer than a week.'

'You're such a dork,' she said.

'See!' he said, triumphant. 'Even you don't really like me.'

5

Walking home from the shop at the end of the day, Elliott chewed over some of the events that had helped shape him, turning him into the bag of complexes and insecurities he was now.

As a child, he had been shy, withdrawn and completely lacking in sporting ability – characteristics that did not rate favourably with his father, who never missed an opportunity to remark on how far short he fell of his ideal of a real man. Elliott had lost count of the number of times his father had told him how 'wet' he was, or that he needed to 'grow a pair'.

Secondary school presented him with an additional set of challenges. In particular, a lad named Rowan Cosby seemed intent on making his life a misery. The persecution began with the almost daily theft of Elliott's lunch, and quickly escalated to direct assault: being regularly tripped up in the corridors, whacked across the head with a book, or bombarded with water balloons.

As all victims of bullying are, he had been painfully aware

of the advice that the only way to put an end to such torment is to strike back. Bullies prefer prey who are compliant. But knowing the theory and putting it into practice can be two very different things.

Elliott discovered this for himself during a game of football. Unexpectedly finding the ball at his feet, and with no players between him and the opposing keeper, Elliott was seized by a sudden impulse to go for goal. It was an error of judgement that received swift punishment when Rowan Cosby arrived seemingly from nowhere, a thundering mass who made no attempt to play the ball but instead had his boot studs aimed straight at Elliott's lower half.

Elliott felt the crunch, the pain, the disorientation as he went spinning in the air. He landed heavily on the sodden ground, spoiling what had been a pristine kit.

And then he couldn't stop himself. There was no conscious thought; it was pure reaction. He jumped to his feet, rounded on his assailant, not caring who it was or how powerful they might be, knowing only at a primal level that he was under attack and needed to defend himself.

The punch was so hard it almost knocked Elliott out.

He was on the ground again, on his backside, wondering what had just happened, his head whirling, his face aching, the shadow of Rowan looming over him, swearing at him, calling him that name.

He remembered it now as he walked home from the charity shop.

Ellie.

It was what the shoplifter had called him, and it was what

Rowan had called him. Telling him he was weak and not a real man.

Sticks and stones, he thought. Names will never hurt me.

But it did. It hurt enormously.

And the physical pain wasn't the worst of it.

He remembered sitting on the staircase, gingerly touching the swollen bruise on his cheek as he eavesdropped on his parents discussing him in the living room below. His mother was telling his father not only that he had been sent home for getting into a fight, but also that she believed he was being bullied.

'Why do you say that?' his father had asked. 'Just because he got into a scrap—'

'No. It's not just that. It's his behaviour. He's not enjoying school. There's something going on.'

'Have you asked him about it?'

'Yes. Of course he denies it, but I—'

'Well, there you are then.'

'No, Jack, you're not listening to me. This could be serious. He might be—'

'Listen,' Elliott's father said. There was a hint of irritation there. 'If somebody's having a go at our Elliott, then he can handle it himself. And if he doesn't – if he's allowing some jumped-up little squirt to make his life miserable – then he's no son of mine.'

And there it was. His father's verdict. A tonne weight placed on top of the needles already digging into him.

He's no son of mine.

Sticks and stones.

*

The relationship between his parents was over just a couple of years later, his dad walking out when Elliott was fifteen. Elliott grew even closer to his mother. Not a natural student, he worked as hard as he could to get the grades he would need for university.

It was at the start of the revision period for his exams that his mother had her first stroke. She wasn't even fifty.

Elliott's life was overturned. His sister was six years older than him, and had already completed her degree, got married, bought a house in Edinburgh, and was expecting her first baby.

The only practical solution was for Elliott to become his mother's full-time carer.

He gave up on his studies, his dreams of going to university, and instead threw himself into the task of helping his mum. He tended to her every need: feeding her, cleaning her, entertaining her, aiding with her therapy. The visits by professional care workers were regular but barely long enough for him to switch off.

His reward was to watch her die before his eyes. Each time it seemed she was improving, she would have another stroke. Frustrated, enraged by the unfairness of it all, Elliott struggled on.

She lasted eight years.

In that time, Elliott had no social life and no respite. When his mother finally passed away, Elliott's sister agreed to forgo her inherited share of the house for as long as he needed it. But he had no qualifications or experience, and therefore no prospects. In the two years since his mother had died, the best he had managed was the job at the charity shop.

Walking home now, he wondered if that would ever change.

6

Elliott's house was nothing special. A shabby little end-of-terrace on an unremarkable street. But it was home. He had lived here his whole life. One day, he would make his fortune, sell the house, give his sister what was due, and move on. But not yet.

As soon as he entered the hallway, Bill showed his face. Well, not just his face, because his customary greeting was to roll onto his back and spread his legs. He lay there, a rug of grey fluff, staring up with eyes that Elliott often described as the colour of the jelly in the middle of a Jaffa Cake.

Elliott bent down and stroked the cat's belly before going into the kitchen. Bill followed him in and then dashed past him to the back door. He had a litter tray, but for some reason he hated using it. Only if there was a hurricane outside would he resort to squatting in the tray, the expression on his rounded features clearly conveying the indignity of it all.

Elliott unlocked the door. Bill sniffed the incoming air as if testing it for optimality, then cautiously stepped outside.

'Don't get into any fights,' Elliott warned him. Not that it was likely. He had seen Bill in confrontations with other cats. Bill would howl at them, a loud undulating cry that sounded like, 'No-no-no-no,' and then he would back down and slink away at a snail's pace.

Not unlike me, Elliott thought.

He sighed, then made a cup of tea before preparing his evening meal. Chicken pie tonight. He ate it in front of the television, hoping for distractions but finding that his mind kept returning to the events of the day, kept mithering him about how he should have handled things.

It'll be better tomorrow, he told himself. A good night's sleep – if that's possible – and I'll have forgotten it all by the morning.

When he took his plate out to the kitchen, he remembered about Bill. He opened the door to let him in, and Bill marched straight to his empty dish and sat next to it, staring up at his owner in expectation.

Encounters with other cats aside, Bill wasn't a very vocal animal. If he wanted something, he would simply seek out Elliott and then sit and stare at him, as if willing Elliott to read his mind. Fortunately, his needs were not complex: any request was invariably for food or a loo trip.

It was only when Elliott opened the appropriate cupboard that he realised something: he was supposed to have bought cat food on his way home.

He looked apologetically at Bill. 'Sorry, fella. I've had things on my mind. Don't go away, I'll be right back.'

He locked the back door, put his coat and shoes back on, and headed out, leaving Bill looking bewildered.

*

Darren thought this had to be the place. It was the only gym near Cardew Park that had come up on his online search, and the only one he could find having walked much of the area.

Today was Monday, which was one of the days that Rebecca always visited the gym. Mondays, Wednesdays and Fridays, almost without fail. Rowing machine and treadmill, followed by weights. She was a very fit woman. He liked that about her. Liked that she wanted to look good for him.

Of course, there was a chance that she wasn't at the gym at all, especially if she'd only just moved to the area. But that was okay. He could wait. If things didn't work out tonight, he'd come back on Wednesday, and then Friday, and then in the following weeks. And in the meantime he'd make other enquiries. This wasn't a huge neighbourhood. He'd find her eventually. And then he'd convince her she'd made a huge mistake.

The gym sat between a second-hand car dealership and a wine merchant. He wondered how many of its patrons worked off their calories and then popped next door for a bottle of wine to replenish them.

Cardew Park was on the opposite side of the street. Darren went in through the gates and walked back along the edge facing the road. When he thought he was at about the right spot, he fought through some bushes to get to the railings. There, he squatted on the earth, peering through shrubbery at the gym across the road. Nobody would be able to see him here in the dark undergrowth.

He waited. People strolled past on the pavement, unaware he could see and hear them. It was strange but also exhilarating to have this power of invisibility.

Rebecca's gym time was usually 7.30 to 8.30. Right now it was 8.35. If she was in there and she was sticking to her routine, she would be out at any minute.

He continued to wait. His buttocks felt damp on the soil and his legs were beginning to ache. It would be worth it, though. Rebecca was worth any amount of discomfort. He would walk through fire to get to his precious Rebecca.

He saw the gym door open. A female figure exited, and his pulse surged. He squinted to see her properly. She was tall like Rebecca, blonde like Rebecca . . .

It wasn't Rebecca.

Something collapsed inside him. He was beginning to think he'd got it all wrong, that perhaps she hadn't gone to the gym at all, or there was a different gym he hadn't found, or perhaps there was another Cardew Park, or maybe he'd misheard the phone message and it wasn't Cardew Park at all, and he was as far from her as he'd ever been, and—

There she was!

He was certain. It was definitely her this time. Even though he couldn't see her face properly from here, he knew her body shape, the way she walked with that slight bounce in every step, how she kept brushing back her hair with her fingers, the way she simply seemed to glow . . .

He exploded out from the bushes, frightening a middle-aged lady walking her dog. She scurried away, dragging her barking mutt behind her. She probably thought he was a

42

pervert, but he didn't give a toss. He knew that his love was pure.

He sprinted to the park gate, terrified of losing sight of Rebecca again so soon after finding her. But there she was ahead of him, strolling along without a care in the world, her sports bag slung over her shoulder.

He had thought long and hard about what he would do next. Great though the temptation was to surprise her immediately, this wasn't the time or place. He needed to find out where she lived and why she had decided to avoid him. Only when he had all the facts would he feel ready to begin repairing the situation.

And so he followed her.

7

The corner shop offered little choice in the way of cat food. Bill liked the sachets of meat in gravy, but they didn't have any, only tins of stuff in jelly. He knew he was setting himself up for a scenario in which Bill would sniff the food and then walk away in disdain, reluctantly consuming it only after a protracted battle of wits in which Elliott would have to make it crystal clear that no alternatives would be brought to the table – or, in his case, to the floor.

It'll have to do, Elliott thought. Damn cat's too fussy.

He picked up a couple of tins, added a bar of chocolate for himself at the counter, paid for them and left the shop.

He unwrapped the bar and started eating almost immediately. He would feel guilty if Bill was staring dolefully at him as he consumed chocolate while his pet was expected to make do with gelatinous gloop.

He almost dropped the remainder of the bar when the beautiful young woman arrived at his side.

His first thought was that he'd done something wrong.

Perhaps forgotten to pay for something in the shop.

'Excuse me,' the woman said. She seemed slightly panicked. 'Do you mind if I walk with you? There's a man behind us. I think he's following me.'

Elliott started to turn around.

'Don't look. I don't want him to know I've seen him. Can we make this look like we're together? Do you mind?'

Elliott didn't have to think twice. He knew that situations like this were hardly uncommon. Women spent much of their lives looking over their shoulders for weirdos who might be stalking them. Of course he would help her. Wasn't that what any real man would do in his shoes?

And besides, there was a certain irresistible thrill in this invitation to step up to the mark.

'Of course I don't mind. You want me to walk you home?'

'No. I don't want him to find out where I live. Can we just keep walking for a bit? He might go away when he sees I'm with you.'

'Okay. Yeah.'

She suddenly linked her arm through his. 'Is this all right? Sorry if I'm being a bit over-friendly.'

'No, it's fine.'

It was more than fine. He took another glance at her. She had the looks of a model. Wavy blonde hair and full lips. She smelt heavenly. He'd never had a girl like this on his arm before. Or any girl, for that matter.

He averted his eyes in case she started to think she'd jumped from the frying pan into the fire.

'How long has he been following you?'

'Just a few minutes, but I know he's doing it. He stays the same distance from me on the other side of the road. When I crossed the road, so did he.'

'Do you think we should call the police?'

'No. I'm sure he'll give up soon. He's not going to try anything with you around.'

Elliott felt like puffing out his chest. Yeah, he thought, that's right. Nobody messes with me.

And then he thought, Wait, are we about to test that out? Is this guy a psycho? What if he gets violent?

He started walking a little quicker.

'Should I look now, see if he's still there?'

'Not yet. Give it a bit longer. We don't want to provoke him.'

Good plan, Elliott thought. Provoking a psycho would be an unnecessary risk. We definitely shouldn't do that.

They walked some more. Elliott offered her a piece of his chocolate.

'Go ahead,' he said. 'Though it's got nuts in. You're not allergic, are you?'

'I'm not allergic. Thank you.' She took a cube and popped it into her mouth. When she did it, there was something delicate and sensual about it.

'This is very sweet,' she said.

'Yeah, I don't even look at the sugar content when I buy chocolate. I worry it might put me off.'

'No, I mean it's very sweet of you – to look after me like this. You're a real gentleman.'

Pride swelled within him again. Look at me, folks, he

thought. A real gent. Like something out of an old film. Cue the music and singing.

And then he realised something.

'Er, this is my house,' he said. 'Do you want us to keep walking?' He was happy to do so, but he wondered how much longer this might continue. Would he end up walking around in the early hours of the morning, carrying tins of cat food as his only defence against a crazed stalker? And what about Bill? The poor guy's stomach must be rumbling.

'This is your place?' He thought he heard a note of surprise in her question, and he hoped that she didn't find his humble abode too disappointing.

She swung round in front of him, stood very close. He wasn't quite sure what she was about to do, but this felt very intimate. And then he saw that her gaze was on some distant point over his shoulder, and he realised she was just performing a subtle reconnaissance.

'He's still there,' she said. 'Shit.'

Elliott went to turn his head, but again she stopped him, this time by cupping his face in her hands. They were warm and soft against his skin.

'No,' she said. 'Look, can I ask you a massive favour?'

He looked into her eyes and gulped. 'Sure.'

'Can I come inside with you? Just for a bit. Just until he goes away.'

He gulped again. 'Inside? In my house?'

'Would that be okay? I don't know what else to do.'

It was an easy one. He was the Good Samaritan, the white knight coming to the aid of the damsel in distress.

'Of course. Yes. Let's go in.'

As he unlocked the door, he tried to remember what state he'd left the place in. He was pretty good at keeping the house tidy, but there was always the chance that he'd left some underwear lying around.

He put some lights on. Bill was in his usual pose, flat on his back.

'Oh, what a beautiful cat,' the woman exclaimed. She went straight to him and started ruffling his fur. Bill stood up to give her hand a good sniff before rubbing himself against her legs.

'What's his name?' she asked.

'It's Bilberry, but I call him Bill.'

'Hello, Bill,' she said, stroking him again. Elliott felt a little jealous.

'Speaking of names, I er, I don't know yours.'

She straightened up. 'I'm sorry. That's awfully rude of me. It's Rebecca.'

Her accent sounded incredibly posh to Elliott – like that of a member of the royal family – and when she proffered a hand, he was tempted to kiss the back of it. As he shook it instead, he recalled Heidi's James Bond jibe, and for the briefest of moments he considered introducing himself with his surname first.

'My name's Elliott Whiston.'

'Pleased to meet you, Elliott. And thank you so much for coming to my rescue. I hated putting you on the spot like that.'

'No, it's fine. I'm glad to help. You can't be too careful. There are so many strange people about.'

'I won't stay long, I promise. If I could just wait here a bit...'

Stay as long as you like, Elliott thought.

'Come into the kitchen,' he said. 'I'll put the kettle on.'

She followed him, looking around as she entered the room. 'Do you live with family?'

'No. You're stuck with just me, I'm afraid.'

'You've got the whole house to yourself?'

'Yup, all mine.' He decided not to go into the technicalities of part ownership with his sister; it would sound less impressive. 'Take a seat, I'll be back in a sec.'

He dived through to the front room. Leaving the light off, he went to the window and peered out. It was so dark out there, but he could swear he could see the figure of a man standing under a tree over by the park.

Elliott went back to the kitchen. As he poured water into the mugs he said, 'I think that guy's still there. Don't you think we should call the police?'

'No, really. He's harmless.'

'Wait. You know him?'

'Yeah. His name's Darren. He lives near where I used to live. He must have seen me on the street tonight. He's got a bit of a crush on me.'

'A crush? Following you around at night doesn't sound like a crush to me. It sounds twisted.'

'He's not crazy. He just has a few ... behavioural issues. He lives with his mum and doesn't get out much. You know how it is.'

'Sure,' Elliott said, feeling a little sorry for the man. He often wondered if people used to think the same about him.

'I broke up with my boyfriend recently and Darren found out about it. Now he thinks he's in with a chance, and he's been sending me some odd messages. I'm not even sure how he got hold of my number.'

'Have you tried putting him straight?'

'Yes. It doesn't seem to sink in. I've given up replying. Now he's seen me with another man, though . . .'

Elliott nodded. 'Good idea.' He wondered if she might suggest reinforcing the deception by going outside to engage in a full-on kissing session. Probably not.

He felt a little more relaxed now. The poor guy outside had problems. He presumably wasn't even aware of the distress he was causing. He just couldn't help himself. That merited sympathy rather than fear, but he could appreciate that a woman would feel threatened by anyone following her, especially after dark. Elliott decided he wasn't going to worry about Darren any longer. Soon enough, the man would give up and go home. In the meantime, Elliott was going to enjoy this rare moment of female company. Well, rare if he didn't count Heidi.

He set down the mugs of tea on the table. 'You're not from around here, are you?'

'No. I'm from Surrey, originally, but I've lived in the north for about ten years. Can't shake the accent, though.'

'You shouldn't. I like it. It sounds posh.'

She laughed. 'One thing I'm definitely not is posh.'

Yes you are, he thought. I bet your parents live in one of those massive country mansions with paintings of your ancestors stretching up the staircase. I bet your servants have bigger and nicer quarters than this house.

'Where do you live?' he asked.

She hesitated, and he realised he'd overstepped. She didn't know him from Adam, so why would she hand over her address?

'Sorry,' he added. 'I didn't mean to pry.'

'It's okay. I'm just renting at the moment. I had to move out when I broke up with my boyfriend, so I'm biding my time until the perfect place comes up.'

He realised she had cleverly dodged his question, but that was fine. Served him right for being so nosy.

'Can I make you something to eat? I haven't got much in, but—'

'No, honestly. I ate earlier, and I've just been to the gym, where everyone's at least a stone lighter than me.'

Elliott thought that might be the cue for a compliment, but he wasn't sure how to frame it without sounding inappropriate. His alternative was to laugh at her self-deprecation, but then he realised he was already running out of things to talk about. He wasn't very good with people he didn't know, especially when they were this attractive.

'What gym do you go to?'

'I've only just joined this one. It's called the Tone Zone.'

Elliott's eyes lit up. 'I go there!'

'You do? I love the rowing machine and the weights. What about you?'

Elliott decided not to mention that he'd tried weightlifting, as he knew his physique betrayed his lack of success.

'Mainly the cross-trainer.'

'Cool. How often do you go?'

'Oh, you know, as often as I can. I find it hard to fit it in these days.' He didn't tell her that his membership had lapsed and that he had no intention of ever going back there.

'Busy social life?'

He nodded. 'Hectic.' He caught a glimpse of Bill, who looked as though he wanted to challenge that claim, and decided to change the subject. 'What line of work are you in?' he asked. Not the best question in the world, but he was struggling.

'I'm a beauty therapist,' she told him.

'Oh, really?' He tried to inject the right amount of interest into his response, but wondered if he'd gone overboard. He didn't really know what a beauty therapist was. He didn't want to come across as an ignoramus after being so enthusiastic.

He took a wild stab. 'Do some of them take a lot of persuasion?'

'Who?'

'Your clients. When you're trying to convince them they're not as ugly as they think they are.'

She stared at him, and then burst into laughter. 'That's . . . not what I do. It's not that kind of therapy. People come to me for various treatments – facials, massages, manicures, that kind of thing.'

'Oh. Right.' *You idiot*. To cover up his embarrassment he blurted out, 'I work with cats.'

She grinned. 'Not facials and massages, presumably.'

'Er, no. I run a charity shop for the Cat Welfare League.'

'What a lovely thing to do. That must be so rewarding.'

The shoplifter came to mind again, and Elliott had to forcibly eject him. 'Mostly, yes. It has its difficult moments, but I love it.'

'That's great. Sometimes I wish I'd done something as ...'
She let the sentence trail off, and he thought he had caught her
in a moment of wistfulness.

'You help people, I help animals. We're both doing our bit.'

'Yes,' she said, brightening. 'You're right. Speaking of helping animals, why does your cat keep staring at me?'

'Does he? I don't— Oh, crap. I haven't fed him. That's his
way of letting us know he's starving.'

Elliott opened a tin and forked the contents out into Bill's
dish. As predicted, Bill sniffed the food and then glared at his
owner, making his disappointment crystal clear.

Come on, Elliott thought, take one for the team. Can't you
see I'm trying to make a good impression here?

'So ...' he said, 'when you're not working or in the gym,
how do you fill your time?'

'Oh, the usual. I like going out. Restaurants, bars, nightclubs. You probably know all the ones round here better than
I do.'

That wasn't the case. He knew a couple of fast-food joints,
but that was about it. He didn't drink much and he couldn't
afford fancy restaurants. The very thought of a nightclub was
enough to trigger his anxiety.

'Yeah,' he lied. 'You should try The Whirligig.' It was the
only local nightclub that came to mind, and then only because
Heidi had mentioned it.

Rebecca's eyes widened. 'That's so weird. I'm in there all the
time. I've never seen you.'

That's because I've never been, he thought. And even if I
had, it's hardly likely that a woman like you would notice me.

'I haven't been for a while. Used to go there all the time, though. I like the music.'

'Me too! What's your favourite?'

He was out of his depth again. He wanted to say Adele, but that hardly seemed to fit the bill.

'Oh, all kinds. I'll dance to anything.'

Much though he would love to see her again, he hoped she wouldn't invite him to go to the club with her. His dancing would be a sight to behold, and not in a good way.

He tried a few more topics of conversation, each ending abruptly as the extent of his knowledge and experience was made painfully apparent to him. He was beginning to realise that Rebecca's world and his were light years apart.

After one particularly lengthy silence, she said to him, 'Do you think he's gone now? Darren, I mean?'

Elliott took this as meaning that any risk of bumping into her stalker was worth it to escape this awkwardness.

'I'll have a look,' he said.

He went back to the window of the front room. There was no sign of anyone. Even though he could happily spend hours with Rebecca, he couldn't lie to keep her here.

'I think he's gone,' he announced as he returned to the kitchen. 'But it's so dark out there. He might be hiding. Are you sure I can't walk you home?'

'Best not. If Darren's still hanging around, I don't want him to see where I live now.'

'I'll drive you. He won't be able to follow us then.' As he said this, he thought about all the junk in his car and the fact that he hadn't cleaned it out in over six months.

'Oh, no. That's a kind offer, though. I'll call a taxi. I'll get them to take me somewhere else before I go home to make it worth their while.'

She cushioned that well, Elliott thought. Darren isn't the only one she doesn't want to reveal her address to.

'Okay, if you're sure.'

While she made her phone call, he washed the mugs and put away the biscuits. He heard her asking the taxi firm to take her across town to Waitrose. Of course she shops at Waitrose, he thought.

While she had her phone in her hand, she said, 'Can I give you my phone number?'

'Your number?' he said, taken aback. He wasn't used to pretty women offering to give him their numbers.

'Yes. If you see Darren again, you can call and let me know.'

'Am I likely to see him again? I don't even know what he looks like. He was too far away.'

'Probably not. If you'd prefer not to . . .'

'No. Sure. Let me have it.'

He took his own phone out, cheap in comparison to her top-end iPhone, and entered her as a contact as she recited the number. He sent her a text and as her phone pinged he said, 'That's me, so you've got my number too. In case, you know, you ever need someone to help you out again.'

She smiled. 'Thank you. It's nice to know I've got a hero I can call on.'

He blinked. Hero? he thought.

'One other thing,' she said. 'On the off-chance that you do bump into Darren, would you mind . . .'

'What?'

'I mean, the chances are slim, but like I said, he's got a few behavioural problems. If he asks about you and me, would you mind telling him that you're my boyfriend?'

'Your . . . boyfriend?'

'Yes. Would that be okay? Darren doesn't understand the subtleties of relationships. If you come right out and say we're a couple, I don't think he'll ever bother me again. I'm sorry, I hate to ask a perfect stranger to lie for me, but—'

'No, that's absolutely fine. And we're not strangers anymore, right? Of course I'll do that for you.'

'Thank you. That's so kind of you.'

The taxi arrived only minutes later. Elliott showed her to the door and escorted her outside, keeping an eye out for the movement of shadows across the street.

Rebecca paused at the car, then suddenly turned and gave him a hug. Elliott froze, not sure how to react.

'You're very sweet,' she said. 'I won't forget this.'

'Neither will I,' he said, and then felt a bit ridiculous.

She got in the taxi. He watched it pull away, saw her wave at him through the rear window. He wondered if he would ever see her again.

Before he went back into the house, he took another long look over towards the park.

He's definitely gone, Elliott told himself.

Definitely.

Darren felt hot tears on his cheeks.

What was going on here? Why was Rebecca with this guy?

Who the fuck was he? They had spent a lot of time in that house. Enough time to—

No. Stop it. It can't be that. There has to be a perfectly reasonable explanation.

But you saw them. Saw that hug she gave him. That was very friendly, very intimate.

Well, maybe not. It could still be innocent. Friends hug all the time. Doesn't mean they're lovers. He might be gay. And even if he's not, look at his house. Would Rebecca go for a guy who lives in a house like that? Looks as though he can't afford a pot to piss in.

And yet . . .

You thought you were out of her league at one time, didn't you? So maybe this isn't so unbelievable. Maybe you and the bastard who lives in this shitty little house aren't so different after all.

But she wouldn't do that. She's got morals. She wouldn't cheat on you. Wouldn't go to bed with another man, ripping off his clothes like she did with you, wouldn't tell him what a fantastic lover he was like she did with you, wouldn't—

NO! She's not doing any of those things! Not with him!

Darren wiped the tears away. He had a pounding headache now, and he was freezing cold. This wasn't doing him any good, speculating like this. He needed answers.

He continued to stare at the house. You could go over there right now, he told himself. Bang on the bastard's door. Force your way inside. You have the knife, right? That fuck-off army knife with the sharp, serrated blade? You could threaten him, get him to tell you everything. You've got nothing to lose now.

Rebecca's nan found that out for herself, the stupid witch. You hadn't wanted that to happen, but it did, and now you're a killer, and one more death won't make any difference. One or a dozen, it's all the same.

But hold on. Let's not be hasty. Rebecca's nan was an accident. Even if you did hide the body, nobody can say her death was premeditated, right? But this would be a completely different ball game. If he fights back and you have to kill him, it would definitely be murder. Even worse, you might not get any answers out of him. You might still not find out what disgusting things he did to your beautiful angel.

So here's what you do. You go back to your car and you find a hotel and you have a nice meal and a beer and you calm yourself down. And then you think and you plan, and you get a good night's sleep, and tomorrow you'll be ready.

Tomorrow you'll get some answers.

8

It sometimes seemed to Elliott that the universe operated in balance. Sometimes things were weighted heavily against you; other times, the scales swung in your favour. More globally, some people lived terribly unfortunate lives, but there were others who seemed to live a charmed existence. Perhaps it all levelled out in the end.

Take yesterday, for example, he mused as he sat behind his desk in the shop. It started off fairly normally, then there was a huge dip when the shoplifter appeared, and then there was an equally large crest when Rebecca came along. One cancelled out the other.

The whole day had seemed ruined after the shoplifter episode. He had been ready to take to his bed for a week. And then along came Rebecca to restore his self-esteem.

There was no indecision on my part, he thought. I rose to the challenge without hesitation. I knew what had to be done, and I did it.

And the result? She called me a hero. A *hero*! Nobody has ever called me a hero before.

It felt good. It felt better than good. Whenever memories of the shoplifter began to creep into his mind, Rebecca provided the ammunition he needed to bat them away.

Balance had been restored.

He was still thinking about Rebecca when Heidi breezed into the shop in the afternoon. The first thing she said was, 'What's wrong with you?'

'Nothing. Why?'

'You're smiling. And there's nobody else here. Why are you smiling?'

'Maybe I'm just overjoyed to see you.'

She shook her head. 'No, that's not it. The smile I get is a polite, *Hello, Heidi, it's nice to see you again* kind of smile. This one's weird. It's all dreamy and a bit freaky. You haven't inhaled the catnip again, have you?'

'Make the tea and I'll tell you.'

'What, you're blackmailing me now? When did you get to be such a cut-throat negotiator?'

'Yesterday.'

'What happened yesterday? When I saw you, you were giving off *Woe is me* vibes. You *are* the real Elliott, aren't you? Do I need to be afraid here?'

'Go and make the tea, and then you'll find out.'

She started slowly towards the back room, staring intently at him as she went. He smiled again. She waved her hand over her own face and said, 'Stop it with the weirdness. It disturbs me.'

She was back a few minutes later with the tea. She pulled up a chair and said, 'Come on, then, clone of Elliott. What's your mission on this planet?'

Elliott sipped his drink, enjoying the moment. 'I had an interesting time last night.'

'If this is about you cutting your toenails, I don't want to know.'

'Nothing so trivial. I met someone.'

'You met someone? Online, you mean?'

'No. In real life. A real person.'

'Okay. And who is this mysterious person?'

'Her name's Rebecca.'

He knew he was smiling dreamily again, but he couldn't help himself. Heidi, on the other hand, had suddenly donned an expression of extreme seriousness.

'Rebecca.'

'Yes.'

'She's a woman?'

'Yes. And not just any woman . . .'

'A Marks and Spencer woman?'

'Better than that. A Waitrose woman. She's gorgeous, Heidi. She could be a model. I've never met anyone like her before.'

Heidi put her mug down. 'All right, I'm going to need a little bit of context here. Models don't generally enter into your life unless they're shop dummies like Myrtle. Who is this Rebecca woman and how did you meet her?'

'I saved her, from a fate worse than death.'

'Yeah, well, now it definitely sounds like we're straying into the realms of fantasy. Get more specific – preferably before I hit you with this tray.'

'Okay. It was after work. I was at home. Alone. Well, except for Bill. And, actually, he's kind of the catalyst for everything because he was hungry and I didn't have anything in for him, so I had to pop out to the shop, you know that corner shop by—'

'For crying out loud, Elliott! Not that specific! Just tell me about the damn woman!'

Elliott blinked, surprised at the outburst, and then decided it might be best to cut to the chase.

'She was being stalked.'

'Stalked? Not by you, I hope.'

'I resent that. Loser I may be, but even I have standards. No, some guy she knows. He won't leave her alone. He was following her last night, so she came up to me on the street and asked if I would pretend to be her boyfriend.'

'Pretend how? Did it involve tongues?'

'Only for talking. She took my arm and we walked for a while, and then ...'

'And then what?'

'She asked if she could come into my house.'

'Your house? Did you let her?'

'Of course I let her. She was being stalked. What else was I going to do?'

Heidi relaxed. 'Yeah, you're right. You did a good thing. What did the stalker look like?'

'I don't really know.'

'What does that mean?'

'I didn't actually see him until I looked out of my front window and he was just standing there by the park.'

'How long did he stay there?'

'Not sure. When I looked later, he was gone.'

'Did she tell you anything about him?'

'A little. Apparently he's just a harmless guy who's got some behavioural issues. Still lives with his mum.'

'If he's so harmless, why was she panicking?'

'She wasn't panicking. She just wanted him to get the message that she's not available. She said I was a hero for helping her.'

'A hero? Well, that's nice. What else did she say while she was getting cosy at your place?'

'We just chatted. I think we really hit it off.'

Heidi nodded slowly. 'I see. What gives you that impression?'

'Well, she gave me her phone number.'

Alarm surfaced on Heidi's features. 'Her number? Why did she give you that?'

'I told you. We hit it off.'

'No. I mean really.'

'Hey, what are you trying to say? All right, if you must know, she gave me her number in case I see Darren again.'

'Who's Darren?'

'Her stalker.'

'Why does she think you'll see him again?'

'She doesn't. But the poor guy's not all there. He might want to confirm her story.'

'Her story being . . .?'

'That I'm her boyfriend.'

9

Darren was starting to build a picture of the bastard, and it was a puzzling one.

He had come here to the house early, grateful for the darkness of the February morning. The guy had left home at twenty past eight, and Darren had followed, assuming that he was on his way to work. What had surprised him was the nature of that work.

A charity shop.

For cats.

So, not only did the bastard live in a shitty little house, but he also worked in a shitty little shop that sold all kinds of crap to old ladies who were crazy about shitty little animals.

That didn't sound right. Didn't sound like his Rebecca at all. Why would she have any interest in a no-hoper like that? She liked nice clothes and jewellery and fast cars and luxury holidays. This scruffy runt simply didn't fit into that picture.

It wasn't even as though he was handsome. Darren didn't

think his own looks were especially remarkable, but compared to the bastard he was Chris Pine.

Maybe he's good in the bedroom, Darren thought as he lurked in the shadows opposite the house. Adventurous. A regular trapeze artist. With a dick the size of a baguette.

But how would it have got that far? How would they have become so intimate in the first place? It didn't tally.

What if he had something on her? What if he was blackmailing her for sex?

The thought of somebody doing that, of forcing her into submission, of hurting his Rebecca in any way, made his blood boil.

He's in there now, Darren thought. Back home after a long day in his sad, pathetic shop.

And what about Rebecca? Is she in there too? Is she doing all the things she used to do for me?

It didn't bear thinking about.

He needed facts.

It was time for a meeting.

Elliott assumed it was Heidi. Whenever his doorbell rang at this time of the evening, it was usually Heidi. In fact, whenever anyone came to his door it was usually Heidi.

He assumed she wanted to know more about Rebecca. For long after he had described the events of last night to her, she had continued to probe him about Rebecca. What did she look like? How did she dress? And even: what perfume was she wearing?

Elliott had no idea about perfumes. He only knew that she smelt heavenly. Heidi hadn't liked that answer.

So this was bound to be her again, armed with a list of further questions he wouldn't be able to answer to her satisfaction.

Except that it wasn't.

The guy at the door was in his late twenties, of slight build – perhaps even weedier than Elliott himself. He was wearing a leather jacket over a woollen sweater and jeans. He seemed apprehensive.

'Hi,' he said. 'I, er, I'm looking for Rebecca.'

Ah, Elliott thought. So this is Darren. Yeah, he does look as though he's not all there.

He remembered what Rebecca had asked of him. Time for a little acting.

'She's not here at the moment, I'm afraid. Can I take a message?'

The man digested this for a long time. 'A message? Well, I don't know . . . What kind of message?'

The question threw Elliott. Poor guy definitely isn't with it, he thought.

'I mean, do you want me to tell her something?'

'I . . . I'd really prefer to talk to her in person, if that's okay.'

Elliott wondered how he was going to let the man down lightly. He hated the thought of having to upset him.

'Actually, she doesn't live here. You should probably go to her house.'

'That's the problem. I don't know where she lives.'

'You don't? I'm sorry, who are you again?' He knew perfectly well, but thought it best to feign ignorance.

'My name's Darren. I'm Rebecca's boyfriend.'

Elliott smiled beneficently. 'Ah, I see. Rebecca told me about you.'

Darren brightened. 'She did?'

'Yeah. Look, Darren, this isn't easy for me to tell you, but Rebecca isn't your girlfriend.'

Darren stared, as if waiting for a punchline. 'Sorry, I don't know what you mean.'

Elliott found his voice stepping up in volume to get the message across. 'She's not your girlfriend. She wants you to leave her alone now.'

'No,' Darren said. 'That's not right. She . . . she made a mistake, you see. She needs me.'

'No. She doesn't. Sorry, but she told me so herself.'

'She said that?'

'Yes. I know it must be really tough to hear, but that's the way it is.'

A curious thing happened then.

Darren began to cry. He stood there on the doorstep while tears welled in his eyes and cascaded down his cheeks.

Elliott didn't know what to do. The guy was obviously in some distress.

'Hey, don't cry. Rebecca wouldn't want that, would she? You need to be strong.'

'You . . . you don't understand. I love her. She loves me too. I can't live without her.'

'Don't talk like that. You'll find someone else. I know you will.'

'No. She's everything to me. She's—'

Darren broke down then, lowering his head and covering his face with his hands, sobbing as his shoulders heaved. Elliott felt his pain. He knew he couldn't send the poor guy away in this state.

'Listen, you want to come inside for a minute? If it'll help, I'm willing to talk about it.'

Darren wiped his face with his hands and sniffed wetly. He nodded without looking up.

'Great,' Elliott said. 'Come on in.'

He guided Darren into the kitchen and sat him down at the table.

'That's it,' he said. 'Do you fancy a cup of tea or a coffee or something?'

Darren nodded again. 'Tea, please. One sugar.'

Elliott put the kettle on for his second visitor in two nights. The house had not seen so many strangers in a long time.

'What's your name?' Darren said.

'My name's Elliott.'

'Like in *ET*?'

'Yes, except I'm not hiding an alien in my wardrobe.'

'Are you hiding anyone else in your wardrobe?'

Elliott knew what he was getting at, but stayed silent.

'You live here alone?' Darren asked. Déjà vu. Rebecca had asked the same thing. This time, though, it felt more like an interrogation.

'I do,' he said. Then he added, 'Except for this little fella.'

As he said this, Bill sauntered into the room. Darren looked at the animal with distaste.

'He's your pet?'

'Yes. This is Bill. Do you like cats?'

'No. And Bill is a weird name for a cat.'

Well, that was brief and to the point, Elliott thought.

'Rebecca doesn't live here with you?' Darren asked.

'She . . . visits. But no, she doesn't actually live here.'

'I see. Could you tell me where she lives now, please?'

It seemed such an innocent request, as if asked by a child.

'I don't think that would be a good idea, do you?'

'Why not?'

'It . . . As you know, Rebecca is a very private person. I don't think she would want me to give out her address.'

'Even to her boyfriend?'

Wow, Elliott thought. He really is deluded. He's already forgotten what he's just been crying about.

He decided not to answer. In silence he made the tea and then joined Darren at the table. He felt like a counsellor, not unlike the way in which he regarded Heidi as his own therapist. The reversal felt good, gave him comfort to know that there were some who were more messed up than himself.

'What made you come here?' he asked.

'To see Rebecca.'

'Yeah, I know. I mean, what made you think she might be here in my house?'

Darren came straight out with it. 'I followed her. I saw her on the street and I followed her. She came inside.'

'Yes, she did. You do know it's not nice to follow people, don't you? Especially women.'

'I didn't have a choice. I needed to know where she lives now.'

'I see.'

'Yes. But you said she doesn't live here.'

'No.'

'So, then, why did she come here?'

Elliott took a sip of his tea while he thought about the best way to put this. He didn't like to deceive, especially someone so vulnerable, but sometimes a little white lie was the best option.

'Darren, I should probably tell you that Rebecca is my girlfriend.'

Darren stared at him. Elliott was ready for more tears, but got a wholly different reaction.

Darren laughed. A high-pitched shriek of amusement at first, and then he threw back his head and screamed with laughter.

Elliott tried to ignore the stab of irritation. And then he remembered who he was dealing with and resolved to be more objective.

'Your girlfriend?' Darren said. '*Your* girlfriend?'

'Yes, Darren. Why do you find that so funny?'

'Well . . . look at you. I mean, come on.'

Annoyance began to bubble up again. So much for that resolution. 'None of us is perfect, Darren.'

He regretted his words as soon as he uttered them. They were barbed, and Darren seemed to feel their sting. His smile disappeared.

'Have you been to bed with her?' he asked.

Elliott tried to recover from the surprise question. No filter, he thought. The guy can't help himself.

'I'm not going to answer that. All you need to know is that she is my girlfriend and you should respect that.'

'Where did you meet her?'

'Darren, I—'

'What's her favourite colour? What's her favourite film? What type of car does she drive?'

'Darren, please. This has—'

'Her favourite colour is pink. The film she watches constantly is *Les Miserables*, and she drives a Mercedes. You didn't know any of that, did you? You're not her boyfriend. You're lying to me.'

Elliott boiled over. 'We met in a nightclub because she loves to dance. When she goes to the gym she uses the rowing machine and weights. She shops at Waitrose. She likes cats. She was born in Surrey. She—' He stopped himself. This was getting out of hand. 'I'm sorry, Darren. You need to start accepting the truth.'

Darren looked to be on the verge of tears again.

'Does she talk about me much?' he asked.

Elliott tried to be diplomatic. 'She doesn't talk a lot about her past. I think she prefers to live in the present.'

'But I'm not really her past. I'm still here, aren't I? I must be in her thoughts.'

Damn, Elliott thought. How can I put this without destroying him?

'Listen, Darren. Don't you think it would be better if you stopped torturing yourself like this? Rebecca is happy being with me, and if you want her to stay happy, then you should let her go. What do you think?'

Darren considered this for some time. His face exhibited a range of emotions.

'Do you love her?'

Elliott paused. He had never been in love, and claiming

so seemed such a leap. But what else could he say that would deter Darren?

'Yes. Yes, I do.'

'And does she love you?'

'Yes. We're very close.'

'I see.'

Elliott waited.

'I think I should go now,' Darren said. He got up from his chair, taking Elliott by surprise.

'Oh, okay. Are you . . . I mean, are you all right?'

'Me? Yes, I'm fine, thank you.'

'But about me and Rebecca. You're okay with that? You understand what I said to you about us being a couple?'

'Yes. You made it very clear. Thank you.'

He started out of the kitchen. Elliott followed, somewhat flustered by Darren's abrupt acceptance of the deceit.

At the front door, Darren paused. 'I hope you enjoyed your time with Rebecca,' he said, and then he walked away.

Elliott watched him go for a few seconds, and then he closed the door. Darren's parting words had puzzled him, but he took it as yet another sign of the man's limited social skills.

Poor guy, he thought once more. Poor deluded guy.

Poor deluded bastard, Darren thought to himself. He really believes he's got something there with Rebecca. A couple? He thinks they're a couple? What a joke!

Darren had no doubt that there was a relationship of some kind there. He didn't like to contemplate the potential depth of it, but whatever it was, it couldn't be love, not like the bastard claimed. You couldn't be in love with two people at the same time. Sure, you could *love* two people – you could *love* dozens of people – but you couldn't be *in love* with more than one. That was just a fact of life. And if Rebecca was in love with Darren – which she was – then she couldn't also be in love with that idiot, no matter how much he wanted to believe it.

It made Darren feel a little better that the bastard was clearly out of touch with reality. Couldn't he see that he was punching way above his weight?

But still, there were a lot of unanswered questions. A key one being why was she even hanging out with him?

He had often wondered if something had gone badly wrong in Rebecca's life. Something she couldn't bring herself to talk about, even to her boyfriend. Maybe she'd had some sort of breakdown. That would explain why she'd just walked out on him. It might also explain why she was spending time with the bastard. He looked like one of those 'good listener' types: the ones who would offer a girl a shoulder to cry on when what they really wanted to do was get in her pants.

He congratulated himself on putting on a pretty good act back there. The crying, especially. Well, except that it hadn't been entirely fake. It was the bastard's fault. Saying that Rebecca didn't want him anymore. That had been cruel and unnecessary. He could easily have sliced the man's throat for that remark.

He thought he might still do that one day.

Right now, though, he was buoyant. What the last few

minutes had proven to him was that he had no real competition. It shouldn't be hard to convince Rebecca of that.

And then she would come running back to him.

Elliott sat on the sofa, Bill curled up on his lap. He was staring at his phone, almost dreading making this call.

He tried to analyse why he felt so anxious, and realised that it was because he feared she might already have forgotten about him, that he was such an insignificance in her life. Perhaps she had swapped phone numbers with him simply out of courtesy, and had now blocked him for ever.

Just do it, he told himself. If she doesn't want to know you now, then take it on the chin. You've had worse rejections.

He called her, and it was quickly answered.

'Hi, Elliott,' she said, and he was already picturing her back in his kitchen, drinking from the mug that he had contemplated never washing again.

'Hi,' he said. 'Did you get home okay last night?'

'Yes, no problem, thanks. What's up?'

'I thought you should know, I saw Darren tonight.'

There was a long pause, and then, 'Darren? Where?'

'At my house. He knocked on my door.'

'Right. Okay. And . . . how did it go?'

He thought she sounded very strange, as if she expected the worst kind of news.

'It was fine. I put him straight. Told him we were a couple.'

'Do you think you got through to him?'

'Actually, I think I did. He didn't seem such a bad guy. A bit mixed up, and he got upset at one point, but I think he's got the picture now. I don't think he'll be bothering you again.'

'That's ... that's great to hear, Elliott. It sounds like it all went smoothly.'

Something weird in her voice again. A note of relief, as though she'd expected it to go disastrously wrong?

'Yeah. By the way, if you're ever passing the charity shop, you're always welcome to drop in for a cuppa and a quick chat.'

'You know what, I might just do that.'

She sounded positive. Keen even. But he didn't expect anything to come of it. Story of his life.

'Great. Okay then, I'll let you go. I just thought I should give you an update.'

'Thank you. It was very thoughtful. And I'm glad Darren has seen sense at last.'

'Yeah. No problem. I'm glad I could—'

'Bye, Elliott.'

'Er, yeah. Bye.'

The call ended. Elliott looked down at Bill, who had one eye slightly open.

'What do you think, buddy? We're not going to see her or speak to her again, are we?'

Bill closed his eye, as though the topic was not worthy of further discussion.

'No, I thought not.'

10

It had come to Darren as a flash of inspiration. One of those rare mental light-bulb moments.

He had gone to bed in his hotel last night thinking he would have to wait till the following evening to see Rebecca, because that was the night she would probably go to the gym. His plan was to find her there, make it clear to her how much he understood the mistake she had made, and then welcome her back into his life, her sins completely forgiven.

Two things had bothered him about the plan, though. Firstly, he hadn't really wanted to hang around outside a gym, maybe for hours. Secondly, she might not even go to the gym at all, especially if Elliott had told her about their meeting last night.

But now he had a new plan. It might not pay off, but at least he would be doing *something*.

He knew that Rebecca was living somewhere near Cardew Park. And, unless she had changed it since he last saw her, he also knew what car she drove and its registration. He would search the area around the park, on the lookout for her Mercedes.

His concern was that it was a huge search area. He had no idea what Rebecca had meant when she had said she lived 'right by Cardew Park' or how far she was willing to walk to get to the gym. And it was also possible that her car might not even be visible from the street.

But then his brainwave had arrived, and that's what had led him here.

The estate agency was called Blackwell and Byrne, which to Darren's mind sounded like perverse cooking instructions. It was the third one on his list, all located on this same street in the centre of Ebbington. The first two hadn't been of any help at all, and his frustration was starting to build, but he forced himself to remain cheery as he entered the premises.

There were no other customers inside. The sole occupant was a fresh-faced young man in a cheap grey suit and loud tie, seated behind an expansive desk and huge padded chair that together conspired to make him appear tiny. He jumped up immediately, like a puppy full of nervous energy.

'Hello,' he said. 'How can I help you today?'

Darren hated him already. Everything about the man felt false, and that he was merely working through a set of corporate instructions he had been given.

'Hi. I'm looking to rent a house.' Rebecca would definitely go for a house again rather than a flat. She hated the idea of strangers living above or below her.

'Cool. I'm sure we can do something for you. Take a seat.'

Darren guessed that the word 'cool' wasn't in the instruction manual, but he took a seat and also the proffered hand.

'My name's Jeremy, by the way. If we could just start with a few details. What kind of area are you looking at?'

'I want to be by Cardew Park. And I like going to the gym, so if it could be within walking distance of that one at the top of Tennyson Road?'

'Cool. That's a desirable area. How many bedrooms do you think you'll need?'

'I don't mind. But I'd like at least one.'

Jeremy laughed too hard at the lame joke. 'And what sort of price range are we looking at?' He rolled his hands in the air as he said this, as though it meant something.

'I don't want a dump. Other than that, you can surprise me.'

'Cool. Let's see what we've got here . . .'

He typed and mouse-clicked on his computer, then swivelled the screen to give Darren a better view.

'Well,' he said. 'We've got a couple of nice properties here. There's this beautiful semi-detached on Ringdale Avenue . . . and then there's this one on Vernon Street . . .'

Darren had stopped listening. He had no interest in properties that were available, but he allowed Jeremy to keep scrolling through them and telling him how amazing they were.

'What do you think?' Jeremy asked. 'I can pull up more details on any that take your fancy.'

Darren pulled a face. 'To be honest, they're not really doing it for me. There was a house I saw online recently, just a week or so ago, in fact, but I couldn't see it on your screen there.'

'It may have gone. Let me see . . . You don't know what road it was on, do you?'

'No, sorry.' And then another thought occurred to him.

'Did I mention I need it to be fully furnished?' He had almost forgotten that Rebecca's last rental contained very little that belonged to her. She didn't like to be tied down to a place.

'Oh! We don't get so many of those. Could this be it?'

Darren leant forward to get a better view of the on-screen gallery. The house looked to be about a hundred years old – solid, full of character, and tastefully decorated and furnished. Exactly the sort of thing Rebecca would go for.

'I think so. Is that near the park?'

'Definitely. Winsford Place. But, like I say, it's already taken. In fact, the tenant moved in just a few days ago.'

'I see. Is that the only one you've let in the past week?'

'In that area and in that price bracket, yes. I could look for other—'

'No, it's okay. That's the one I want.'

'Yes, but unfortunately—'

'Thank you for your help.'

Darren got to his feet. He had no more to say to this man.

'Okay,' Jeremy said. 'Cool.'

Darren put Winsford Place into his car's satnav and followed its directions. It took him to a tree-lined street running down from the park. About a ten-minute walk from the gym. It had to be Rebecca's new address. Had to be. He knew her tastes, and it was exactly where she'd told her nan it was.

Except that there was no sign of her car.

Might not mean anything, he thought. He approached the door, rang the bell.

Nothing.

He waited for a few minutes, then gave up. He drove away, went for a coffee, came back.

Still no sign of her.

He continued like this for the rest of the day, returning to the house every hour or so. At each failed attempt he didn't become angry or upset; he simply vowed to keep on trying. God loves a trier, he told himself.

At about five thirty, his tenacity paid off.

Rebecca's Mercedes was parked on the driveway.

Elation surged through him as he stared at the house. She was in there, behind one of those windows. Almost within touching distance.

Reinvigorated, he walked up to the door and rang the bell. Within seconds a shape materialised through the leaded glass. Despite all its distortions, he knew it belonged to Rebecca.

When she opened the door and he saw the shock on her features, he regretted not bringing her flowers. That would have been the right thing to do. But that could come later. Anything she wanted could be brought to her later.

'Darren,' she said.

He beamed, ecstatic at the vision of her. She was dressed casually in leggings and a tight pink sweater, emphasising her curves.

'Hi,' he said. 'Surprised?'

'A little. How did ... how did you find me?'

'I did a little detective work. It wasn't hard. I'd find you anywhere.' He decided not to mention that his efforts had involved the death of her grandmother.

'I see. Well ...'

'Can I come in? We've got a lot to talk about.'

She looked behind her, into the depths of the house.

'I'm sorry,' Darren said. 'Have you got company?' He braced himself for her answer.

'No, no. It's just . . .'

'We really should talk, Rebecca. I don't think it will take long.'

She hesitated but then relented. 'Okay. Come in, Darren.'

He followed her into a hallway and then through a door into a long living room with French windows looking out onto a mature garden. Music was playing. Ariana Grande.

'Nice place,' he said.

'I think so.'

'Fresh start?'

'Well . . .'

'That's okay. It's allowed. We all need a reboot now and again.' He gestured towards the plump sofa. 'May I?'

'Of course.'

He thought she seemed apprehensive, and he wondered if she was afraid of someone finding out about her male visitor. Not Elliott, though. She couldn't possibly be afraid of that dork.

He sat down. He had hoped she would join him on the sofa, but she chose an armchair instead, keeping her distance. On the table between them was an opened bottle of red wine and a half-filled glass. He was glad there was only one glass.

'Please,' he said. 'Don't let me stop you drinking.'

She shook her head. 'It's okay. I was just winding down.'

'Tough day?'

She shrugged. 'Not really.' A pause. 'Darren—'

'You not doing the gym tonight? I'm asking because of the wine. You wouldn't normally drink before going to the gym.'

'No, I thought I'd give it a miss tonight.'

'But it's Wednesday. Your gym night. You always go to the gym on a Wednesday.'

'Yeah, well, call me crazy, right?' She paused. 'Darren, I—'

'I've missed you, Rebecca. I've missed you so much.'

She stared. 'I know. And I'm sorry. I didn't think it would affect you this much.'

He laughed without humour. 'Why wouldn't it? I was in love with you. I still am. I can't stop thinking about you.'

She took a while to choose her words. 'You need to move on, Darren. Coming after me like this – it's not healthy.'

'I don't want to move on. We're good together. You know that. We make a perfect couple.'

'Nothing's perfect. And nothing lasts for ever. Things change. People change.'

'I haven't changed. I feel exactly the same as I did before.'

'Then maybe it's me who's changed. I don't know. It's hard to explain.'

'Then try. We never really had a proper conversation about this. One minute everything was fine, and the next you said you had to end it. I still don't understand what happened.'

She shook her head. 'I don't think I do either. I got scared. I'm not very good with commitment.'

He nodded. 'I get that. But we can work on it. I'll prove to you how much better things will be when we're a couple again.'

She seemed to agonise over her next choice of words, which made Darren think he didn't want to hear them.

'Darren—' she began.

'My offer still stands, you know.'

She seemed puzzled. 'Offer?'

'Of marriage. I want to marry you. I don't have a ring here with me now, but if you want me to get down on one knee and—'

'I'm not sure you just heard what I said. If I can't be your girlfriend, then I certainly can't be your fiancée.'

'Well, okay, but what then? What can I do to get you back? Name it and it's yours.'

'It's not as simple as that. Feelings don't work that way.'

'But they don't just switch on and off either. You were happy with me. We had some great times. Not one argument. And then suddenly you ran away. You didn't even give me a heads-up.'

'That's not quite true, Darren. I told you I didn't think it was working between us. You're the one who couldn't accept it.'

'And I still don't accept it. It doesn't make any sense. Not unless . . . something happened.' He looked at her pointedly.

'What do you mean?' she asked. 'What are you suggesting?'

'Another guy? Did you meet another guy?'

'There was nobody else, Darren. I told you that at the time. I wouldn't have done that to you. I'm not a horrible person, despite what you might think of me.'

He felt chastised, ashamed that he had allowed himself to throw hurtful accusations at her.

'I don't think you're horrible. I think you're the nicest person I've ever met. I'm just trying to understand what went wrong.'

Tears filmed his eyes. This wasn't going as he had hoped. He seemed to be on the verge of losing her for ever. He had to fix it, but to do that he needed to get inside her head, and right now she wasn't letting him in.

'Darren,' she said softly, 'you can't keep torturing yourself like this. I'm not the right person for you, and that's all there is to it.'

'What about *him*? Is *he* the right person for *you*?'

Rebecca stared. 'Who are you talking about?'

'You know who I mean. The cat guy. Elliott.'

'How . . . how do you know about Elliott?'

He studied her face, trying to work out if the question was genuine. He could believe that she hadn't seen him following her on Monday evening, but surely the bastard would have told her about the meeting last night?

'I saw you with him. You went into his house. You seemed very . . . friendly.'

Rebecca hesitated. 'How do you know his name, and about the cat charity?'

He continued to wonder if she was feigning ignorance, but he played along. 'I asked him.'

She looked irritated. 'You asked him? When?'

'He didn't tell you? Yeah, I knocked on his door last night. We had a good chat.'

'That's not cool, Darren. You shouldn't have done that.'

'Why? What's he to you?'

'A friend.'

'Just a friend? That's not what he told me.'

'What did he say?'

'He said he's your boyfriend.'

She waited a few seconds before replying. 'Okay, so now you know.'

Darren shook his head. 'He's not your boyfriend.'

'Yes, Darren, he is.'

'No. He's not your type.'

'I don't have a type.'

'So what's he got that I haven't?'

'It doesn't work like that. Elliott is—'

'STOP telling me how things work!'

Rebecca jumped, and Darren immediately regretted his forcefulness. He hadn't come here to frighten her, but she was making him act that way. He softened his voice. 'I'm not an idiot, Rebecca. You shouldn't patronise me. I've come here to forgive you.'

It was Rebecca's turn to raise her voice. '*Forgive* me? Now who's being patronising? I don't need your forgiveness. I haven't done anything wrong. We had a fling, and now it's finished. Get over it, Darren, because that's what I've done. I've started a new life with a new boyfriend, and we're both really happy together.'

'Do you sleep with him?'

'That's . . . that's not an appropriate question. Do you really expect me to answer that?'

'You slept with me, so I assume you're sleeping with him.'

'Assume what you like, Darren. I'm not talking about this

anymore, and I'd be grateful if you'd leave now, please.'

She got to her feet, waited for him to do the same. He stayed put.

'Rebecca, please. I don't want to fight. I'm trying to fix things. I'll do whatever you want. Just ... just come back to me. Please.'

'It's too late for that. I'm really sorry.'

He stood up. Moved slowly towards her. He thought she looked apprehensive. There was no need. He wouldn't hurt her. This was about love, not hate. It was about finding the good things in life. She needed to realise that, needed to understand that she couldn't run away from her destiny.

'You're so beautiful,' he told her.

She said nothing. Wouldn't even look him in the eye.

'Can I hold you?' he asked.

'I don't think that would be a good idea.'

'Just a quick hug. Nothing weird. Like friends do.'

'No, Darren. I don't feel like hugging you right now.'

Still he went towards her. 'Why not? We hugged a lot before. Did a lot more than hug. Do you remember? Remember what we did in bed? It was so good, wasn't it?'

'Darren, please. I'd like you to go now.'

He closed in. She stepped back until she was against the chair and could go no further. He brought his hands to her waist. He had always thought his hands fitted perfectly there.

'No, Darren. I'm not doing this.'

He ignored her, pulled her closer to him. Her scent was intoxicating, her flawless beauty staggering.

'No,' she said again. She brushed his hands away, went to

89

step past him. He grabbed her by the arms this time, not hard at first, but then she tried to pull away and he had to tighten his grip, had to keep her there with him, because she was his, she belonged to him, and he wasn't about to give her up easily.

'Darren!' she said, and she twisted and writhed, and he had to restrain her, to wrestle with her, and they fell back onto the armchair, he was on top of her, pressing against her, feeling her soft curves beneath him, and overwhelming desire surged through him, he had to have her again, and he brought his lips down to hers, but she turned her face away and so he had no choice but to take hold of her hair and bring her towards him again, because they had to be together, they needed each other, they were two inseparable parts of a whole. He kissed her, gently at first as he savoured the give of her plump lips, but then harder when she tried to speak, stifling her voice because words were not important now, they were just sounds that meant nothing in comparison to the timelessness of their love for each other.

He wanted more, and knew that she craved it too, and so he brought one hand up beneath her sweater, quickly found her warm breast and squeezed it hard, just like she had asked him to do in the past. Noises caught in her throat, and he knew she was enjoying herself, knew that she had been waiting for this moment for such a long time. She was trying to move beneath him, and he wished they were on a bed or even on the sofa so that they had more room to manoeuvre, but this would have to do, it would still be wonderful for both of them. He pressed his mouth harder against hers, flicked his tongue out, probing, finding at first only a barrier of smooth enamel, but

90

then she allowed him in, clearly desperate to feel him inside her again, and so he bowed to her wishes, began to explore the warm wetness of her mouth.

The pain was excruciating. His whole body catapulted backwards as the agony shot through him. He brought his hand to his mouth and caught what seemed to be a geyser of blood, and his mind froze in terror at the thought that his whole tongue might be gone, that he might never be able to speak properly again.

And then there was more pain as Rebecca's knee was rammed into his groin. All thoughts of being amorous vanished in an instant. He didn't know which injury to concentrate on first, and that led to his next oversight as Rebecca freed her leg and launched a foot into his face. He fell back and landed hard on the floor. Rebecca threw herself from the chair and tried to jump across him. It was all he could do to reach up and snag her ankle. She fell awkwardly onto the coffee table and he heard glass shattering, and he hoped he hadn't hurt her badly even though she had been so violent with him, because she was his angel, he wouldn't hurt her for the world, and he was already preparing his apologies, his pleas for forgiveness, when he caught a glimpse of the wine bottle being swung in a wide arc towards his head before everything turned to black.

11

He awoke coughing and spluttering in a furnace of pain. His mouth, his groin, his head – all on fire. He lay on his back, staring at the ceiling which seemed to be pulsating slowly in and out, making him feel seasick.

He raised his head and blinked. He could see two of everything, so he blinked some more, but the images still didn't coalesce properly. He tried sitting up. He heard the tinkle of broken glass, and there was an intense whiff of wine that wasn't helping his nausea.

Sitting there on the floor, he looked down at himself and tried to remember what had happened. Why he was so wet and so red?

And then the pieces began to reassemble. He recalled how Rebecca had taken such a strange and aggressive turn against him for no reason, lashing out wildly. And then, yes, the wine bottle . . .

He looked again at the dark fragments around him. It must have hit him with some force because wine bottles don't break easily.

He turned his eyes on the coffee table. Rebecca's wineglass was also broken, and again he hoped she hadn't been hurt in the fall. It had been a simple misunderstanding, that was all. He didn't want her to suffer because of her confused state of mind.

He tried getting to his feet and almost fell over again, so he settled on the armchair and waited for the seasickness to abate before making another attempt.

Where was Rebecca? Had she gone to get help for him?

'Rebecca?' he called. '*Rebecca?*' His voice sounded strange to him, as if muffled. He wondered if it was because of the blow to his head, but then he remembered what had happened to his tongue in the throes of their passion for each other.

He put his hands on the arms of the chair and pushed himself up, then stood there swaying for a minute before trying to walk. He staggered over to the window, glass crunching beneath his shoes. There was no sign of Rebecca's car.

He turned, saw a mirror on the wall, made his way to it slowly.

He looked like he had just walked out of a war zone. Blood ran down his head and from the corners of his mouth. It had mixed with the red wine and drenched his shirt. He turned his head to one side and studied the massive bump he saw there. He touched it gingerly, winced with the pain. Then he opened his mouth and examined his tongue. It was massively swollen and there was a deep laceration near its tip, still oozing blood.

He wondered what had led Rebecca to act so out of character. Was she ill?

Or was it something to do with the bastard Elliott?

She had said he was her boyfriend now, but that wasn't the case. That couldn't possibly be true. Besides, she had performed her disappearing act before she had even heard of Elliott.

Hadn't she?

Darren gave this some more thought. Could she have known Elliott back then, when they were still in a relationship? Could she have begun an affair?

The thought infuriated him, but he quickly dismissed it. For one thing, Rebecca wasn't like that; she was too moral. For another, he would have known. He could read her like a book. It would have been so obvious.

So what was happening?

More answers were needed. More data.

He would have to speak to her again.

He toyed with the idea of waiting in Rebecca's house. She would have to come home sometime. But there was also the possibility that she wouldn't be alone – that she would return with the police or somebody who might do him harm. Her confused state made her actions unpredictable. He couldn't take that risk. Best to retreat and lick his wounds for now, then come back later. He would definitely bring flowers next time.

He went upstairs to the bathroom. At the sink he washed the blood from his face, then wiped his jacket down with a wet flannel. He rinsed his mouth out with cold water numerous times until the water appeared more pink than red.

He descended the stairs and left the house, pausing for a minute on the driveway when the world seemed to sway around him and he thought he was going to vomit. Eventually, he made it to his car. He drove slowly back to his hotel, praying he wouldn't black out again and crash.

Before wandering through the hotel lobby, Darren zipped up his jacket to hide his stained shirt. He still got the impression that people were staring at him. He had to share the lift with a large middle-aged woman who kept glancing at him and wrinkling her nose as though she thought he was a wino.

When he was alone in his room, he stripped and showered and tended to his wounds. The lump on his head showed no signs of subsiding, and it felt as though someone was inside his skull trying to batter their way out, but at least it had stopped bleeding and he could focus his eyes again. So that was something positive.

His tongue was another matter. Looking at it in the bathroom mirror, it seemed to have a large gobbet of red jelly at its tip. He hoped that was a good sign, and that it didn't indicate that part of it was about to drop off, or that it would end up being forked like a snake's.

Wrapping a towel around his waist, he returned to the bedroom and sat on the edge of the bed, his mind consumed by Rebecca.

What had got into her? She liked a little bit of play-acting, but this was way over the top. Was she aware of how much she had hurt him? And where was she now?

He wondered if she had joined some kind of cult. That Elliott guy looked like someone who might be in a cult. Those people fuck with your mind, make you do strange things. Yeah, that was a possibility.

Darren swung his legs onto the bed and lay back against

the pillows. Tiredness washed over him, and his head was still pounding. He closed his eyes. Seconds later he was asleep.

When he awoke again, he wasn't sure how much time had passed. An hour? Two? He checked the bedside clock and was surprised when he saw that it was almost half past eight. Rebecca would normally be at the gym now. Except that she had said she wasn't going tonight, which was weird. She always went to the gym on a Wednesday. Further evidence that her life had become messed up.

He decided it was time for another little chat. Nothing physical this time, though, no matter how much she might demand it from him. She would just have to be patient. He would satisfy her needs later, once they'd got to the bottom of what was affecting her so badly.

He dressed and left his room. Down in the hotel lobby, the smell of cooking drifted to him from the restaurant, nauseating him again. He hadn't eaten for hours, but knew he'd throw up just to look at a plate of food.

Outside, he was grateful to fill his lungs with the cold air. It seemed to clear both his body and his mind. He went to his parked car and unlocked it. Inside, blood was caked on the seats and the steering wheel. He didn't want to waste time cleaning it off, so he ignored it and drove away.

When he got to Rebecca's house, there was still no sign of her car. No lights showing in any of the windows either. Still worth checking, he thought, so he went to the front door and rang the bell. Tried knocking too. No answer.

He returned to his car. I can wait, he thought. She's got to come home eventually.

He put the radio on to help pass the time. After a few minutes he switched on the interior light and flipped down the visor to check himself out in the vanity mirror. He still looked like shit. The lump over his temple was like a billiard ball, and his complexion was as pale as a vampire's. He hoped he wouldn't scare the crap out of Rebecca. He would have to be extra nice to compensate for his appearance.

Flowers! Shit, he had promised himself he would bring flowers. Too late now. The only place he'd get flowers would be a supermarket or petrol station, and Rebecca hated cheap shit like that. No good getting chocolates either, because she was always watching her weight.

She had looked so good earlier. Svelte – was that the right word? He thought it was. She was certainly shapely. Soft and yet firm at the same time. Darren held up his hand, recalling the way it had cupped her breast earlier. To be continued, he thought.

He switched the light off and settled into his seat. He was tired again, but knew he couldn't allow himself to drift off to sleep. This was too important.

An hour later, he began to worry. She's not coming back, he thought. Even though part of her wants to see me again, her brain is too screwed up to allow it. Or maybe something bad has happened to her. She could be in trouble. Maybe other cult members have kidnapped her. She might be desperate for my help.

Don't panic, he told himself. Give her time. Everything might still be okay.

Another hour passed. His stomach was rumbling, but he

couldn't think about food. His head was throbbing again, too.

Shit, where was she?

He heard footsteps. He turned as a figure drew alongside the car. An elderly man walking his dog. The man lowered his head to peer into the car as he passed, locking eyes with Darren. After the man had moved on a few metres, both he and the dog turned to look again at the car.

He suspects something, Darren thought. Might have noticed me when I first arrived, and how he's wondering what I'm up to. Nosy old git.

He let it go, but about twenty minutes later the man came back. He stared challengingly at Darren through the windscreen. When he had passed, Darren checked his rear-view mirror and saw how the man paused for a few seconds, watching the car.

He's looking at my number plate, Darren thought. He's going to report me.

The man began walking again, tugging at his dog to follow. Darren saw them disappear into a house further down the road. He imagined the man at one of the windows of the house, studying him, phone in hand as he debated whether to call the cops.

Darren didn't want to have to explain himself to the police. Especially not with blood all over his leather upholstery. He would have to move.

He started up the car, put the lights on, drove away.

You can relax now, you old fart, he thought.

He decided he would come back later. Much later, once all the interfering busybodies were safely tucked up in bed.

In the meantime, he wasn't planning to be idle.

There was someone else he could talk to – someone who knew a lot more than he'd already admitted.

12

Elliott was in a buoyant mood. Trade at the shop had been unusually brisk, and he had felt very managerial in the way he had handled each and every customer. It seemed to him that the business with Rebecca and Darren had bolstered his self-confidence. He had handled things perfectly and with great maturity. And even though it was highly unlikely that he would ever encounter the lovely Rebecca again, her praise had stayed with him for the whole day, propping him up. For once, he felt in control – the driver rather than a passenger.

He was watching reruns of *The Big Bang Theory*. Bill was on the sofa next to him, curled up asleep. Occasionally he would snore, and Elliott would pause the programme just to listen to him. It was too cute and funny to ignore. Later, when Elliott went up to bed, Bill would probably follow. He would settle at the foot of the bed, refusing to budge and making it difficult for Elliott to find a comfortable position for his legs.

Speaking of bed, Elliott was already yawning. He decided he'd get to the end of this episode and then turn in. He needed to be refreshed in the morning when he donned the mantle of Manager Man once more.

The doorbell rang. Bill raised his head in alarm. Elliott groaned his displeasure. Not now, Heidi, he thought. I don't want any more questions about Rebecca.

He plodded to the front door in his slippers. Opened it. Sighed inwardly when he saw it was Darren.

'Darren!' he said. He tried to sound cheery about it, because his rule was to be as nice as he could to everyone, even when they were preventing him from going to bed.

'Hello again, Elliott. Mind if I come in?'

'Well, actually—' Elliott began, but Darren was already moving past him. Elliott sighed audibly this time, but he closed the door and followed Darren inside. He hoped this wouldn't take long.

He showed Darren into the living room and offered him a chair. Darren sat down and eyed Bill, who was glaring back at him with apparent disfavour. Elliott resumed his seat on the sofa and picked up the remote. He paused playback rather than stopping it, to make it clear he was in the middle of something. It was only when he turned to Darren again that he noticed the bump on the side of his head.

'What happened to your head?' he asked.

Darren started to raise a hand to his temple, then changed his mind. 'An accident. I had an accident.' When he spoke, it sounded like he had a mouthful of cotton.

'That looks nasty. Have you seen a doctor?'

'No. I'm okay. It's fine.'

'How'd you do it?'

Darren hesitated. 'It was an accident.'

Elliott realised he wasn't going to get any further with this line of conversation; and besides, his bed was calling him.

'What can I do for you?'

'I think you know.'

Of course, Elliott thought. What else could it be?

'You mean Rebecca?'

'Yes. Rebecca. Is she here?'

'Here? No.'

Darren glanced towards the ceiling. 'Upstairs, maybe?'

'No. She's not in the house. We . . . we don't see each other every single day.'

'Uh-huh. Then where is she?'

'I don't know. Probably at home.'

'She's not at home.'

'How do you know?'

Darren ignored the question. 'I need to talk to her.'

'Darren, we discussed this, didn't we? Rebecca has made it clear that—'

'But it's urgent now.'

'Urgent? Why?'

'You tell me.'

This was making no sense to Elliott. But then he wondered why it would. The guy obviously had some issues. His thought processes probably weren't like everybody else's.

'I . . . I'm not sure what you want me to tell you.'

'Just the truth. I think that's always the best approach.'

'I already told you the truth. Have you forgotten? Remember when we spoke yesterday, and I said to you—'

'I saw her today.'

'Saw who? Rebecca?'

'Yes.'

'You saw her today?'

'Yes.'

'Okay. Where was that?'

'At her house. She invited me to her house, so I went.'

Elliott stared at his visitor. He wasn't sure what to believe. Darren was living in a fantasy world. Dealing with those fantasies without upsetting the man might require some delicate handling.

'Why did she invite you?'

'To talk. And . . . you know . . .'

'No. What?'

'To have sex.'

And now Elliott knew how delusional Darren was.

'You had sex?'

'Not exactly. I put a stop to it. I wanted to sort things out first.'

'And did you?'

'No. That's why I'm here. To sort it out.'

'Well, I'm not sure I can help you with that. If Rebecca won't talk to you, I can't make her.'

'I'm not sure that's true.'

Irritation started to build in Elliott. 'Why do you say that?'

'You told me you're her boyfriend.'

For a moment, Elliott debated whether to come clean, to back out of this ridiculous situation, but he still felt an allegiance to Rebecca. He didn't want to saddle her with being continually persecuted by Darren.

'Yes, that's true.'

Darren twisted his mouth into a doubtful smile. 'So you can talk to her.'

'Talk to her about what? I don't know what you expect from me.'

Darren suddenly lurched forward, causing Elliott to think he was about to launch himself at him, but he moved no further than the edge of his seat.

'You said you were her boyfriend. And when I went to see her, she said the same thing. She said you're a couple. A *couple*. Do you know what it means to be a couple?' His face had contorted, become ugly.

'Darren, you need to relax. I'm not trying to upset you. I want to help you, but I really don't—'

'A couple do everything together. Each one knows what the other one thinks. We had that, me and Rebecca. If you've got it too, then you can persuade Rebecca.'

'Persuade her to do what?'

'To come back to me.'

'Why would I do that? Why would any man talk his girlfriend into going back to her ex? That's not reasonable.'

And then Darren jumped to his feet, and Bill scarpered out of the room, and Elliott was starting to feel uneasy about this.

'I am reasonable. I am more than reasonable. I need her back. And I need her to explain it all to me. I need . . . the lies . . . to stop.'

He was becoming increasingly agitated, as if on the edge of some kind of breakdown. Elliott had never had to deal at such a personal level with someone who had problems like this. He didn't know what to do to calm the situation down.

'What lies?'

'*Her* lies. And . . . and *your* lies.'

'Darren, I'm not lying to you. Neither of us wants to hurt you.'

'You do. You both do. You're working against me, and I don't know why. I don't . . . know . . . what . . .'

He clutched at his head and grimaced, as though experiencing an intense pain. Elliott wondered if he was having a stroke. He stood up and moved towards Darren.

'Are you okay? Can I do something?'

Darren let out a shriek and then proceeded to make hawking noises in his throat. He rolled something round in his mouth and then spat it out. A large globule of what looked like red jelly splatted onto Elliott's rug.

Elliott felt his stomach turn. He had never seen anything like this. Was it a medical emergency?

'Should I call an ambulance?'

Doubled over, Darren held up a palm in objection. Elliott watched as the man appeared to recover slowly, but his eyes were continually drawn to the congealed mass on his rug.

'I'm okay,' Darren said. As he did so, blood poured from his mouth.

'That's not okay,' Elliott answered. 'You're bleeding.'

'I bit my tongue, that's all.' He said it as though it was an everyday occurrence, but it seemed a lot more than that to Elliott.

And then things started to come together in his mind. The bump on the head, the bleeding . . . and his visit to Rebecca, a woman who would never have invited Darren to her house and who now seemed, for some unfathomable reason, to be out of his reach.

'Darren, did something bad happen today?'

'What do you mean?'

'Something between you and Rebecca? Did it get violent?'

Darren shook his head. 'She's not herself. She's confused. You've fucked with her brain.'

'Where is she, Darren?'

'I don't fucking know, okay? That's why I'm here. Because *you* know, and you're not telling me. I need you to sort this shit out. She doesn't love you; she loves me. She has to come back. We have to be *together*.'

This was way beyond social awkwardness. This was a man deranged. Dangerous, even.

'All right. Listen to me. I'll make you a promise, okay? I'll talk to Rebecca, and then I'll see if I can get her to explain things to you. How does that sound?'

Darren thought about this as he swayed unsteadily on his feet. 'Yeah. Sounds good. I . . .'

He stopped speaking and lowered his head again, and it took a few seconds for Elliott to realise he was crying.

'Hey, don't cry. I'm sure we can sort this out.'

Darren lifted his gaze, sniffed wetly. His face was bathed in blood and snot and tears, and he looked about ready to keel over at any second.

'Are you in a cult?' he asked.

'A what?'

'A cult. Like, with a bunch of religious nutcases?'

'No,' Elliott answered. 'I'm not in a cult.'

Darren studied him for a while, then said, 'I should go home now.'

Elliott wanted to breathe a sigh of relief. 'Yeah, I think that's a good idea. Would you like me to call your mum?'

'My mum? Why would you want to call her?'

'Well, I just thought—'

'No, I don't want you to call my mother. How old do you think I am?'

'Sorry. I just thought—'

'You want to know something?' Darren said.

'What's that?'

'I think of you as the bastard. That's kind of my name for you.'

Elliott didn't know what to do with this information. 'Oh. Okay.'

'But you could prove me wrong. If you help me, I would be in your debt for ever.'

'I'll, er, I'll see what I can do.'

Darren nodded again, then moved past Elliott, banging into him as he went.

Bill was sitting in the hall, watching the departing stranger with wide eyes. Darren looked down at the animal.

'Your cat has the eyes of a fucking devil,' he said. 'Ugly little shit.'

Elliott contained his anger. He was very protective of Bill. He put his hand on Darren's shoulder as he escorted him to the door, and when he got there, he had to resist the impulse to push him out into the street.

When he had stepped outside, Darren stopped and turned.

'You'll talk to Rebecca?'

'I will. I promise.'

'She has my number. I'll be expecting her call.'

'Great.'

'I hope you can convince her.'

'I'll certainly try.'

'Either way, I'll come back here tomorrow night.'

'What?'

'To thank you. Or not, as the case may be. Eight o'clock okay?'

'What?'

'I'll see you at eight.'

And then he turned and staggered down the road, and Elliott wondered what the hell he'd got himself involved in.

13

He was expecting Rebecca to sound tired and not a little displeased at the lateness of the call, but in fact she sounded remarkably upbeat.

'Hi, Elliott,' she said. 'What's up?'

'Sorry to call you so late, and for ringing you yet again – I don't want you to start thinking I'm another stalker or anything...'

'Don't worry about it, Elliott. What can I do for you?'

'Yeah, well, it's just that he came to my house again.'

'Who? Darren?'

'Yeah. And he was acting pretty weird.'

'Oh, I'm really sorry about that. I didn't want this to happen. Did he give you a hard time?'

Elliott thought about this. Was he given a hard time? Or was he just being the wuss that he usually is, unable to deal with a minor drama?

'Not exactly. I just... I don't know what to do with the guy, you know?'

'Yeah, he's a character, isn't he? Harmless, though.'

'Yeah, about that. I mean, he won't get violent or anything, will he?'

She laughed, and he felt embarrassed to have asked. 'No. He just needs to be told what's what. You have to be firm with him.'

'Uh-huh. Only ... he had a few things wrong with him tonight.'

'Like what?'

'Like a massive bump on his head, and he was spitting up blood.'

'That doesn't sound good.'

'No. He wouldn't let me call a doctor, though. I don't suppose ... you might know anything about it?'

'Me? Why would I know about it?'

'He says ... he says he saw you today, at your house.'

'At my house? He doesn't even know where I live now.'

'He said you contacted him and invited him over.'

'Why on earth would I do that? I'm doing my best to avoid him.'

Elliott decided not to mention the sex that Darren had thrown into the conversation. This was already getting too ridiculous.

'That's what I thought. I just wanted to check it with you. So you haven't seen him, then?'

'No. Not since Monday night when you came to my aid, kind sir.'

The flattery distracted Elliott for a moment. God, what he wouldn't give to spend a few more hours in her company.

'All right, but . . .'

'Yes?'

'I was just wondering . . . Darren is obsessed with you.'

'I know.'

'I mean *really* obsessed. Unhealthily obsessed. And I was thinking, after what you said about being firm with him . . .'

'Yeah?'

'I wonder if you could have a word with him. You know, to set him straight, once and for all.'

Silence. And then: 'I'm not sure that would be a good idea.'

'You don't? I mean, I don't want to push you into anything you don't want to do, but he's getting pretty insistent. He made it clear he's not giving up on you until you talk to him.'

'I understand, but you have to see it from my point of view. I've known Darren for a while. I know how he thinks. If I talk to him, it will just encourage him, and if he finds me again he'll make my life a misery. You wouldn't want to put me through that, would you?'

'No. Absolutely not. It's just . . . I don't know what to do with him. The guy needs help that I can't give him. He even said that if you don't call him, he'll come back to my house again tomorrow.'

'Shit, I'm so sorry. You did such a good thing for me, and now it's causing you all kinds of trouble.'

Elliott felt a stab of guilt. 'No, it's okay. I can handle it. I could just do without him dropping in at my house every night for the foreseeable future.'

'I'm sure he'll give up soon. Be firm. Stick to our story. I'm your girlfriend. If you want to be more convincing, you can

113

tell him about the birthmark I've got high up on the inside of my left thigh, and the flower tattoo on my bum.'

Elliott suddenly felt very hot, and when he next spoke, his voice was a little higher in pitch than it had been.

'Er, okay. You think that'll work?'

'If we can convince him that you and me are an item, he'll definitely give up. I've told him the same thing, so we just need to keep our stories straight.'

'Okay,' Elliott said. 'I'll try that.'

'Thank you. You're so sweet. Do this for me, and when he drops off the scene I'll definitely take you for a drink.'

Elliott was glad she couldn't see the huge daft smile on his face. 'No problem.'

'Speak to you soon, Elliott. Goodnight. And good luck.'

'Night, Rebecca.'

He ended the call. She was right. He could handle this. He was Manager Man. He just needed to be assertive, even if that was something usually beyond his reach. If he and Rebecca could carry on singing from the same hymn sheet then

Something struck him.

The same hymn sheet.

What was it Rebecca had said?

I've told him the same thing.

When? When did she tell Darren that? She explicitly said that she hadn't seen Darren since Monday evening, so where and when did this discussion take place?

Rebecca had done a good job of raising his temperature earlier, but now he felt distinctly chilly.

14

Darren had slept for nearly ten hours without interruption, and felt much better for it. Not that his appearance reflected any improvement. The lump on his head had turned very dark and had scabbed over, making it even more noticeable, and his skin still looked incredibly sallow. More positively, the split in his tongue seemed to have healed again, despite the pink spittle stains on his pillow.

He'd thought he was going to die at Elliott's house. The pain in his head had been immense – as though his skull was about to explode because of a build-up of uncontainable pressure. Had the blow with the bottle done some permanent damage – fractured his skull, maybe? Might he have another attack?

At least he was hungry. That was a good sign. He hadn't eaten last night, partly because of his extreme fatigue but also because of his tongue.

He washed, dressed, and went down to breakfast. He was fully aware that the member of staff who showed him to his table was stealing glances at his head wound. He ordered coffee, then ventured to the buffet tables. There were more surreptitious peeks at him as he piled all the components of an English breakfast onto his plate.

Back at his table, the coffee was already waiting. He poured a cup, added milk, and took a sip. His tongue burned like it had been dipped in acid, and he almost shrieked with the pain.

He gathered himself, waited for the pain to diminish. He wasn't going to be defeated, wasn't going to allow himself to die of starvation. He cut off a sliver of fried egg, blew on it until it was cool, then put it in his mouth. His tongue protested but it was bearable, and the taste was divine. He grew bolder, pushing increasingly substantial forkfuls of food down, until he was going at it like a man who had just been rescued from a desert.

As he neared the end of his meal, he noticed that a boy of about five or six years old was staring intently at him from the next table. Darren didn't know whether it was because of the way he was eating or his swollen head. In any case, he sent the kid a friendly smile.

The boy recoiled in horror and squeezed up against his mother for reassurance.

Darren took out his phone and switched on the front-facing camera. He bared his teeth and saw the blood staining them, as though he'd just used them to rip open the flesh of a living animal.

Shit.

He let out a sigh, then abandoned the table and went back to his room, where he hung the 'Do Not Disturb' sign on the door handle before locking himself in.

He had no plans to go anywhere today.

In the bathroom, he rinsed the blood from his mouth, then brushed his teeth. Best to skip lunch.

He returned to the bedroom, occupied the sole armchair and turned on the television. Before getting too settled, he checked his phone. No messages, no missed calls.

She would phone eventually, though. Elliott had promised, hadn't he? He said he would talk to Rebecca. If he and Rebecca were as close as they claimed, she wouldn't deny him.

He couldn't possibly leave the hotel today, not with such an important call about to come in. He wanted to be alone when he spoke to her, didn't want anyone hearing him pledge his undying love to her.

He turned up the ringer volume on his phone to maximum, then placed it on his lap in readiness.

Won't be long now, he told himself.

Elliott spent the day worrying.

All he wanted was a boring life. No drama. No unforeseen events. Certainly no blood-spouting stalkers. What had he done to deserve that?

The paradox was that he knew he'd done the right thing. Given the same situation again, he would act in exactly the same way. What he hadn't bargained for, of course, was Darren.

There's no need to be afraid, he told himself. Darren's harmless. Eccentric, yes, but also harmless. Rebecca told you so.

But still he dreaded the thought of tonight's meeting. Confrontation wasn't his strong suit, especially with someone whose behaviour might be unpredictable. He certainly could never have predicted last night's events. It's not often that a random stranger comes into your house, spits blood on your rug and demands that you give up the girlfriend you never had in the first place.

And about that girlfriend . . .

That was worrying him too. Had she lied to him about not talking to Darren? If so, why? And what else might she have lied about?

He jumped when the shop door opened. Heidi again. She of the swishing ponytail and the sunny smiles.

'Hey, Elliott!' she said. 'How's it hanging, fella?'

'If you mean the noose that's around my neck, I think it's probably hanging exactly as it should.'

'Uh-oh. Someone's on a downer. What's up?'

'For one thing, I never understand how you can be so insanely happy all the time. For another, I'm in a bit of a pickle and I need your advice.'

'Pickles are my speciality. Except for dill pickles. Can't stand them. If you ever buy me a burger, ask them to leave off the dill.'

'I'll remember that. Can we get back to my problem now?'

'We may. Shoot.'

'Okay. It's about Darren.'

'Who's Darren?'

'I told you about him. The guy who was stalking Rebecca.'

'What about him?'

'Well . . . I think he's stalking me now.'

'He's not choosy, is he?'

'I'm serious. He came to my house.'

Heidi's expression became suddenly graver. 'What?'

'Yeah. Twice. He seems to think I can hook him up with Rebecca.'

'And presumably you told him you can't do that?'

'Of course. I don't think he believes me.'

'Did you tell him you really don't know anything about this woman?'

Elliott hesitated. 'Not exactly.'

'What does that mean?'

'It means . . . it means I told him kind of the opposite. I told him she's my girlfriend.'

'Your *girlfriend*? For fuck's sake, Elliott. Why the hell did you do that?'

'I told you. That's what Rebecca asked me to do. That's our story.'

'Why? Why is it your story? If she'd told you to say you were her long-lost sister in drag, would that have been your story?'

'No, that's just silly.'

'Whereas this isn't, right? Telling everyone you're dating a supermodel is perfectly normal.'

'It's not outside the realms of possibility.'

'Yes, Elliott, it is. And besides, that's not the point. What you've told this freak is simply not true, and now it sounds like you've landed yourself in a ton of shit because of it.'

'Well, I wouldn't say it was as much as a ton.'

Heidi stared at him. 'You're unbelievable,' she said. She walked away from him, turned, walked back again.

'This guy . . .'

'Darren.'

'This guy Darren. What's he like?'

'What do you mean?'

'Well, I'm hardly interested in his star sign or his favourite colour of Smarties. What's he like? Is he an axe-wielding maniac or just your average serial killer?'

'Neither. He was exactly as Rebecca described him. A harmless guy who's a little eccentric.'

'Harmless?'

'Yes.'

'Are you sure?'

Elliott thought about this. Could he really be sure, after only two brief meetings, that Darren would never cause him harm? The man definitely looked as though he'd already been in a fight. Maybe he wasn't as inoffensive as Rebecca claimed.

'I think so.'

'Thinking so is not good enough, Elliott. In a situation like this, you have to assume the worst.'

'Why?'

'If you were a woman, you wouldn't even think of asking that question. We have to protect ourselves constantly from men like him.'

'I'm sure he's not as bad as that.'

'Elliott, he was stalking a woman. However you want to try and defend him, acting like that is simply not acceptable. Banging on your door and insisting that you become his dating agency is not acceptable either.'

'So what do you suggest?'

Heidi thought for a moment. 'Where did you leave things with him?'

'He said he wanted to talk to Rebecca, and he asked me to have a word with her and get her to ring him. And then he went away.'

'Okay, and did you contact Rebecca?'

'I did.'

'And?'

'She said she wanted nothing to do with him.'

'I'm sure she did, but that's no reason to leave you to deal with the fallout.'

'That's not what she's doing. I helped her because she was in trouble. I've only got myself to blame for any fallout. What I don't know is what to do about it.'

Heidi took some time to think about it. 'All right. Darren wants to talk to Rebecca, but Rebecca won't talk to Darren. Did Darren say what he'll do if things don't go his way?'

Elliott shrugged. 'I guess I'll find out tonight.'

'Tonight? What happens tonight?'

'He said he's going to come to my house again. Eight o'clock.'

'To do what?'

'To talk about the situation. Rebecca said that I should be firm with him, tell him again that she and I are a couple, and that he needs to stop pestering us.'

'Okay, well, no offence to Rebecca, but I think you should ignore her advice.'

'I'm not sure that's—'

'Second of all, call the police.'

'The police?'

'Yes, Elliott. The police. There's a crazed stalker turning up at your house tonight. If anything justifies calling the cops in, it's that.'

'I really don't think I should be bothering the—'

'Elliott! Stop pretending this is nothing, just because you can't see past a pretty girl's looks. She probably didn't mean to, but Rebecca has royally dropped you in it, and this is the only way to dig yourself out. Maybe you're right and Darren is just a bit slow on the uptake, but he's more likely to listen to the cops than he is to you. If they have a quiet word with him, you'll probably never see him again.'

Elliott considered her advice and could find little fault in it. On top of that, there was still the nagging suspicion that Rebecca may have lied to him. He had already decided not to share that information with Heidi. He wanted to cling on to the hope that it was all a misunderstanding.

But still, what Heidi said made a lot of sense.

'All right,' he said.

'You'll call them?'

'Yes.'

'Go on, then.'

'What, now?'

'No time like the present. Go ahead. I'll mind the shop if you want to go into the back room to do it.'

'I—'

'Go! Go now!'

He got up from his chair. 'You know, you can be very bossy,' he said.

15

It never rang. Not a peep out of it the whole day.

Darren looked at his phone screen again. No missed calls, no messages.

He was very disappointed.

Elliott had made him a promise. Which meant one of two things: either the bastard had not called Rebecca or Rebecca had said no.

Either way, he thought, it's me who suffers. And that just isn't fair.

His phone told him it was almost six o'clock in the evening. He doubted that she was going to call now. He couldn't just sit here waiting. Besides, he was famished.

He decided to ring down for room service, order something soft and mushy that wouldn't damage his tongue.

And after that, if he still hadn't received the promised call, he would pay another visit to the bastard.

*

The police turned up at a quarter to eight, which Elliott thought was cutting it a bit fine, given that his unsolicited appointment with Darren was at eight.

But that's okay, he told himself. They're busy people, and this must be a low priority for them. In fact, I really don't know why I went along with Heidi on this, but here we are, so let's just go through the motions.

'Cup of tea?' Elliott asked.

'No, ta,' one of the uniformed officers said. There were two of them, both male, one with a beard. Elliott didn't know why, but he felt intimidated by them. More intimidated than he had been by Darren, in fact.

As they all took their seats in the living room, Bill came in and did his staring act.

'Here comes the Old Bill,' Elliott said. Then he quickly added, 'His name's Bill, you see. And he's getting on a bit.'

The officers stared at him in bemusement.

'I'm PC Lincoln,' said the bearded one, 'and this is PC York.'

'A tale of two cities,' Elliott said with a smile.

They didn't smile back.

'Sorry?' Lincoln said.

'Your names. A tale of— Never mind.'

They continued to stare, emanating contempt, and Elliott was already wishing this ordeal was over.

'So,' Lincoln said, 'if you could just give us a little background on this situation you're in . . .'

'Certainly,' Elliott answered. He decided to play it straight from now on. Stick to the facts and avoid trying to be amusing or clever.

He launched into his story, starting with the initial meeting with Rebecca and ending with a reminder that Darren was due to darken his door again in the next few minutes. The officers listened intently and made occasional notes, their faces impassive.

'This Rebecca woman,' York said. It was the first time he had opened his mouth. 'Have you got a surname for her?'

Elliott thought about it and realised he hadn't. 'No, sorry.'

'Address?'

'No, I haven't got that either.'

'What about Darren's surname?' Lincoln asked.

'Er, no.'

'His address?'

Elliott shook his head.

'Phone number?'

'Sorry.' He was beginning to feel ill-equipped and inadequate.

'Okay. But Darren threatened you, yes?'

'Well, not exactly.'

'What does that mean?'

'He didn't threaten me as such. He just wants me to help him get together with Rebecca. He's infatuated with her.'

'And you think he's mentally unstable?'

'Well, they're not the words I would use.'

'What words would you use?'

'Like I said before, he has behavioural difficulties.'

'What type of difficulties?'

'I . . . I don't know. I'm not a psychologist.'

'But you would say he's a danger to others?'

'I . . . Probably not, no.'

'So he's not dangerous and he's not mentally unstable?'

'Not that I can tell.' Elliott realised this wasn't going well. 'But I don't know him well enough. The very fact that he's been harassing a young woman on the street—'

'Harassing? You're sure about that?'

'Well . . .'

'Or just walking in the same direction as her?'

'No, it was much more that. He stood outside for ages, just watching my house while she was here. If he wasn't harassing her, why is he now harassing me? Why would he keep knocking on my door and asking about her?'

'Perhaps because he has behavioural difficulties?'

Hoist with my own petard, Elliott thought, or whatever that phrase was they'd learnt when he did *Hamlet* at school. He shifted uncomfortably in his chair.

'Look,' said Lincoln, 'I'll be honest with you. In terms of any criminal offence being committed, you haven't given us a lot to go on.'

'But—'

'That being said, we'll hang around for a bit and have a chat with this Darren guy when he shows up. Fair enough?'

'Yes,' Elliott said. Despite the awkwardness he felt, the outcome was what he'd hoped for. A few stern words from this menacing pair would surely be enough to send Darren scuttling for cover, never to return.

'So,' York said, 'if that offer of a cuppa still stands?'

'Absolutely.' Elliott jumped up and went to the kitchen. It took him a while to select mugs that seemed manly enough for his visitors – nothing with cats on, for example, and certainly not the *Mamma Mia* mug that Heidi had bought him. He could hear the rumble of voices coming from the living room, but not what was being said. He imagined they were dismissing this exercise as a complete waste of time, and decided not to venture back in there until he'd finished making the tea.

When he carried in the tray of drinks, complete with a plate of assorted biscuits to help keep the law on his side, he saw Lincoln checking his watch. Elliott glanced at his wall clock: five past eight, and no sign of Darren.

'Penguin?' he asked.

'Sorry?' Lincoln said.

'There are some Penguin biscuits there, to go with the tea. Or are you more of a Hobnob aficionado?'

'We're okay, thanks.' Lincoln said this just as his partner was stretching a hand towards the plate, causing him to withdraw immediately, a look of dismay on his face.

'I'm sure Darren will be here any minute,' Elliott said. 'He seemed very determined.'

As he resumed his seat, he considered the possibilities. In a fit of optimism, he wondered whether Rebecca had changed her mind and decided to ring Darren after all, in which case Darren might have decided there was no need to come over. Or maybe Darren had just come to his senses. Either of those scenarios was fine by Elliott.

On the other hand, the more likely possibility was that Darren was simply not very punctual.

But then five past became ten past, and ten past became a

quarter past. The policemen put their empty mugs back on the tray, PC York still eyeing up the biscuits.

Lincoln said, 'Looks like your friend is a no-show tonight.'

The officers got to their feet. Elliott followed suit.

'I think he'll still come. Couldn't you hang on a bit longer?'

Lincoln frowned. 'If he does show up, and you think things are getting a little out of hand, you could always give us another call. And maybe if you told him you've spoken to us, that might persuade him to leave you alone.'

Elliott wasn't convinced, and he really didn't want to allow things to get to the point of being 'out of hand', not even 'a little'.

'Hasn't he already overstepped the line, though. I mean, harassing me and stalking a young woman . . .'

'Not really. From what you've told us, he's just had a couple of chats with you, and you can't tell us where he lives or even what his full name is. And without some corroboration from the lady involved—'

'Wait. I have her phone number. What if you rang her now, got her side of the story?'

The officers looked at each other, then Lincoln nodded and produced a mobile phone. 'What's the number?' he asked.

Elliott found Rebecca in his contacts and reeled the number off while PC Lincoln typed it in. He waited hopefully while Lincoln brought the phone to his ear. It felt to him that the situation had escalated somewhat. Heidi had convinced him that it wasn't something to be dismissed lightly, and that it might in fact be downright dangerous. He just wanted out of it now. Let the police, Rebecca and Darren sort it out between themselves.

'Hello?' Lincoln said. 'Am I speaking to Rebecca? ... My name's Police Constable Lincoln ... Yes, that's right. I'm at the home of a Mr Elliott Whiston. I believe you know him? ... Right. He's made a complaint about a man called Darren ... Yes, Darren. The complaint involves an allegation of stalking committed against you by Darren on Monday evening, and that since then, Darren has been harassing Mr Whiston to discover your whereabouts. I wonder what more you can tell us about it?'

Lincoln listened for a while, throwing in an occasional 'I see'. Then he said, 'And is that something you'd like to press charges on? ... Okay, that's very helpful. Thank you very much ... Yes, I'll pass that on. Goodbye now.'

He ended the call. Elliott thought he had a graver look on his face now, as though he finally appreciated how serious this was.

'Well?' Elliott urged.

'She said she doesn't know anyone called Darren.'

It took a couple of seconds for Elliott to recover. 'What? Of course she does. Why would she say that?'

'Perhaps I should be asking you that question.'

'I ... I really don't know. It doesn't make any sense. His name is definitely Darren. He told me that himself. So what is the name of her stalker, then?'

'You tell me, Mr Whiston.'

The tone was accusatory now. Both officers looked ready to clap him in irons.

'Why do you keep asking me? I don't understand what's going on here. You asked Rebecca if she wanted to press charges. Whether her stalker's name is Darren or not, you need to put a stop to it.'

'Well, perhaps this little chat with you will do just that.'

Elliott opened and closed his mouth like a goldfish. 'What do you mean?'

'Mr Whiston, the young woman I just spoke to suggested that if anyone is stalking her, it's you.'

16

Elliott was dumbfounded. What the hell was going on? How had he been shifted from hero to villain in an eye-blink? And why would Rebecca do that to him of all people, the man who had rescued her, the man whom she promised to take for a drink when this was all over?

'What?' he said to the officers. 'Rebecca told you I've been stalking her?'

'It wasn't the word she used. She said you've been pestering her, phoning her constantly.'

'Really? And did she explain how I magically got hold of her name and number in the first place?'

'She said you spoke to her at the gym she goes to, and that you must have got her number from a staff member or by sneaking a look at their database.'

'That's ridiculous. I—'

'Have you ever been to a gym called the Tone Zone?'

'Well, yes, but not for ages. Way before she started going there.'

'I see.'

Elliott detected a lot of unsaid meaning in those two words. A mountain of doubt about his version of events. The reversal was beginning to panic him.

'No. You don't see. This is all arse-backwards. I'm the good guy in this. I helped her out, and now you're leaving me to deal with the real troublemaker.'

'Ah, yes, the mysterious Darren. The man you don't know anything about except for his name. The man you were meeting at eight o'clock.'

'Okay, well, obviously he's late or he's changed his mind or whatever, but I haven't been lying to you. Everything I said is the truth.'

Elliott heard the high-pitched desperation in his own voice, and knew it was doing nothing to persuade the two policemen. It was time to cut his losses.

'All right,' he said. 'Forget it. Forget I said anything.'

Lincoln looked at his colleague, and then the pair headed for the door. 'One other thing,' Lincoln said before they left. 'Rebecca said to tell you that she'd like you to stop phoning her.'

The policeman's sternness left Elliott in no doubt that this was intended as a warning. He nodded, watched them leave, then closed the door behind them.

The first thing he did next was to rush back to the living room, grab his phone and call Rebecca.

'What the hell?' he said when she answered.

'Have they gone?' she said. 'The police?'

'Yes, they've gone. And I'm lucky they haven't taken me with them in handcuffs. I'll say it again: what the hell?'

'I'm sorry, Elliott. I really am. You didn't say anything about getting the police involved.'

'And you didn't tell me what I'm getting myself into. I *had* to call them.'

'Why? Why did you have to call them?'

'Because I don't know what Darren is capable of. I don't know what he's going to do when I see him next.'

'I told you. He won't do anything. He just wants to ask you about me. All you had to do was tell him to go away, not call the police.'

'Well, that was my decision. What I don't get is why you felt the need to lie to them.'

'Because the way you're reacting is unnecessary. It's overkill. Darren is harmless—'

'So you keep saying.'

'Because it's true. He doesn't deserve to have the police on his back. And I don't want them interfering with my life either.'

'And so your only solution was to make them think I'm some kind of pervert?'

She laughed, but it wasn't mocking; it was her particularly delightful laugh that reminded him of how beautiful she was, and he wished she hadn't laughed because it was defusing his temper, and right now he needed to be angry.

'I'm sorry,' she said. 'I wasn't expecting them to call, and I just blurted out the first thing that came into my head. I didn't call you a pervert. I just said you were keen on me and that you were . . .'

'Pestering you.'

'Well . . . yeah. Sorry. Can you forgive me?'

He didn't want to forgive her, but he had a feeling he was heading that way.

'Depends.'

'On what?'

'On your answer to my next question.'

'Which is?'

'When we spoke yesterday, you said you'd told Darren that you and I were boyfriend and girlfriend. But you also said you hadn't spoken to him since Monday. Both of those can't be true, Rebecca, so which is it?'

There was a silence, and Elliott guessed that she was coming to terms with being caught out. She was falling from the pedestal on which he had placed her, and it saddened him.

'Elliott,' she said quietly, 'I didn't lie to you.'

'You need to explain,' he said.

'What I actually said to you was that I hadn't *seen* Darren since Monday. I didn't say anything about speaking to him. I called him, on the phone.'

Elliott tried to cast his mind back to their conversation. Had she said 'seen' or 'spoken'? He wasn't certain.

'Why didn't you mention that at the time?'

'I said I'd told him about us. I didn't feel it necessary to state that I used my mobile phone to do it.'

'No, I mean before that. When I was asking about whether you'd seen him. Wasn't that a natural moment for you to say something like, *No, I haven't seen him, but I did ring him*?'

'I don't know. Maybe. Does it matter? The point is, I haven't lied to you. You do believe me, don't you?'

134

'I don't know what to believe.'

'That . . . that's a little bit hurtful, Elliott.'

There was something in her voice, like she was genuinely upset. He was starting to feel like a scumbag.

'I'm sorry,' he said. 'I'm not trying to upset you. You put me in an awkward position with the police—'

'And I've apologised. I don't know what more you want me to say. It was you who decided to bring the police into this without discussing it with me first.'

Yeah, he thought, I'm definitely a scumbag.

He said, 'I'm also worried about Darren. I don't know how he's going to take this.'

'Didn't you say he would come over tonight?'

'Yes. Eight o'clock.'

'It's way past that now. He hasn't shown up?'

'No.'

'Well, there you go, then. Maybe he finally gets it. He probably won't bother you again.'

'Maybe.'

'Elliott, you're making far too much of this. I came to you because you looked like the sort of guy who might do a girl a simple favour. I really didn't think it would cause you this much distress. I hoped you'd be able to handle it.'

Elliott sensed his character was under fire here. Was he making too much of a fuss about nothing? Had he allowed Heidi to push him in that direction without any direct evidence?

'I *can* handle it. It's just . . . well, I've never been in a situation like this before, you know? I don't know Darren as well as you do. I thought he might be a psychopath or something.'

'You've met him. Does he seem like a psychopath?'

'Well …' Elliott answered. He'd never knowingly met a psychopath before, but didn't most of them come across as perfectly normal people until they chopped your head off and put it in their fridge? Not that Darren could be described as 'normal'. Normal people don't spit blood onto your rug or convince themselves that you've stolen their girlfriend.

Before he could voice any of these thoughts, Rebecca seduced him with her laugh again. 'You're so cute, Elliott. I'm glad I met you.'

He could feel the heat rising to his cheeks. 'Yeah, well, me too. Meeting you, I mean.'

'We'll get that drink together soon. I promise.'

'Sure. Great. I look forward—'

'Night, Elliott.'

'Yeah, okay. Goodnight.'

He dropped his phone onto the sofa and looked down at Bill, who had finally ventured back into the room.

'Explain women to me, Bill,' he said.

Darren sat on his hotel bed, brooding.

He'd been lucky, he realised. Extremely lucky.

He had arrived at Elliott's house at twenty to eight. He'd had no intention of announcing his presence immediately: the appointment was for eight, so that was when he would ring the doorbell. On the dot.

He'd waited in his car.

And that was how he had come to see the two policemen arriving.

They had obviously thought they were being clever, parking their brightly coloured vehicle around the corner like that. They hadn't reckoned with this early bird catching those worms.

He had decided not to hang around after that. Best to come back to the hotel and reconsider.

He realised now that he had underestimated Elliott. The bastard had set a trap for him. A *trap*! That wasn't sporting, not at all.

Darren's head was throbbing again. He went to the bathroom, tossed down two paracetamol, came back.

He wondered what Elliott had told the police, probably without even consulting Rebecca. She wouldn't have gone along with it. No way would she have even thought about getting her other half into trouble with the law.

But Elliott hadn't minded dropping him in the shit. In fact, Elliott probably thought it was an easy way to take his better-endowed competitor out of the picture.

Oh, Elliott, he thought. You are so out of your league. I will do whatever it takes to get my girl back.

Even if that means death.

17

Elliott welcomed being in the shop again on Friday. He hadn't slept well last night. Kept thinking Darren would come knocking. The guy didn't seem the type to respect social norms.

Bill wasn't bothered. He had slept soundly at the bottom of the bed, his snoring not helping his owner's mood.

Elliott had been relieved to get out of the house, away from possible encounters that, in his lively imagination, had grown terrifying. Despite almost shouting at himself to 'man up', and despite Rebecca's assurances that Darren was a pussycat, he wasn't convinced he could manage another meeting. He knew pussycats. He knew they had claws and fangs and could switch tempers in a heartbeat.

Bill hadn't supplied the requested explanations about women, either.

On one of Elliott's shoulders sat Rebecca, so apologetic and lovely and disarming. Last night, he had ended up feeling incredibly guilty for doubting her, such was her power over him. She thought he had nothing to worry about when it came to Darren.

On the other shoulder sat Heidi – his close friend, his confidante, his counsellor. She was firmly of the opinion that Rebecca had landed him on the wrong side of a man who was capable of dishing out actual bodily harm.

Which of those two was he supposed to listen to?

His phone pinged and he glanced at the screen.

Speak of the devil. A message from Heidi: *How did it go with the police?*

No use pretending, he thought. He typed out his reply: *Terrible. They didn't believe me.*

He wasn't surprised when his phone rang only seconds later.

'What do you mean?' Heidi yelled. 'How could they not believe you?'

'I don't know. Maybe I don't have a trustworthy face or something. I told them the whole story and got the feeling they thought I was living in a fantasy world.'

'What did they say to Darren?'

'He didn't turn up, which didn't help my case, especially when I couldn't tell them anything about him.'

'Did you tell them about the stalking?'

'Of course I did. I even gave them Rebecca's number so they could ring her.'

'And?'

He really didn't want to reveal this, but it was the truth after all. 'She . . . she denied all knowledge. She told them that I was the one who was giving her a hard time, and not some Darren person that she'd never heard of.'

There was a moment's silence during which Elliott could easily imagine the shock on Heidi's face.

'The fucking bitch,' Heidi said.

'In her defence, she said she lied because she was trying to protect Darren. She didn't think he deserved to be hassled by the police.'

'Don't defend her, Elliott. You did a wonderful thing. You protected her when she needed it. But the least she could have done was be straight with you about the situation with Darren. There's clearly a lot more to this story, and for whatever reason, she doesn't want it to get out. That's simply not fair on you. If you ever see Darren again, you need to tell him the truth about what really happened the other night. Get them both out of your hair.'

'Well, it looks like it's over now anyway. They seem to be keeping away from me, and I'm happy for it to stay that way.'

'Good. It's no longer your concern. Let them sort it out between themselves. I can't believe those cops, though.' She paused. 'Look, I've got research meetings all day today, so I won't be at the shop, but we'll talk later, okay?'

'Sure. And thanks.'

'You're welcome. I don't even charge. Bye, Elliott.'

'Bye.'

The shop got suddenly busier after that, and he was grateful for it. For a good couple of hours he was able to concentrate on the needs of others rather than his own problems. When a lull finally hit, he considered the prospect of taking a couple of days off, spending some time up at his sister's. Heidi wouldn't mind looking after Bill, and—

The shop door opened again. He prepared to affix a smile and appear helpful.

Until he saw that it was Darren who had entered.

He came straight over to the desk. Stood there looking down at Elliott.

'Hey, Elliott,' he said.

Be strong, Elliott told himself. This is your domain. You're in charge here. You have to show him who's boss.

'Hey, Darren. How can I help you?'

'Oh, I think you already know the answer to that one, Elliott.'

'Then I take it you haven't come here to buy something or make a charitable donation?'

'No. I hate cats. They're sly and sneaky. Like some people I could name.'

Elliott was quickly gaining the impression that Darren wasn't in the best of moods. That angry-looking lump on his head probably wasn't helping.

'How did you find out where I work?'

'I followed you from your house the other day. You don't seem very aware of your surroundings, Elliott. You should always be aware of what's coming up behind you. Might save your life one day.'

It seemed to Elliott that Darren's words were beginning to sound a lot more like threats. He was unnerved to learn that Darren had been spying on him.

'Okay, Darren, I think we need to have a talk about your behaviour. You—'

'About *my* behaviour? Are you serious? You're the one who tried to set a trap for me.'

'A trap? What are you talking about?'

'The police. I saw them go into your house. You were trying to trap me.'

So, Elliott thought, he was there all along. Watching the house. Watching me.

'It wasn't a trap. I wanted them to have a word with you, that's all.'

'I don't need to have a conversation with the fucking pigs. I need to have a conversation with Rebecca. *That's* what you need to arrange, but you don't seem to have got that into your thick head.'

There was real agitation there. A sense that he could go off the deep end.

'All right, let's stay calm here. Let's talk about this sensibly.'

'I already spoke to you sensibly. You didn't listen. You haven't done what I asked.'

'Actually, I did. After you left on Wednesday night, I phoned Rebecca and I told her you needed to speak to her.'

'Uh-huh? So then where's her call? Why hasn't she been in touch? I waited all day for her.'

'She . . . she said she didn't want to contact you.'

Darren stared, blinked, shook his head. 'Nah. You're lying again. She wouldn't do that to me. If you told her how much I was hurting, she would try to help me.'

'I'm sorry, Darren. That's just how it is.'

Darren nodded, but without conviction. Elliott was worried what he might do next, and was surprised when he started wandering around the shop.

'What do you do here?' Darren asked.

'I look after the shop. We sell second-hand goods, and the money we raise goes to the Cat Welfare League.'

'The Cat Welfare League? You spend all your time looking after cats?'

'Yes.'

'But what about humans? Don't you think they need help?'

'Some do, yes.'

'But for you, cats are more important?'

'No. Not more important. Why can't both be helped?'

'I'm just saying. You spend all day in this shitty place so that a few cats get a tin of Whiskas or whatever. Don't you think that's such a waste? Think of all the people you could help instead.'

'What people do *you* help, Darren?'

Darren flashed an angry glare. 'You don't know anything about me.'

'You're right, I don't. Why don't you tell me about yourself? I don't even know your full name.'

Darren ignored the prompt and continued to meander, inspecting items as he went. 'I'm more interested in you, in what you're doing with my girlfriend.'

Elliott could feel the two women on his shoulders again. Rebecca telling him to repeat the lie that she was *his* girlfriend now. Heidi advising him to confess the truth. He was having a hard time deciding which guidance to follow.

For the moment, he bided his time.

Darren took down a man's cloth cap from its hook, holding it gingerly between finger and thumb.

'People really buy this shit?'

'They do.'

'But it's used. It's been worn, probably by some smelly old bloke with a scaly scalp.'

'We clean everything thoroughly. Most of our stuff is as good as new.'

Darren tossed the cap aside onto a table and pressed on with his patrol. He took a striped tie from its rack, held it up to examine it, then draped it casually around his neck. Elliott wasn't sure what to say next, but he felt he wasn't taking charge in the way he'd imagined he would.

'Why don't you come over here and talk to me properly?' he asked.

Darren ignored him again. He approached the shop mannequin.

'Who's this?' he asked.

'We call her Myrtle.'

'Yeah?' Darren circled the mannequin. 'Did you dress her?'

'No. My assistant did it.'

'But you do it sometimes?'

'Sometimes.'

Darren smiled lasciviously at him. 'I bet you enjoy that, don't you?'

'Not particularly. Actually, I—'

Darren grabbed the front of the button-up lacy top that Myrtle was wearing and ripped it open, sending buttons pinging onto the floor.

'What the hell?' Elliott said, getting to his feet. He watched as Darren began fondling the mannequin's breasts.

'Do these remind you of Rebecca?' Darren asked. 'So firm and smooth.'

145

'That's enough, Darren. I think it's time for you to leave.'

Smiling, apparently unconcerned, Darren strolled back towards Elliott. 'Are you good in bed? Are you well hung or something? Because I'm having a hard time understanding why Rebecca would go near you. Maybe you could explain it to me.'

Elliott sat down again. Squaring up to the other man seemed too confrontational. Besides, it felt more comforting to have the few feet of desk between them.

'This is all getting a bit silly now,' he said. 'You're talking to the wrong person. I can't help you.'

'You *can* help me. All I want is for me and Rebecca to be together again. That's not a lot to ask, is it? And don't start giving me your bullshit about you two being in love, because I'm not buying it. There's something else going on, and to be honest, I don't really care what the fuck it is as long as you end it and send Rebecca back to me.'

Elliott decided he was going to have to demolish one or two of Darren's pet fantasies.

'Darren, you and Rebecca were never a couple. You know that, don't you? Rebecca finished with her previous boyfriend, and then you heard about it and decided you'd like to be with her. Now, I can understand that – she's very beautiful – but you can't just go after women like that. It's not right, and it can frighten people.'

Darren gave him a long, hard stare, and Elliott wondered what thought processes had been triggered in his brain. He started to worry that confronting Darren with harsh reality might have been a step too far and that it would lead to some kind of horrible meltdown.

And then Darren threw back his head and let out a huge roar of laughter. When he looked down again, there were actual tears in his eyes.

'You're a riot, man. Where do you get this stuff? How do you even invent nonsense like that?'

He wandered away across the shop again, still laughing. Elliott failed to appreciate the humour but it was a better reaction than rage. And yet there was still the problem of convincing Darren to allow reality through his filters.

He watched as Darren plonked himself down on a customer chair and continued to chuckle to himself while fingering the tie that was still hanging loosely around his neck. It was beginning to look as though he had no intention of leaving. Elliott glanced at the phone on his desk and debated whether to call the police. The worry was that Darren might not find that so funny. And after Elliott's last encounter with the cops, he wasn't really sure he wanted to reach out to them again.

It was while he was considering his scant options that the shop door opened and his troubles instantly multiplied.

In came the bearded man from earlier in the week.

The shoplifter.

18

The lowlife glanced first at Elliott and then at Darren, and then he walked casually over to the DVD section. Elliott stared after him in disbelief. The sheer temerity of the man!

Elliott side-eyed his phone again. Surely he would have to call the police now? But he had no proof of anything, against either of these men. And by the time the police got here—

'All right,' Darren said, approaching the desk again. 'Enough of the weird talk. We need a plan you might actually stick to this time.'

Elliott's attention was split. He did his best to listen to Darren while also keeping his eyes on the bearded man.

'First of all,' Darren continued, 'you need to face some facts. This thing you think you have with her, it's not going anywhere, so if— Are you listening to me?'

Elliott switched his gaze back to Darren. 'Er, yeah. Darren, look, this isn't a good time, okay? There's a guy over there . . .'

Darren glanced over his shoulder at the man, just as he was

slipping a DVD into his pocket. 'Great. This shithole has an actual customer.'

'You don't understand. He's stealing.'

'I don't give a toss. I'm the customer you're dealing with, and I have a serious complaint. What are you going to do about it?'

Elliott's heart began pounding furiously as he noticed the bearded man drop two more DVDs into his pockets. He knew he had to take action. He couldn't keep allowing the shoplifter to come in here and walk out with his stock. And it had to be swift and decisive; it had to prove to Darren that he was not a man to be trifled with. If he didn't, Darren would think he was weak, and then Elliott would never be able to shake him off either.

But, on the other hand, taking a pounding from a petty thief was unlikely to do him any favours in that regard.

Darren raised his voice. 'I said what are you going to do about it?' Behind him, the shoplifter started making his way towards the shop door.

Elliott made his decision. He jumped to his feet. 'Hey!' he shouted.

As on his last visit, the man made no attempt to flee. He simply stopped walking and looked across at Elliott.

'Can I help you?' he asked.

'You . . . you took some DVDs again.'

'What do you mean?'

'You keep stealing DVDs from the shop. They're in your pockets. You need to pay for them.'

The man looked to Darren. 'Can you believe this guy?'

Darren gave no reply to the man, but kept his gaze on Elliott. 'You haven't dealt with my complaint. Sort out this bloke another time.'

'Yeah, Ellie,' the man said. 'What kind of manager are you? Calling me a thief, in front of a customer.'

Elliott felt the familiar tremor in his legs, the sickness in his stomach.

'I saw you.' He pointed towards Darren. 'He saw you, too.'

The man looked at Darren. 'Is that right, mate?'

Darren put his hands up. 'Keep me out of it. I'm just trying to—'

The shoplifter whirled on Elliott again, cutting Darren off. Elliott could see how irritated it made him.

'See? It's only you accusing me. Why are you trying to embarrass me, Ellie?'

Elliott straightened his back and tried to appear imposing. The other man was still several inches taller than him.

'Y-you took the DVDs. Put them back or pay for them.'

The thief moved closer, a snarl on his lips, the smell of weed emanating from his clothes.

'Or what?' he asked. 'Will you go running home to your fucking mummy?'

Elliott found his hand moving as if of its own accord. He raised his palm, placed it flat against the man's chest.

'I'm asking you nicely to step away now,' Elliott said. 'Then we can discuss this properly.'

The thief looked down at Elliott's hand. 'Take your fucking hand off me before I break your fingers.'

Elliott froze, not sure what to do.

And then he heard Darren's voice: 'Excuse me. We hadn't finished.'

The man turned to him and snarled, 'Fuck off', then faced Elliott again. 'I'll give you three seconds. One . . .'

Elliott licked his parched lips. He felt on the verge of collapse.

'Two . . .'

Darren came and stood right next to the man. 'You don't understand. This is about my girlfriend. It's urgent. I need to—'

Without even looking at Darren, the shoplifter pushed him away. 'Fuck you and fuck your girlfriend.' Then, to Elliott, he said, 'Three. Time's up.'

Elliott dropped his hand. And with it went everything he thought made him a decent human being.

'Good girl,' said the shoplifter. 'Now go back to work and—'

His next words were cut off as the striped tie was looped over his neck and yanked tightly into a noose. He reached for his neck, but the grip from Darren behind him was too firm. Elliott stared in horror as the man's face turned purple and his mouth opened and gasped for air, weird croaking noises coming from his throat. Darren's own face had now twisted into something manic and terrifying.

'You don't get to say that about Rebecca!' Darren yelled. 'Nobody gets to say that about her.'

Even as the man fell to his knees, Darren kept up the tension, his knuckles white with the effort.

'Stop it,' Elliott said. 'Stop it, you're going to kill him.'

'You didn't listen,' Darren said to his victim, his voice rising in pitch. 'I tried to tell you, but you didn't listen. Why won't anyone listen to me?'

Elliott put a hand on Darren's arm. 'Let him go. *Let him go!*'

The shoplifter stopped struggling and went limp, and it was only then that Darren released his grip and allowed the man to flop to the floor.

He's dead, Elliott thought. He's killed him!

But then the still figure suddenly found life again, announcing it with a huge intake of breath. He clambered to his feet, coughing and spluttering, and then made a break for the door and raced out of the shop. Darren didn't try to stop him.

Elliott stared in disbelief at Darren, who stooped over the desk, apparently exhausted by his outburst. This wasn't simply a man with unspecified 'behavioural issues'. Darren was certifiable. A violent psychopath.

He was afraid to speak but he felt he had to. 'Darren, why did you do that?'

Darren turned. 'He tried to get between me and Rebecca. Did you hear what he said about her? That wasn't right.'

'Darren, you almost killed that man. You—'

'What do you care? He's a thief.'

'I know. But that's no reason to . . . to *execute* him!'

'I . . . I don't like violence. But sometimes, you know, when people try to destroy what I have with Rebecca . . .'

He gave an accusing look as he said this, and Elliott began to worry that his own life might be at risk. It was time to own up. Heidi was right: Rebecca had been playing him like a fiddle. She must have known what Darren was capable of. She no longer deserved his protection.

'There's something you should know,' he said. 'Rebecca is not my girlfriend.'

Darren rubbed his cheek. 'Go on.'

'I don't know anything about her. We'd never met before Monday night. She came up to me because you were following her, and she asked me to pretend to be her boyfriend so that you would leave her alone.'

'Go on,' Darren repeated.

'That's it. We made up a story to keep you away from her.'

Darren stared at him, then nodded gravely.

And then he laughed.

'Nice try, Elliott. You almost had me going there.'

'It . . . it's true. I don't know the woman.'

'Sure, sure. That's why she spent so much time in your house the other night. It's why you've got her phone number.'

Elliott picked up his mobile phone from the desk. 'I'll call her now if you like, and pass it over to you.'

'Don't even bother. She won't talk to me on the phone, and even if she did, she would just repeat the lies. What I don't know is why. Why did she lie to me, and why do you keep changing your story?'

'I was trying to help her. I thought I was doing a good thing. She's frightened of you, Darren.'

Darren shook his head. 'No, she isn't frightened of me. I would never hurt her, and she knows it. Something else is going on, and nobody will tell me what it is.'

'Nothing else is going on, at least as far as I'm concerned. Whatever happened between you and her has nothing to do with me.'

'It has *everything* to do with you. She told me so. You've got some kind of control over her. You've turned her against me, and I don't like that. I don't like it one bit.' Darren's voice was growing higher in pitch again.

'I haven't. I swear to you. I—'

'Bring her to me. Set up a meeting so that I can get a full explanation from her and you can convince her that she needs to come back to me.'

'I can't do that. I have no idea where she is.'

'I don't believe you. For whatever reason, she trusts you. Give her back to me.' Darren moved towards the shop door. 'I'll come and see you tonight. No police. Just you and me and Rebecca. Let's sort this thing out once and for all.'

Elliott watched as Darren left the shop. And then he thought about the scene he'd just witnessed and felt he was going to be sick.

19

Elliott didn't even attempt to prepare an evening meal. Simply opening a pouch of Bill's foul-smelling mush had been enough to send his stomach into convulsions.

Seconds were ticking away, and at some point enough of them would have ticked away and Darren would arrive. What made it worse was that Darren hadn't said when. Every moment was filled with the dread of a death-knell ring of the doorbell.

And Darren had huge expectations. He expected Rebecca to be here. If she wasn't, he was liable to start cutting off air supplies.

Elliott had never before witnessed such an extreme act of violence. His appraisal of Darren's potential had been radically transformed. He'd viewed Darren as little more than an irritation – a weak unfortunate who had an obsession but was not malicious. Hell, the guy had even cried when they first met. Heidi had done her utmost to shift Elliott's perception into more hazardous territory, but he suspected that had more to do with her inexplicable dislike of a woman she had never met rather than an evidence-based risk assessment.

But now it seemed that even Heidi had underestimated the danger.

Who does that? Who strangles people almost to the point of death?

Psychopaths, that's who.

Elliott had never met a real psychopath before. At least not knowingly. He hadn't the faintest idea about what behavioural signs to look out for. But this was surely one.

A psychopath is visiting me tonight, he thought. A man who is willing to employ extreme violence is coming here, and he is going to be very angry when I don't give him what he wants, and I don't know what I can do about it.

It was all Rebecca's fault, of course. This whole mess was on her.

She was the subject of another considerable change in Elliott's viewpoint. He had seen her as the innocent party in all this – a beautiful but desperate individual who had reached out to him in her time of need. He had believed every word she had uttered, without question.

Sure, his devotion had suffered a bit of a wobble over that mix-up about her denying and then admitting to speaking to Darren, but he had been willing to grant her the benefit of the doubt.

But not now.

Now he was convinced that she had cynically manoeuvred him into an impossible situation. For her to claim that Darren was harmless was admission enough that she knew him well.

And if she knew him well, then she knew the truth and had refused to reveal it. Compounding this with her blatant lies to the police was the cherry on the cake.

He needed an explanation from Rebecca just as much as Darren did.

And therein lay the problem.

Elliott had been calling her ever since Darren left the shop. She wasn't answering. Every call went straight to voicemail, so he'd left messages. He had also sent a load of texts. No reply.

Elliott's current frame of mind was such that he would quite willingly drag Rebecca kicking and screaming to his house if only he knew where she was, but convincing Darren of that was another matter. He was doubtful that Darren would accept any excuse for her absence.

He had considered calling the police again, but what was he going to tell them? He knew no more about Darren than he had before, other than that he was mentally deranged, and Rebecca had already cast severe doubt on any version of events that Elliott might allege. It seemed highly unlikely that the cops would be willing to act as his nursemaids this evening or any other.

Which left . . . what?

And then the doorbell shattered the silence.

He got to his feet slowly, his legs rubbery even before he had taken a step. When he reached the hallway, it crossed his mind to pretend he wasn't at home. I could just sit in a corner and hide, he thought. Like a complete wuss.

But he knew he couldn't hide for ever. Darren would catch up with him at some point.

You can do this, he told himself. Stick to the truth from now on. At some point even Darren will have to accept it.

Elliott got to the front door. Swallowed loudly. Opened up.

'Ta-daaa! What took you so long? You haven't eaten, have you?'

Heidi. Bearing pizza boxes.

She barged through without waiting for an invitation. 'Get some plates,' she said. 'And napkins. Do you have any salad? No, never mind the salad. Who wants healthy shit, right?'

'Er, do come in,' Elliott said.

He followed her through to the kitchen, where she went straight to the fridge.

'I forgot to get coleslaw. You got any?'

'No . . . Heidi, what are you doing here?'

'I told you on the phone. I said we'd catch up later. Well, now it's later.'

'I didn't think you meant tonight.'

She eyed him with suspicion. 'What's wrong with tonight? You're not hiding that Rebecca here somewhere, are you?'

'Of course not. She's the last person I'd invite over after what's happened.'

Heidi seemed pleased at this. 'Good. I'm glad to hear it. What about beer? You must have beer?'

'You know I never drink at home.'

'Jeez, what kind of establishment is this? All right, just get the plates.'

Elliott opened a cupboard and took down a couple of plates. Despite the lack of forewarning, he was actually glad of

Heidi's arrival. She had a calming effect, and only now did he realise how hungry he was.

He watched as Heidi dished out some slices of the pizza.

'I got one pepperoni, one Hawaiian. You like both, right?'

He nodded.

'Good. Because there is a large group of people who assert that pineapple does not belong anywhere near pizza. They're wrong, of course.'

Elliott was already wolfing down a slice, even though he was still on his feet.

'Er, can we not be a little more civilised about this? Trays on our laps in front of the TV, at least.'

'Sorry,' Elliott mumbled. 'I'm suddenly starving. Too much nervous energy.'

'Nervous? Why are you nervous?'

'Because I'm about to become the victim of a psychopath.'

Heidi blinked at him. 'What?'

'Darren. He's a psycho. And he's coming to see me again.'

'Has something happened today?'

'Everything has happened today. None of it good.'

Heidi gestured to a chair. 'Sit. Talk to me. What's going on?'

So he told her. Recounted every awful minute of the encounter in the shop. And all the while Heidi sat there transfixed.

'What the fuck?' she said finally.

'I know. Not exactly your normal day at work, right?'

'Elliott, this has gone too far now. You need to talk to the police again.'

'And tell them what? They already think I'm pathetic and a timewaster.'

'But that was before you knew you were dealing with a maniac. Things have changed.'

'For me, maybe, but not for them. Why would they believe me now, especially after Rebecca told them I'm a stalker?'

Heidi shook her head in despair. 'You really need security cameras in that shop. They would have given you all the proof you need.'

'We *have* cameras.'

'I meant cameras that *work*.'

'The owners don't want to pay out for a new system. They see it as money taken away from the cats.'

'Yeah, well, the cats don't have to worry about homicidal stalkers, do they?' She took a bite from her pizza. 'What exactly is Darren expecting you to do for him?'

'He expects to come here and find Rebecca waiting for him.'

'And then what? What's he going to do with her?'

'Talk to her. Win her over.'

Heidi raised an eyebrow. 'Are you sure about that?'

'What do you mean?'

'Look, it's obvious that this Rebecca person has been using you, but if Darren is as wacko as you say he is, then she can hardly be blamed for not wanting to be within a mile of him.'

'I suppose. Doesn't help me, though, does it?'

The conversation stalled. They filled the time stuffing their faces.

'Okay,' Heidi said finally. 'We need a plan.'

'You mean like a funeral plan?'

'I was thinking of something a little more optimistic. We

need to get the two of them to talk to each other. Cut out the middleman, that being you.'

'Well, duh. That's what I've been trying to do. Rebecca is refusing to play ball. She won't even answer my calls now.'

'*Nil desperandum*. You've got a secret weapon now.'

'Which is?'

'Me. I'll call her on my phone.'

'Why? What good will that do?'

'In case you hadn't noticed, Elliott, I'm a woman. That means I can talk to her on a woman-to-woman basis.'

Elliott frowned. 'You're going to tear her apart, aren't you?'

'No, I'm not. I'm going to appeal to her sensitive nature, if she has one. Only if that doesn't work will I rip her to shreds.'

'I still don't think she'll be willing to phone Darren.'

'Maybe not, but that brings in the other part of my cunning plan. I'll put the call on speaker, and you record the whole conversation on your phone. We'll try to get her to explain why she split up with Darren and why she doesn't want to see him again. That way, even if she refuses to talk to Darren directly, we can play the recording back to him. He'll hear exactly what he needs to hear to make him leave you alone.'

Elliott thought about it. 'I'm not sure it'll work.'

'Have you got a better idea?'

'No.'

'Then let's give it a try. What have you got to lose?'

'Only my life.'

'Just give me Rebecca's number and then get your phone ready.'

Heidi pushed the plates aside, then took out her phone and entered Rebecca's number as Elliott recited it.

'Ready?' she asked.

Elliott tapped the red button on his voice recording app. 'Ready.'

Heidi made the call. It was answered almost immediately.

'Hello?'

'Is that Rebecca?'

'It is.'

'My name's Heidi Liu. You don't know me, but I'm a good friend of Elliott's.'

'I see.'

'Please don't hang up. I just want to have a really quick chat.'

'All right. What do you want?'

'I want you to know that Elliott is a good person. Actually, he's one of the kindest and most generous people I've ever met.'

Elliott stared at Heidi. He had never heard her pay him such compliments, and it touched him.

'He did you a massive favour over Darren,' Heidi continued. 'And now Darren is making him responsible. He's trying to use Elliott to get to you, and he's not going to take no for an answer.'

'Darren is ... difficult. He means well, but he has some issues.'

'Yes. Elliott found that out today when Darren almost killed another man in front of him.'

'What?'

'I think you heard me. And I think you've known for some time what Darren is capable of.'

'No. I swear. What did he do?'

164

'Strangled the guy because he got in Darren's way. He's lucky to be alive.'

'Oh my God. I can't believe it. I have never seen Darren do anything like that. I would have told Elliott if I had.'

'Okay. But that's what we're dealing with. That's the situation you've left poor Elliott in.'

'I ... I'm sorry. I really didn't intend for any of this to happen.'

'All right. Well, now's your chance to fix it.'

'Fix it how?'

'By meeting Darren. You could do it at Elliott's house if it makes you feel safer.'

'No, I don't think it would be a good idea for me to go there.'

'Well, call Darren, then. One phone call – that's all you need to do.'

'And say what?'

'Whatever Darren needs to hear to get him off Elliott's back. He wants some kind of explanation from you, doesn't he? Well, why not give it to him?'

'Because ... it's complicated.'

'How complicated can it be? Did you use to go out with him?'

A long pause. 'Yes.'

Elliott's eyes widened. This was the first time Rebecca had admitted to an intimate relationship with Darren. Maybe there was something in this woman-to-woman business after all.

'So why did it end?'

'I'm not going to discuss it over the phone.'

'Okay, well, discuss it with Darren then. Call him and talk to him in the way only you can, from the heart. If nothing else, tell him his problems are with you, not with Elliott.'

'I don't know . . .'

'Please. You've only met Elliott once. You don't know him like I do. He doesn't deserve what you're putting him through.'

Another pause. 'All right. I'll make the call. For Elliott's sake.'

Elliott smiled and punched the air.

'You will?' Heidi said. 'When?'

'I'll do it right away.'

'Thank you. What are you going to say to him?'

'I'll figure it out. Goodbye.'

The line went dead. Elliott ended the recording. 'Yes!' he said. 'Thank you. I don't know how you pulled that off, but it was great.'

Heidi looked up from her phone, her face glum.

'What's the matter?' Elliott asked. 'Didn't you hear what she said?'

'I heard. She's not going to make the call.'

'What . . . what are you talking about? She just promised.'

'That wasn't a promise. She said that to get rid of me.'

'How do you know?'

'I know her type. I know insincerity when I hear it.'

'She sounded definite to me.'

'Okay, well, you keep telling yourself that when Darren is pounding your head against a brick wall.'

'That's . . . I don't understand.'

166

'You don't have to understand. Just accept it. She's leaving you hanging out to dry.'

Elliott shook his head. 'No, she wouldn't do that.'

Heidi jumped to her feet, startling him. 'Oh, for fuck's sake. Get real, will you? Start looking below the surface. Rebecca doesn't care what happens to you as long as it keeps her lunatic ex-boyfriend out of her hair.'

The pizza suddenly lost its appeal. As soon as he had heard Rebecca's voice, he had allowed himself to fall for her charms again. Now he felt angry and foolish. He wanted to continue the argument, to tell Heidi that she was mistaken, but deep down he suspected she'd got it spot on.

'If you're right—' he began.

'I *am* right.'

'—then Darren is still coming here tonight.'

'Probably. Even if Rebecca *does* call him – which she won't – it doesn't mean that she'll manage to rein him in. And she didn't give us anything we could play to Darren.'

Elliott nodded. He now wished he hadn't eaten the pizza, because it seemed on the verge of making a reappearance.

'Okay,' he said. 'Fine.' He got up, went to the sink for a glass of water.

'What does that mean?' Heidi asked.

'It means fine. I'll have to deal with it.'

'You're worrying me, Elliott. How are you going to deal with this?'

'I'll just have to talk to him again. Keep repeating the truth until he gets it.'

'And if he won't listen?'

'I don't know. What else can I do?'

'Have me here as backup. He won't try anything if I'm here.'

'No,' he said. 'Absolutely not. Darren insisted that there should be nobody else here apart from me and Rebecca. It would just aggravate him, and that's the last thing I want.'

'But what if he gets violent?'

'Then I'll run away and lock myself in the bathroom. Look, I really don't think it will come to that. Darren acted like that in the shop because he was already caught up in a confrontation. He's not going to get that from me.'

Heidi stared at him for the longest time. 'I hope you're right about him, Elliott. There are a lot of cats out there depending on you.'

20

Elliott stood in the hallway, staring at the front door. He knew what he had to do; he just wasn't sure he was fully prepared for it.

It had gone ten thirty. Elliott had started to hope that Rebecca had stuck to her word and called off the pit bull. But now here it was at the door, ready to clamp its jaws on a juicy thighbone.

The doorbell rang again, its noise this late at night seeming to shatter the peace of the whole street. Elliott hoped it would provoke dozens of annoyed neighbours to descend on his house and deal harshly with the interloper in their midst.

Realising he could put it off no longer, he stepped forward to answer the door.

Be nice, he told himself. Don't let him rattle you. Deal with him calmly and rationally. And if all else fails, hit him with the iron or the vase or any of the other makeshift weapons you've strategically positioned around the living room.

Darren looked ill. The streetlight lent his complexion a pale yellowish tinge, and the lump on his head seemed even darker than before, giving it the appearance of a huge, malignant mole. His eyes were crazed with capillaries, as though he'd been crying.

He's a mess, Elliott thought. He's weak. If it comes to it, I could beat him in a fight. I think.

As before, Darren didn't wait for an invitation to enter. As they came within inches of each other, Elliott noticed the smell of alcohol on Darren's breath. His gaze dropped to the beer bottle in Darren's hand.

Perfect. Not only insane but drunk.

They went through into the living room. Darren plonked himself down on the sofa next to Bill, who raised his head and sniffed the odours wafting to him from the visitor. Elliott sat in the armchair and glanced casually at the table to his right. On it, next to his phone, rested a heavy stone paperweight that could do some serious damage if necessary.

'So?' Darren asked. 'Where is she?'

'Rebecca? Well, you didn't give us a time. She didn't know when to be here.'

'Uh-huh. So if you ring her now and tell her I'm here, she'll rush right over, yeah?'

Elliott chewed on his lip. 'No.'

'No. I thought not. You haven't spoken to her, have you?'

Elliott considered his reply. He could tell Darren that a telephone conversation had taken place with Rebecca, but he wasn't convinced that revealing further confirmation of her rejection was a wise idea.

'I've tried. She won't answer my calls or texts.'

Darren took a slug of his beer, then shook his head. 'Not good enough.'

'I don't know what else you want me to do. What I told you at the shop was the truth. I don't know Rebecca. I'd never seen her before Monday night. I got dragged into your relationship problems without even being asked.'

'Yeah, yeah. So you said. Problem is, that's not what you told me at the start, is it? So stop trying to bullshit me.'

'I didn't say it at the start because Rebecca asked me not to. She wanted me to pretend to be her boyfriend so that you would leave her alone. I had no idea you'd get so worked up about it.'

'Who's worked up? I'm just sitting having a beer, talking to the guy who's going to help me get my girlfriend back.'

'Look,' Elliott said, 'I was just trying to help someone. That's all. I don't know where Rebecca is, or even how to get her to talk to me. If I could help you, I would.'

Another sip of beer. 'Good to hear. I mean, I helped you out, didn't I? In your little cat shop.'

It seemed a curious way of looking at it. 'Yes. Yes, you did, but—'

'So now you owe me one, right? No offence, mate, but Rebecca isn't right for you.'

'We're not a couple! I keep telling you that.'

'I think you know where she is right now.' He looked up at the ceiling. 'She's not in the house, is she?'

'No. She's not here.'

'Because I'd hate to have to search the place.'

'I promise you, she's not here.'

'Okay. Well, I'll take your word for it.'

It occurred to Elliott that he had already lost control of the situation. He needed to reassert himself. After all, this was his house.

He got up from his chair. 'Good. I hope you manage to find her and sort out your differences. Now, if you don't mind . . .' He gestured towards the door.

'What are you doing?' Darren asked.

'I'd like you to leave now. In fact, I don't want you to come here ever again.'

Darren stared. And then he smiled. 'Sit the fuck down.'

'What? No. You heard what I—'

'I said sit the fuck down before I break your fucking legs.'

Elliott sat, and felt what little resistance he'd possessed drain out of him.

Darren leant forward. He looked almost remorseful. 'I don't want to ruin things between us. You seem like a nice person. Inoffensive, you know what I mean? I don't want to see you get hurt. But you broke something, and now you have to fix it.' He settled back into the sofa, and then he reached out a hand and began stroking Bill's head. 'I mean, if I did something bad to your cat, you'd expect me to replace it, wouldn't you?'

The threat hit hard. Elliott looked across at Bill, who didn't seem to sense the danger.

'Why would you hurt my cat?'

'I wouldn't. I'm just saying. Hypothetical, right?'

Elliott continued to watch Darren's hand. 'Please,' he said. 'You're putting me in an impossible situation.'

'Nothing's impossible. You just have to dig a little deeper. You could have had that prick in the shop, the way I did. You know that, right? It's all a matter of being who you need to be. And right now, I need you to be the man who gives my Rebecca back to me.'

Darren's fingers pushed through the cat's fur on top of its head. His thumb curled beneath Bill's chin. All it would take was a sudden twist of the wrist . . .

'All right,' Elliott said. 'I'll try again, okay? No promises, but I'll do my best.'

Darren smiled and withdrew his hand. 'I knew you'd see sense. Rebecca will see sense too, once you explain everything to her. Tell her how much I miss her.'

Elliott nodded. He would agree to anything to get this lunatic out of his house.

Darren stood, came across to where Elliott was sitting. Elliott glanced again at the objects on his side table.

'You won't let me down, will you? I'm counting on you. You have to put this right.'

Elliott licked his dry lips. 'I'll . . . Yeah. Sure.'

Bizarrely, as if concluding a business meeting, Darren proffered his hand. Elliott took it with reluctance, feeling as though he was entering into a contract without reading the fine print.

'Good seeing you again, man. Once Rebecca sees we're on the same side over this, she'll come round.'

'I, er, I hope so.'

Darren moved to the door. At the front doorstep he turned, finished off his beer, then handed the empty bottle to Elliott.

'One more thing,' he said, his expression grave. 'Don't

underestimate me, okay?'

'I . . . I'm not sure what you mean.'

'The paperweight. If you'd gone there, you'd be dead now, do you understand?'

And then he put his hands in his pockets and strolled away.

Elliott stared at the bottle as if it were contaminated, then he closed the front door and rushed back into the living room. He put the bottle down next to the stone paperweight, then picked up his phone.

The call was still connected.

'Did you get all that?' he said into the phone.

'Every word,' Heidi replied.

It had been a simple plan, as all genius plans are. Even though it wasn't that different from the approach they had tried with Rebecca, it hadn't occurred to Elliott to try it on Darren. The prize for that piece of thinking went to Heidi again.

Elliott had placed the call just after Darren had rung the doorbell. Heidi had listened in and recorded every word on a dictation device she used for lectures. The aim was twofold. First, if things became a little too heated, Heidi would dial 999. Second, they now possessed a record of the whole conversation that they could present to the police in the hope that they would take the matter more seriously.

Elliott realised that he had almost given the game away when he had glanced towards the phone on the side table. Fortunately, all it had done was to draw Darren's attention to the paperweight.

'Is it enough?' Elliott asked.

'He threatened to break your legs, Elliott. How much do

you need?'

'You won't have heard what he said to me at the front door. He told me I could easily be dead now.'

'Doesn't matter. What came across crystal clear was that Darren is one deluded, violent, obsessive dude. Believe me, we've got more than enough for the police.'

Elliott nodded. Finally, he thought, I've got a way out of this.

21

It wasn't enough.

Heidi looked down at the voice recorder on the passenger seat of her car. She hadn't lied to Elliott about that; what they had was good stuff. Anyone listening would realise instantly that Darren was a nut-job. His threats were clear and unambiguous. He needed taking off the streets. At the very least, he should be the subject of a restraining order.

But only if they could find him.

That was the problem. Take this to the police and they would say, 'Okay, so who is this guy and how do we find him?' Without those answers they were no further ahead.

Which was why Heidi was now following Darren in her car.

She hadn't told Elliott about this part of her plan – he would only have made a fuss – but it had been in her head the whole time. It was obvious to her that they needed to know where Darren was living.

She had told Elliott she would be listening to the phone call in her flat, but that had been a lie. Instead, she had raced to her car, driven it to Elliott's house and parked up.

During the telephone conversation her heart had been in her mouth. She had hoped things wouldn't get too dramatic, but at the first hint of violence she had been intending not only to call the police but also to go hammering on Elliott's door herself. She had even agreed a 'safe word' with Elliott in case he became aware of imminent danger before she did. The word Elliott had insisted on was 'ukulele', his reasoning being that it would jump out of the conversation. Heidi's counter-argument was that it would be difficult to work it into the discussion.

When she saw Darren leave the house, it had come as a huge relief. Elliott was safe. She could move on to phase two.

So now she was following Darren. He had walked down a side street and hopped into a large Audi saloon. It made her wonder what kind of job he did to afford a car like that. If he was a boy racer she would have had no chance of keeping up in her little Corsa. As it turned out, he drove at a sedate pace.

She kept her distance – enough to maintain his car in her sights while not alarming him by driving up his arse. In the daytime the roads around here were insanely busy, but it was getting late now, giving her more of a fighting chance of staying on his trail.

As she drove, she questioned why she was taking chances for Elliott. The answer wasn't hard to find. Ever since she had first met him at the charity shop, she had wanted to spend more time with him. He was cute, he was funny, he was interesting, he liked the same things she did, and he wasn't macho.

She had gone out with a macho guy years ago, and while he had been very easy on the eye, she quickly discovered that he seemed to have traded in his personality and intelligence.

The best thing about Elliott was that he opened up to her. Their bond was intimate. He was willing to bare his soul, and one day she hoped she could do the same.

She often wondered when that day might come. Despite all their conversations late into the night, Elliott seemed reluctant to take things a step further. She wanted it, but she had always promised herself that she would not make the first move. She needed to know that she wasn't pressurising him into something he didn't actually want. What irked her was that he seemed to be taking so damn long about it.

She had decided a while ago that she would allow him all the time he needed. Now, though, she wasn't so sure. Rebecca had seen to that.

Heidi had surprised even herself with her depth of feeling about Rebecca. She recalled vividly the shock and sense of loss that surged through her when Elliott first hinted at the possibility of another woman in his life. She hadn't hated Rebecca at first – in fact, she had been so proud of Elliott for coming to the poor woman's rescue – but what she had learnt more recently had put Rebecca squarely in the 'lying and manipulative cow' category.

So now it was time to prove to Elliott just how much she was willing to do for him. And if handing over Darren's address still didn't do the trick, then she was going to have to come right out and tell Elliott exactly how she felt.

They drove into Copperley, a large urban sprawl bordering the river. Up ahead, Darren was signalling a left turn. She got into the same lane, two cars behind him, then performed a scan of the street signs. They were about to head towards the dockland area. There were some nice hotels and apartment blocks along the river, and with a car like his, it seemed an obvious destination.

On the dock road Darren took a right turn. Heidi followed slowly, happy to allow other cars to jump in front of her. All she needed was a good enough view of him turning into the grounds of one of the huge buildings that loomed up on either side of them.

But then those buildings got left behind. The surroundings became darker and dingier and absent of life. This was not a place to stop, let alone to reside in. Darren had to be heading out of town. This could be a long night.

It came as a huge surprise when Darren suddenly indicated another right turn. No other cars were going that way, so Heidi had to slow right down, hoping that Darren would manage to complete the turn before she closed the gap between them. Behind her, a van blared its horn at her and overtook, and she caught a glimpse of the driver gesturing obscenely.

Darren turned. Heidi speeded up and followed. The road ahead was on a steep incline. The buildings on either side lay squat and forlorn. Most were boarded up and adorned with graffiti. Nobody walked these pavements.

Yet another right turn from Darren, this time into a narrow one-way street. Heidi stepped on the accelerator so as not to lose him, prepared to turn . . .

Darren had parked up, just few metres along from the corner.

She abandoned the turn, continuing straight on instead, then went down the next side street and stopped her car.

She was mystified, but also disappointed. This surely couldn't be where Darren was living, but then what possible reason could he have for coming here?

She decided she needed to find out.

As she got out of her car and locked it up, she realised there were no other cars in sight, and wondered whether hers would still be here when she got back. These dark side streets were dripping with foreboding. She imagined only criminals ever ventured here. What was Darren playing at?

She walked back down the hill, stopped at the corner, cautiously poked her head around it. Darren's car sat in front of a pair of tall, spike-topped metal gates. The gates were open. Beyond them was an empty concrete parking lot and then a single-storey building with large sliding wooden doors and a smaller customer door. Faded and rusted signs on the walls indicated that it was once a garage.

Heidi moved closer. She confirmed that the car was empty, then passed through the gates and began walking towards the building. She could feel her pulse thudding in her ears.

She was startled by a sudden noise to her left. She squinted into the darkness, saw the eerily glowing eyes of a cat staring back at her.

The customer door ahead of her was slightly ajar. There was a sign at eye level that said 'Reception'. She wondered what kind of reception might be in store for her. And yet the place clearly held something of interest for Darren. What the hell could it be?

She stepped closer, listening intently for any clues. She brought one eye to the gap between the door and the jamb. She could see nothing inside but inky blackness.

She didn't hear a thing. Didn't hear him come round the corner of the building. Didn't hear him come up behind her.

The first she knew of the trap he had sprung came only when he clamped a hand over her mouth and touched a cold blade to her throat.

22

'Who are you?' he asked.

He had dragged her into the garage, tied her hands together around a concrete post behind her, bound her feet. He had taken her keys and phone, and then he had fetched her car, slid open the garage doors and driven it inside. Then he had brought his own car in, put a padlock and chain around the gates and closed up the building. On the off-chance that anyone would choose to venture down this forbidding street, they would never know the building was occupied.

Darren sat on a wooden stool, staring down at her. Among other items on the bench next to him, a battery-operated lamp provided the only source of light. Heidi wondered why he had brought such things – the lamp, the rope he'd used to tie her with, a roll of duct tape, scissors, a box of snacks, bottles of water. The answers her brain conjured up were not pleasant.

'Who are you?' he said again.

'N-nobody. My name's H-Heidi. I was just walking past

183

and I saw your car and the open gates. I w-wondered what was going on.'

'Well, H-Heidi, the first thing you should know about me is that I don't like people who lie to me. So cut the fucking bullshit and tell me why you followed me all the way from Elliott's house. And if you say "Who's Elliott?" I am going to slice your fucking ears off. Okay?'

Her swallow was audible in the echoey chamber. She could smell grease, oil and dirt but the garage was clearly no longer in use. The shelves were bare and there were no vehicle maintenance tools or equipment on show. Just a couple of ragged tyres sitting in one corner. Heidi guessed there was no longer any power or running water.

She'd thought she had made a good job of tailing Darren. Clearly not. No point lying now.

'I'm his best friend,' she said, doing her utmost to control her nervous stutter. 'I was trying to help him.'

'Help him do what?'

'I was trying to find out more about you. Find out where you live.'

'Why?'

'To get you off his back.'

'Did Elliott ask you to follow me?'

'No. He doesn't know anything about this. In fact, he'd be annoyed if he knew.'

'So why did you do it?'

'I told you. I wanted to help him.'

'You normally go around *helping* people like this? Sticking your nose in where it's not wanted?'

'No. But Elliott means a lot to me.'

'What does that mean? You fucking him?'

The expletive rattled her. It was a demeaning view of the relationship she wanted with Elliott.

'No.'

'You and Rebecca both fucking him?'

She shook her head. 'There's nothing between him and Rebecca. He already told you that.'

'Yeah, but he's just as much a liar as you are. Seems like I'm surrounded by fucking liars.'

Darren got off his stool, then picked up his knife and began pacing. It was a big knife. A hunter's knife. Heidi could still feel its icy bite at her throat.

'We're not lying,' she said. 'We—'

'Shut up.'

She paused, then tried again. 'All I was trying to do—'

He rounded on her, the knife poised. 'I said shut up. I'm thinking.'

Heidi went silent. She watched him walk to and fro. How unhinged was he? Was he going to hurt her?

She told herself that he had nothing to gain from hurting her. But then why tie her up? Why did it feel like he planned to keep her here for a long, long time?

'Do you love him?' Darren asked suddenly.

'What?'

'Elliott. Do you love him?'

'I . . . I don't know.'

'But you'd do anything for him, right? The way I'd do anything for Rebecca.'

'Yes. Yes I would.'

'And would he do anything for you?'

'I don't know. I'd like to think so.'

Darren thought about this, nodded, resumed pacing.

'How often do you see him?' he asked.

'Most days.'

'Where?'

'At the shop. I help him out sometimes.'

'For pay?'

'No. I don't do it for the money.'

'Ever go to his house?'

'Yes. Lots of times.'

'When? When do you go to his house?'

'A couple of times a week. Or when he goes up to see his sister. I go in and look after his cat.'

Darren smiled. 'You've really got the hots for him, haven't you?'

'I wouldn't put it like that.'

Darren looked down at his knife and gingerly touched a finger to the tip of its blade, as if wondering how best to make use of it. A combination of fear and the cold sent shivers through Heidi's body.

'Why are we here?' she asked.

Darren looked up. 'What? Oh, this place. You like it? Took me a while to find somewhere as quiet as this. I've searched all over town in the past few days. Nobody ever comes here. A perfect hideaway.'

'You're living here?'

'Me? No. I like my creature comforts. I'm going to bring Rebecca here.'

Heidi's chills suddenly intensified, scurrying across her body. 'Why?'

'To talk things over with no distractions. Away from people who could influence her. She needs the freedom to be herself.'

Heidi looked again at the knife, the rope, the duct tape. Darren didn't want to give Rebecca freedom; he wanted to abduct her.

Darren had stepped way beyond the bounds of reason.

'I hope you and Rebecca can sort things out,' she said. 'But it's nothing to do with me or Elliott. Please let me go.'

Darren tapped the flat of the blade on his palm. 'Sorry, but it has everything to do with you and Elliott. He stole my girlfriend. He's keeping her from me and he needs to give her back. What you've done tonight has made you his accomplice. You're as guilty as he is.'

'I'm not guilty of anything. Nobody is trying to hurt you. You've got it all wrong, can't you see that?'

Darren suddenly raised the knife and stabbed it down into the benchtop with a bang. He left it embedded there as he advanced on Heidi.

'Don't you fucking dare! I'm not wrong. People don't just leave their loved ones for no reason. Something happened, and I need to know what. Elliott knows. Maybe you know, too.'

'I promise you, I don't know. If I knew where Rebecca was, I'd tell you. But this isn't the right way to do things, is it? Please, Darren, just let me go before you get into serious trouble.'

Darren stared with wild eyes, then shook his head. 'You

don't understand. I'm already in trouble. I've gone too far to stop now.'

Heidi could tell it wasn't a throwaway comment. He was talking about something concrete. Something grave.

'How have you gone too far, Darren?'

His mouth opened and closed, and in the dim glow of the lamp she thought she could see tears welling in his eyes.

'Doesn't matter. Have to move on, right? Have to fix things.'

'I agree. So let me go. That would make things better between *us*, wouldn't it?'

'What would you do if I let you go?'

'Nothing. I'd just go home. I wouldn't say anything, not even to Elliott.'

'LIAR!' He spat the word at her. 'You'd tell him everything. That's what people do when they're really in love. I've been there. You'd tell him and then you'd both tell the police. They'd come after me and they'd stop me from finding Rebecca. That wouldn't be making things better.'

'So . . . you're going to keep me here?'

'You haven't given me a choice.'

The horror of his pronouncement ran through her brain. 'Think about this carefully. Don't do anything you'll regret.'

He became agitated again. 'I regret *everything*! I regret being me. I regret my life. I regret not being able to hold on to the one person who means everything in the world to me. Doesn't matter what I do now, I can't possibly make things any worse.'

'That's not true. It—'

'*Shut up!* Let me think.'

He went back to the bench, levered out his knife, began pacing again.

'Where do you live?' he asked.

'Why?'

'Just answer the fucking question!'

'I rent a flat, not far from Elliott's house.'

'You share it?'

'No, I live alone.'

'And where do you work?'

'At the university. I'm a research student.'

'So you can come and go as you please, right? You can work from home?'

'Sometimes. But I have to be there for meetings and I do some teaching. What's this got to do with—'

It hit her then. He was trying to figure out who might notice her absence.

'It won't work,' she said. 'People will start wondering where I am pretty soon. They'll come looking for me.'

'You're that popular, huh? Well, let's see.'

He put down the knife and picked up her mobile phone, then came across to Heidi and turned the screen towards her. She wondered what he was showing her, and then it struck her that he was simply using the device's facial recognition to unlock it.

Darren strolled back to the bench, his fingers already flying across the phone.

'What are you doing?' she asked.

'You said you're a research student. Well, now it's my turn to do some research.'

She watched, her dread mounting. Darren was going through her texts, her WhatsApp messages, her emails, her social media, her diary, her calendar, her contacts.

Her life was on that phone.

Soon he would know everything about her.

23

Elliott almost bounced out of the bed when his phone started ringing. He had been dead to the world, his mind calmed by the knowledge that he finally had some proof of Darren's harassment.

He scrabbled for his phone, groaned when he saw the call was from Heidi. Why couldn't it wait till morning? And why the hell was she making it a video call? He wasn't sure he felt comfortable about her staring at him in bed, especially while he was wearing his pyjamas.

He answered nonetheless. Heidi didn't look her usual self. She appeared haggard, even upset.

'Hey,' he said. 'Are you okay?'

She burst into tears. Elliott was suddenly wide awake.

'Heidi?'

'I'm sorry, Elliott. I'm really sorry. I've made a big mistake.'

'What are you talking about? Heidi? Heidi?'

He heard some fumbling, rustling noises. The phone's camera was all over the place. Something bright and reflective came into view. It touched Heidi on the lips, then hopped to her cheek, then came to rest below her eyeball.

It was a knife blade.

Elliott sat up. 'Heidi? What the hell?'

And then another face intruded, pressing up against Heidi's to fit onto the screen.

'Hello, Elliott,' Darren said. 'I hope we're not disturbing you. It's pretty late, I know. Sorry about that.'

'Darren? What's going on? What are you doing with Heidi?'

'Your little friend decided to pay me a visit. I've been getting to know her really well. Better than you do, in fact. You should hear some of the stuff she's written about you on her phone. It'd make you blush.'

'Darren, please, don't hurt her. She's got nothing to do with the Rebecca thing.'

'Two girls on the go at once, Elliott? Or is it more than two? You're such a dark horse.'

'Did you hear what I said? She can't help you get Rebecca back.'

Darren side-eyed his captive, his knife still hovering dangerously below her left eyelid.

'Hate to disagree, but I think you're wrong.'

'How? I just told you—'

'You haven't been taking me seriously. Now things are going to change.'

'Darren, this is getting out of control. You're going too far. Please, let Heidi go. We won't tell anyone about this.'

'Yeah, that's what she said. Unfortunately, I don't believe either of you. I trusted you to do the right thing, Elliott, and you let me down. Now we do things my way.'

'Meaning what?'

'Meaning a swap. You bring me Rebecca, and I give you Heidi. I think one woman is enough for any man, don't you?'

Elliott's mind was reeling. This was nuts. It seemed so much the stuff of nightmares that he wasn't even sure he had woken up.

'Darren, listen to yourself. You're talking about kidnapping someone and holding them hostage. You can't do that.'

'She came to me. I didn't invite her. I'm just making her feel welcome.'

Elliott looked into Heidi's eyes. She didn't appear to be feeling welcome. She was terrified.

'It's not going to work. You can't keep her there. People will start to wonder where she is.'

'Yeah, about that. Seems your little friend here doesn't have much of a social life apart from you. Quite sad, to be honest. She's really into her work, but as it's the start of the weekend, nobody at the university is going to miss her for a while. That will give you long enough to sort things out with Rebecca. It'll have to be, because that's all the time I'm giving you. You've got until midnight on Sunday.'

'Darren, please! I'm begging you to let Heidi go. I really don't know where Rebecca is, and she won't answer my calls.'

'Your problem. You sort it out. Send a message to this phone when you've got some good news. And don't get any stupid ideas about tracing Heidi's phone. I'll be switching it off straight after this call. And if I see one police officer around here, if I notice anybody else following me, then I will kill her. Is that clear?'

Elliott knew it was not an empty threat.

'Yes,' he said quietly. 'Perfectly.'

He realised he was crying. He had experienced powerlessness many times before, but never in a situation that might involve sacrificing someone else's life. What frustrated him most was that no amount of that elusive quality called bravery would help him now. He so wanted to be strong, to put on a Liam Neeson act and tell Darren that he would find him and kill him. Instead, he shed tears.

'Don't cry, man,' Darren said. 'Just fix this and get your friend back.'

'Elliott!' Heidi yelled, but she was cut off. The screen went blank as the call was ended, but the scream was still echoing around his brain. His biggest fear was that it might be the last word he would ever hear her utter.

Elliott wiped his eyes, telling himself to convert his anguish into anger. He needed to focus on ridding himself of that lunatic for ever, instead of bowing down to his will as he always seemed to do.

Easier said than done, though, right?

He recalled the blade on Heidi's face and struggled to keep thoughts of her being mutilated out of his mind. Darren had the upper hand. One mistake and her life could be ended with a flick of the wrist.

He thought again about turning to the police, and quickly rejected it. He didn't trust them. He wanted to believe that they were a highly organised group of finely honed experts, making use of the most advanced technology to track down and take out criminals, but he suspected that was the stuff of movies. If the pair who had turned up at his house the other night were anything to go by, Heidi would be as good as dead the moment he rang 999.

Which left . . . What?

Himself, basically. Just him and whatever ability he might possess to persuade either Rebecca or Darren – neither of whom he knew how to find – to see things his way.

It seemed hopeless.

24

'What happens now?' Heidi asked.

'Now?' Darren said. 'That depends on Elliott. If he brings Rebecca back to me it all ends happily ever after.'

'No, I mean right now. Tonight.'

Darren smiled, then stretched his arms. 'Good question. I think it's time for bed, don't you?'

Heidi drew her legs up, looked around for a mattress or somewhere more comfortable that he might be intending to take her.

Darren laughed. 'Don't flatter yourself. You're not a patch on Rebecca. I'm going back to my own bed. You're sleeping here.'

'Y-you're leaving me here?'

'Yup. Just you and the spiders. And possibly some rats. I don't think they'll bother you too much, though.'

He picked up the scissors and duct tape from the bench, then started towards her.

'What are you going to do with that?'

'Just a precaution. I don't want you making too much noise.'

'Please. You seem like a decent guy. You don't need to hurt me.'

'Quiet now. This won't hurt. And I don't have a choice.'

'Yes, you do. Let's talk about this.'

'I've done enough talking for tonight.' The tape gave out a high-pitched squeal as he peeled it open.

'Wait! What if I need . . . you know?'

He looked mystified. 'What?'

'The toilet. What if I need to go?'

He hesitated, and then he said, 'You can go now.'

'I don't want to go now.'

'You go now, or not at all. What's it to be?'

Heidi considered the offer. To enable her to visit the toilet, Darren would have to untie her. It might give her the opportunity she needed to escape. At the very least, it would allow her to get a proper look around her for something she might use as a weapon.

'Hurry up!' Darren said. 'I need my bed.'

'Okay, okay. I'll go.'

Darren nodded, then took the tape and scissors back to the bench and retrieved his knife.

'Don't try anything,' he told her. 'I don't want to get your blood all over me.'

He untied her feet first, then walked behind her and untied her hands, releasing her from the post.

'Stand up,' he commanded. He pointed with the knife. 'Toilet's over in the corner there.'

She started moving towards the door, Darren just a couple

of steps behind her. She scanned her surroundings as best she could without giving the game away. The garage had been pretty much emptied out. Bulky items of furniture like cupboards and shelving had been left in place, but no wrenches or hammers or anything else she could use to cave in this bastard's skull.

The lamplight became ever dimmer as she neared the far corner of the garage. When she pushed open the toilet door and peered inside, she could see only blackness.

'I can't go in there,' she said.

'You said you wanted to pee.'

'I know. But I can't see a thing. I can't see what I'm doing.'

'What's there to see? It's not like you have to stand when you're doing it.'

'I can't even see where the toilet is. Please, can I have the lamp, just for a minute?'

'Jeez,' Darren said. 'Why do you have to make everything so fucking complicated? Don't move.'

He went for the lamp, brought it back, handed it to her.

'There. Don't take all fucking night about it. And don't flush unless you're taking a dump. There won't be any water to refill the cistern once you empty it.'

She grimaced. There was something deeply intrusive about his reference to her bodily functions.

Entering the tiny space, she pushed the door closed behind her, noting that its lock and handle had been removed. Darren could shove his way in at any time. The room contained just a toilet and hand basin. No mirror that she might break to create shards of glass. She looked up at the tiny window set high in the top of the wall and saw that it was reinforced with wire mesh. There was no way she'd be able to break through it even if she could get up there.

She bent down, manoeuvring the lamp to give her a better view of anything that might be hiding beneath the cistern.

The lamp . . .

It was a modern version of a miner's lamp, steel and glass, with a handle on the top. Heidi hefted it up and down. Not as heavy as she would have liked, but beggars can't be choosers.

She put the lamp on the floor and thought about her options as she squeezed out what little fluid there was in her bladder.

'You done yet?' Darren called.

'Just about.' She readjusted her clothing and picked up the lamp.

One shot, she thought. Just one clean shot. Enough to stun him, enough to get the knife off him . . .

Darren kicked the door open. The bang of it slamming against the wall was like a gunshot.

'Come out,' he ordered.

She stepped towards him, gripping the lamp tightly in her fist, readying her arm muscles to take an almighty swing at his head.

Darren moved back, out of reach.

She took another step towards him.

'Stop,' he said.

He knows, she thought to herself. He knows what I'm thinking.

'Put the lamp on the floor,' he ordered.

'W-what?'

'Put the lamp on the floor and walk back over there.'

Decision time. Could she rush him now? Could she overpower him?

He had a knife. A big fucking knife. She had a measly little lamp.

'Are you deaf? Put the fucking lamp down and do what I say!'

Don't be stupid, she told herself. Reluctantly, she lowered the lamp to the floor.

Darren escorted her back to the concrete post, told her to sit, then tied her up again. If anything, the restraints were even tighter than before.

She watched as Darren fetched the lamp, and then the duct tape and scissors. Tears stung her eyes as he wrapped a long piece of the tape around her head, covering her mouth.

'I'll be back in the morning,' he told her. 'Unless your boyfriend tries anything silly. If anything happens to me, nobody'll ever find you here.'

She had assumed that he would at least leave the lamp here with her, but even that was too much to hope for. When Darren had opened the shutters and taken his car outside, he turned the lamp off and then closed her in.

She listened to him lock up the outer gates and drive away. The silence became total, the blackness complete. She was already aching all over, the bindings cutting into her wrists and ankles, her arms stretched behind her and around the post, the concrete floor hard against her buttocks. She didn't know how she was going to cope for the many bleak hours ahead of her.

Optimism seemed unreachable. The thought of police cars and helicopters combing the streets for her was a pipe dream. Darren was right about her. All told, hers was a pretty sad and lonely existence. Nobody would miss her. She'd be lucky to get even a single phone message over the weekend. She had put on a pretence with Elliott. Gave him the impression that she went out partying and on dates with other guys. The truth couldn't have been more different.

The tears poured out of her then. She was proud of the strength she had shown to Darren, but now, with nobody to witness it, she could cry freely.

Her one hope in the whole world – the one person who might possibly get her out of this mess – was Elliott. And, reluctant though she was to admit it, he seemed the unlikeliest of saviours.

25

It had been well over a year since Elliott had last visited the gym – probably more like two years. It was just another source of anxiety. When he had originally signed up at the Tone Zone, his trepidation had been outweighed by the high hopes that it might make him look more manly and aid his self-esteem. What actually happened was that the prime physical specimens around him made him feel even more puny, and even though he stuck at the workouts for over a month, his pain and breathlessness diminished at a rate consistent with the increase in his muscle mass, which is to say hardly at all.

And now he was back.

He had racked his brain all night for answers. Well, except for when he was worrying himself sick about Heidi. Weirdly, the forcible removal of her from his life had made him suddenly realise how important she was to him, and how little he had appreciated her. He was worried sick. Where was she? Was Darren hurting her? Was she even still alive?

In his search for solutions, he had naturally focused on

Rebecca, but not in any flattering way. His opinion of her had been flipped on its head. She could help him and she knew it, but was refusing to do so. He had phoned her multiple times throughout the night, and each of his calls had been blocked.

But that focus had caused him to revisit the short time he had spent with Rebecca – to run through whatever snippets of conversation he could recall that managed to filter into his consciousness through the awe he had experienced in her presence. One that had stayed with him was that, immediately prior to the event that was to turn Elliott's world upside down, Rebecca had been to the gym.

This gym.

Story at the ready, Elliott pushed open the door and entered. Even at this early hour of the morning he could hear the clanging and pounding of the equipment, along with the grunting and panting of its users. It all made him want to go back to bed.

Behind the desk facing Elliott was a square-jawed young man wearing a T-shirt stretched tightly across muscles the size of basketballs. As the man looked up at him, Elliott could swear he could see pity in his eyes.

'Hey, man,' said the jock. 'How's it going?'

'Good, thanks.'

'You looking to get fit? You've come to the right place.'

Elliott resented the implication that he looked severely out of shape, however true it might be.

'Actually,' he said, 'I'm trying to find someone.'

'Yeah? Who might that be?'

'A girl. Her name's Rebecca. She's just joined this gym.'

'Uh-huh.'

Elliott wasn't sure what to do with that response. He had been hoping for something a bit more helpful.

'The thing is, I've got something that belongs to her.' He reached into his pocket. 'This wallet.'

The wallet was bright pink. Elliott had dashed to the charity shop an hour ago and picked out the most girly-looking item he could find.

'Yeah? How'd you end up with it?'

'I met her in a bar on Monday night. She mentioned that she'd just been to the gym. Anyway, when she went, she left this behind.'

'You met her in a bar?'

Again Elliott felt resentful. Why wasn't it believable that he could talk to a woman in a bar?

'Just briefly,' he said, almost apologetically. 'All I got was her first name.'

The jock seemed satisfied with a version of events that went nowhere near a vision of Elliott actually being successful in picking up a woman.

'There's no ID in the wallet?'

Elliott opened it up, showing the money and the junk he had stuffed into it.

'Nah. Just some cash, old train tickets, some receipts, that kind of thing.'

The man looked doubtful, as well he might. Who doesn't have something with their name on in their wallet? A driving licence? Credit card? Elliott knew it wasn't a great cover story, but it was the best he could come up with.

'Okay, man. You want to leave it with me? I'll check our system, find this Rebecca who was here on Monday, and give it back to her. Sound good to you?'

Elliott had expected this. He frowned. 'Actually, I was hoping to give it back to her in person, if that's possible.'

'What, you don't trust us?'

'No – I mean yes. Of course I trust you. Absolutely. It's just that, well, you know . . .'

The man shook his head. 'What?'

'I was hoping . . . I mean . . . The other night, in the bar, I thought we were getting on pretty well . . .' He thought about winking, decided against it.

'Ah,' said the jock. 'Gotcha.' He said nothing else for a while, and Elliott began to wonder if the penny really had dropped, and what more he might do to push it over the edge.

And then the man suddenly yelled out 'Enya!', startling Elliott. A woman appeared from a back room and glided silently up to her colleague. She was clad in dark Lycra that made it crystal clear that body fat was not permitted within its confines.

'What can we do for you today?' she said to Elliott. The pair of them gave Elliott the creeps. It was like they had been manufactured by aliens working from a blueprint of idealised humans.

'He wants a woman,' the jock said.

'I see,' Enya said, still staring at Elliott. 'That's . . . an unusual request.'

'To be clear,' Elliott said hastily, 'not just any woman. A particular woman. Her name's Rebecca. She's a member of your gym. Only just joined.'

'I see,' Enya said again. 'Well, we do have a new joiner called Rebecca here at our fitness suite.'

Elliott noticed how she corrected his use of the word 'gym'.

'Yes, and as I was just saying to your friend here—'

'Bryce.'

Bryce. Of course it was.

'Yes. I've got Rebecca's wallet. I was hoping to return it to her.'

'Did Bryce explain that we'd be happy to—'

'Yes, yes, he did explain that.' Elliott's frustration was mounting, particularly as he suspected that Enya had already overheard every word that had been uttered since his arrival. 'But I'd like to speak to her myself, if that's okay.'

There was a long silence. Once again, Elliott wondered if he was the one who was expected to break it. He had felt awkward enough telling Bryce in as near a man-to-man way as he could manage that he wished to pursue Rebecca romantically; saying it to Enya would sound so creepy that she'd probably feed him his own testicles.

It was Bryce who spoke. 'What exactly would you like us to do for you, sir?'

The word 'sir' was usually a term of respect, but coming from Bryce's mouth made it sound to Elliott like he was being awarded a badge of inferiority.

'Well, I thought maybe if you could let me have Rebecca's address . . .'

There was a sharp and simultaneous intake of breath from both trainers. Then they shook their heads in slow and perfect synchrony. Definitely androids, Elliott thought.

'We can't give out client details,' Enya said.

'That would be a severe breach of data protection,' Bryce said.

'I'll tell you what, though,' Enya said brightly, 'I'm sure we must have Rebecca's number on file. Why don't I give her a call and tell her you're here with her wallet, and we take it from there?'

'No,' Elliott said, his voice rising. 'You don't understand. I need to see her alone. You need to tell me where she lives. Please. I—'

He stopped when he saw the concerned expressions and realised how desperate he sounded.

'Sir,' Bryce said, his voice far less welcoming now, 'I think you need to leave.'

'Look,' Elliott said, 'I know this must sound ridiculous, but you just need to believe me when I tell you that this is actually a matter of life and death. If I don't see Rebecca soon, somebody is going to die.'

Bryce and Enya looked at each other as if wirelessly exchanging data, then turned back to Elliott.

'Do you even know her full name?' Enya asked.

Elliott stared at her.

'No,' he admitted. 'As I just told Bryce here, I don't know her full name. And I can't tell you what this is really all about. I'm just asking you to trust me. I'm not crazy, and I'm not going to hurt her. I just need her help.'

In response, Bryce reached for the phone on his desk. 'I'm calling the police.'

Elliott took a stride towards him, halted when he saw the potential for bone-breaking violence in the man's eyes.

'No. Please. Don't call the police. It'll only make matters worse.'

'For you, maybe.'

'Yes. For me. But also— Okay, forget it. Forget I was ever here.'

He turned away. As he reached the door, he heard Bryce say, 'Man, you need serious help.'

Back on the street, Elliott thought about how true those words were. He needed help. The problem was that nobody was willing to give it to him.

And time was ticking away.

26

Heidi felt like shit.

Each muscle and sinew was either on fire or completely numb. She had slept hardly a wink, partly because of the discomfort but also through fear. Darren had been right about the unwanted creatures: she had heard them scurrying about in the darkness, scratching and nibbling. On several occasions she felt they were on her – a rat's whiskers touching her foot or a spider crawling across her scalp. She was cold, too. The chill had seeped right into her bones, adding further to the woes of pain, hunger and a need to use the toilet again.

And then there was the added dread of what Darren might do to her when he came back. When he learnt that Elliott had failed to find that bitch Rebecca.

She was never more grateful than she was this morning for the intrusion of daylight. Seeping under the doors and through a grimy skylight, it was weak and without warmth, suggestive of a bleak sky outside, but it least it returned sight to her. She scanned the garage again, more slowly and carefully this time, scrutinising everything for its possible utility. Top of the list was her car. She tried to visualise the contents of its glovebox and boot, tried to see beyond the confectionary wrappers and tissues and other junk to find something that might actually help her. That was assuming she could even get to it. In the night she had run through all kinds of scenarios that involved overpowering Darren and then leaping into her car and using it as a battering ram to break through the doors and gates on her route to freedom.

Now, in the cold light of day, they all seemed far too fanciful.

They felt even less realistic when Darren turned up again.

She heard the squeal of the outer gates first, then the car being driven onto the forecourt and the gates being relocked. Her heart was pounding furiously even before he slid back the heavy wooden door.

After he had brought in his own car and closed the door, he removed the tape from her mouth and smiled down at her.

'Good night?' he asked.

'What do you think?'

'Hungry? Want some breakfast?' He held up a plastic bag he'd brought with him. 'I bought some pastries.'

She nodded. 'I need the toilet again.'

'Yeah, I thought about that, too.' He reached into his bag and took out a pair of toilet rolls. 'I bet Elliott never bought you toilet paper.' He laughed.

He put the bag down on the bench, then took out his knife and came back to her. As before, he removed the rope from her ankles before untying her hands.

'You can get up. Just remember I'm the one with the knife.'

Heidi stood, grateful for the freedom to move around once more. She shook her limbs and stretched, hoping to banish the pain from being kept constrained in a single pose for such a long period.

Darren tossed a toilet roll across to her. 'Knock yourself out.'

While she was in the washroom, Heidi took another look up at the tiny window and felt the disappointment as she confirmed to herself that it wasn't a feasible escape route.

When she returned, Darren was already stuffing his face with a croissant. He beckoned Heidi over to the bench. He slid a bottle of water and an open box containing two more pastries towards her. He made no attempt to offer up the only wooden stool, but she would have declined it anyway. She had no doubt that she would be back on the floor again soon.

While she downed her meagre breakfast, Heidi used the opportunity to take a closer look at the other items on the table. Aside from food and drink and the lamp, the only things she wanted to get her hands on were the knife or the scissors. She would do anything within her power to get away from this man, including ramming a sharp object through his eye.

'Just so you know,' Darren said, 'I think Elliott's already forgotten about you.'

Heidi shook her head. 'He hasn't forgotten about me.'

'No? I checked your phone this morning, and there's nothing from him yet.'

'It's still early. He wouldn't have been able to do much overnight.'

'Hmm. I also drove past his little cat shop, and guess what?

He was serving his sad customers, acting like it was just a normal day.'

The words hit her hard. She didn't know what she had expected Elliott to do, but it didn't involve turning up for work.

'It's like he doesn't think you're important,' Darren said. 'Doesn't he give a shit about you?'

Heidi said nothing. She had suddenly lost her appetite, and tears were stinging her eyes. Had Elliott given her up as a lost cause? Would he do that to her?

'Eat up,' Darren said. 'Looks like you could be here for a long time.'

Saturday dragged. Elliott did his allotted hours in the shop because he didn't know what else he could do. But his mind was never on his work; it was always on Heidi and Rebecca and Darren – the triumvirate that seemed to govern his life now. He found himself having to ask customers to repeat their requests – often more than once. Several went away empty-handed, disappointed with the uncharacteristically poor standard of service. Some were more concerned, asking if he was okay.

But he wasn't okay. Not at all.

He was in the very definition of a no-win situation. It wasn't even as though he had avenues he could explore. The last of those had been the trip to the gym, and that had been a complete disaster. He knew that the staff there had only been doing their job, but couldn't help feeling that if he had handled things differently, explained himself better, then maybe they would have tossed him a bone. Instead, he'd come across as a pervert.

Elliott's nerves were shredded. Where was Heidi? What was Darren doing to her?

A part of him still wanted to call the police. That portion of his brain kept insisting that the police were the experts and would know exactly what to do in a situation like this. And then he would picture Heidi with the tip of a huge knife against her face, and he would abandon the notion.

So what else was there?

How do you find a person when they don't want to be found and you don't even know their name?

Okay, he thought, what *do* I know about her?

She's blonde and beautiful. She used to go out with a maniac. She likes to shop at Waitrose.

He paused to focus on that. Could he drive to Waitrose, try to describe her to the staff? Use a cover story like he did at the gym?

He shook his head. Waste of time, and liable to end up with the security guards descending on him.

So what else?

She drives a Mercedes. Contact the dealerships?

Hardly likely to be successful without at least a registration number. He didn't even know the colour.

Moving on . . .

She has a birthmark on her inner thigh and a tattoo on her buttock.

There you go! I just wander around the streets asking random strangers if they've seen what's under the skirt of a beautiful blonde called Rebecca. That won't get me arrested, will it?

The tattoo, though. Didn't she say it's a butterfly? Call some tattooists?

Again he shook his head. Everybody has butterfly tattoos, and often on their butts. And she probably had it done years ago, in a completely different town.

Surrey? She said she was born somewhere in Surrey.

Yeah, but Surrey's such a big place, and she also said she'd lived up north for the last ten years, and 'the north' is even bigger than Surrey. So that doesn't help.

What else? Think, for Christ's sake!

There was the beauty therapy. She had mentioned that as her occupation, and it had stuck in his mind because he didn't know what it was. But he had already spent hours searching online for a beauty therapist matching her name or description. Even called many of them.

Nothing.

He suspected now that it was a lie anyway. It hardly seemed to fit with her driving a Mercedes.

Okay, what does she like?

She likes cats, but lots of people like cats, so that doesn't narrow it down. Her favourite film is *Les Miserables*. Again, too wide a net to cast. She likes dancing. Yeah, right, because that's such a niche thing to do. Hardly anyone likes a good dance, right?

Jesus, where is this getting me? What is the point of—

Dancing.

A club. She mentioned a club she goes to. What the hell was it called?

Wait. It's the same one Heidi has been to.

The Whirligig.

27

Darren had come back to the garage at lunchtime, but that had been hours ago. It was dark. The noises had started up again – the creatures of the night venturing out. She guessed they had probably caught scent of the food that had been consumed here recently and were scavenging for crumbs. She hoped they didn't have a taste for human flesh.

An image still haunted her – of Elliott at work, as though it were any normal day. She kept telling herself that Darren had probably exaggerated. In a quick drive-past there was no way he could have assessed Elliott's state of mind. Maybe he really was frantic with worry. Maybe he was just trying to keep himself occupied so that he didn't fall apart.

Yes, it had to be that.

But still . . .

He was in work, when he should have been out looking for Rebecca.

And yet, in practical terms, she didn't know what 'looking for Rebecca' might mean. Where would Elliott possibly start?

Maybe he would surprise her. Maybe he was a lot more resourceful than she was giving him credit for.

Because if not . . .

She heard the car arrive again. Darren brought it inside, locked up, switched on the lamp.

'What time is it?' she asked after he'd removed the tape from her mouth.

'Nearly nine o'clock,' Darren said. 'You want to hear my news?'

Elation surged through her. Elliott's done it, she thought. He's found Rebecca!

'Yes. Tell me.'

Darren smiled. 'There's no news. Not a peep out of your boyfriend. He's a real loser, isn't he?'

She said nothing. She wanted to reject the accusation, but somehow she couldn't find it within her.

'I think we should call him. Would you like to hear his excuses?'

She so wanted to see Elliott again, to hear his voice. But more than that, she needed to know that he hadn't abandoned her.

'Yes. Please.'

'Same rules as before. You say anything about where we are, and I will finish you in a heartbeat. You understand?'

She nodded.

Darren sat next to her on the floor, the knife to her face and the phone held out in front of him. Then he called Elliott.

The video call was answered immediately.

'Heidi!' Elliott shouted. 'Are you okay? Please tell me you're okay.'

'Elliott, I'm fine. I'm so glad to see you.'

'All right,' Darren said. 'Enough of the cringey stuff. What's going on, Elliott? I don't suppose you have Rebecca with you, do you?'

'Darren, I'm trying. I swear to you. What you've asked me to do is next to impossible, but I'm doing my best.'

'Really? Because I don't think Heidi here believes you. I think she's losing faith in you.'

'That's not true!' Heidi called out. 'I trust you, Elliott.'

'Is she mistaken?' Darren asked. 'Are you going to get hold of Rebecca for me? Because it didn't look like you were trying very hard when I saw you in the shop today.'

'You . . . you saw me?'

'Several times. You weren't out looking for Rebecca.'

'I . . . It's not straightforward. You have to give me more time.'

'I gave you a whole weekend. And you've already wasted half of it.'

'I haven't wasted it. I'm following up on things.'

'Yeah, sure. Looks like it. I wasn't kidding, Elliott. You know what will happen to Heidi if you don't deliver on time tomorrow.'

Heidi couldn't hold back her doubts any longer. 'Elliott, please tell me you're trying to help me.'

Elliott's eyes shone with sincerity. His voice began to crack. 'I promise. I'll get you out of there. I won't let him hurt you.'

'Not really much you can do to stop me, is there?' Darren said. 'Get off your arse and find Rebecca. You have one day left. So does Heidi.'

When the screen went blank, Elliott screamed. On the sofa, Bill raised his head and stared at him for daring to interrupt his sleep.

It had crossed Elliott's mind to tell Heidi what he was doing to find Rebecca, but he feared that saying his plans out loud would make them sound so lame, and the last thing he wanted to do was lower her spirits.

Because, he admitted to himself, as plans go, this one *was* pretty lame. It was also last-ditch. If nobody at The Whirligig could point him in Rebecca's direction, then that would be the end of it. Whether it put Heidi's life in danger or not, he would have to go to the police.

He had decided he would get to the club at one in the morning. Most of the clubs didn't really get going until after the pubs closed, and he didn't want to stick out. The one thing in his favour was that it was Saturday night, which would surely be any club's busiest night. If Rebecca really was a regular, then it would give him his best opportunity of finding someone who could put him on the right track.

He kept telling himself that it could work. It *had* to work. Heidi was depending on him.

He checked his watch. Just under four hours to go.

28

As he stood in the queue outside The Whirligig, Elliott's anxiety had already reached almost unmanageable proportions.

He didn't know anything about nightclubs. While everyone else his age had been clubbing, he had been nursing his mother. He had no regrets but it made him feel totally out of place. For one thing, he was sure his clothes marked him out as a complete outsider. His shirt and trousers were what he normally wore to work. He also wished he hadn't brought a jacket with him, because it seemed that everybody else had swallowed some magic anti-freeze instead. The girls in particular didn't seem to care how much of their flesh was exposed to the chilly night air.

When he eventually reached the front of the queue, the doorman looked him up and down, smiled, then nodded him in. Elliott suspected that he had instantly been labelled as being incapable of causing any trouble.

At a desk just inside the door, most of the arrivals showed a membership card and went straight through. Elliott had to pay a hefty entrance fee that was a big dent in his finances.

But then he was in, and it was every bit as bad as he had expected.

The noise was intense. The music involved a steady and thunderous beat that felt as though someone was using his head as a drum. It was accompanied by a cacophony of voices that made him wonder how anything was actually heard and comprehended.

There was neon and LED lighting everywhere, along with spotlights that rotated and changed colour, frequently dazzling him. It took him a while just to locate the bar, and then he began the long uncomfortable trek to get to it, forging his way through densely packed bodies.

It was at least three deep at the bar. Elliott patiently waited his turn, even though it seemed that many others didn't. He wasn't much closer after almost ten minutes. Eventually he spotted a gap and dived into it, apologising profusely as he stood on a girl's toe.

He watched as the young bartender closest to him flipped bottles into the air and then caught them before pouring streams of brightly coloured alcoholic beverages from great heights into a cocktail shaker. When his display was finally over and the drink had been served, Elliott waved a hand and managed to catch his eye.

'What can I get you?' the bartender shouted at him.

'Actually,' Elliott shouted back, 'I'm looking for someone.'

'I only make drinks. What can I get you?'

Elliott realised he needed to get the man on his side, and that he wouldn't achieve that in the short time it would take to be served a bottle of beer.

'Er, okay. I'll have whatever that girl just had.'

'A Six-Fingered Hand Job?'

'Er, yeah. One of those, please.'

The man started his routine again. After one particularly tricky manoeuvre that would have ended up with broken glass everywhere if Elliott ever attempted it, he tried his questioning once more.

'You mind if I ask you about this person I'm looking for?'

'You can try. I doubt if I'll know them. You know how many thousands of customers come through here every week?'

'No. How many?'

'I don't know, but lots. I don't know any of their names.'

'You might know this one. She's called Rebecca.'

'Rebecca what?'

'I don't know.'

'That's not a lot of help.'

'Best I can do. Do you know any Rebeccas?'

'Maybe.'

'This one's very blonde and very beautiful. Could be a model.'

The bartender said nothing for a while as he concentrated on his juggling. Elliott wanted to tell him not to bother for his benefit – he'd be perfectly happy if the drinks were poured in the normal fashion – but he thought it might upset the guy.

'Why are you looking for her?'

'I found something that belongs to her. It's valuable.'

'You found it here, in the club?'

It hadn't occurred to Elliott that this might be part of his story, but he thought it sounded much better than the version he was about to relate.

'Yeah. Last week. We got talking. I only got her first name. She had to go, but she left something. I'd like to return it to her.'

The bartender finished shaking the drink and began pouring it into a glass.

'I only know one Rebecca that comes in here.'

Elliott's eyes lit up, and this time not because of the spotlights.

'Is she blonde? And beautiful?'

'Oh, yeah.'

'Know how I can find her?'

A pause. 'Maybe.'

Elliott had seen enough films to know what to do now. He took out his wallet, edged a couple of notes out. The bartender waited. Elliott showed the corner of another note.

The bartender put out his hand. Elliott slipped him the cash and watched as the man went over to the till and then returned without change. This was getting to be an expensive night.

'So?' Elliott said.

The man lowered his voice, making it difficult to hear what he was saying. It sounded to Elliott that he said, 'The booze.'

'The what?'

The bartender shifted his eyes to the right, looking across to the far side of the club. 'The booths. If it's the same girl, she was over there the last time I saw her.'

Elliott followed the gaze. He saw a seating area containing well-padded semicircular booths, mostly occupied. From this distance he couldn't see Rebecca, but his pulse was racing.

Could she be over there right now, just metres away from him?

'Don't forget your Hand Job,' the bartender said.

'What? Oh, yeah.' Elliott picked up his drink, took a sip, winced. It tasted like rocket fuel.

He moved away from the bar, his eyes on the booths. He hadn't counted on this. Best-case scenario, he'd hoped that someone might give him a useful pointer, a direction to follow, someone else to ask in a long chain of enquiries. Could it be as easy as this? And if his quest really was over, what was he going to say to her?

He took another sip, more for courage this time. No point overthinking it. He'd have to play it by ear. He prayed that it wasn't a different Rebecca. Not after his hopes had been raised so dramatically.

Drink held aloft to avoid it getting knocked, he approached the seating area. The decibel levels abated slightly here, and there seemed to be less chance of unwanted laser eye treatment, but it was gloomier, and he found himself having to get up close to each booth to examine its occupants, some of whom seemed perturbed by the close scrutiny of the nerdy stranger in their midst.

And then he saw her.

Rebecca.

The booth at which she was sat was tightly packed; others stood around her. But she was not the centre of attention. This prize went to a handsome dark-haired man in a designer suit, regaling his onlookers with an anecdote that had them captivated as they sipped their expensive champagne. Rebecca sat next to him. Well, not merely *next* to him, but practically on his lap, one of her hands clutching his thigh. She was wearing a strappy cleavage-revealing sparkly dress, and Elliott marvelled at how she looked even more stunning than he remembered. But her own eyes were fixed firmly on her male friend as she hung on his every word.

Elliott came right up to the group, drink still in hand. Nobody seemed to notice him at first. He didn't have their confidence, their presence. He was an irrelevance to them.

The man finished his story with the punchline, 'And then he looked down at his feet and realised he was still in his fucking slippers!' Elliott had no idea what he'd just missed, but the man's disciples seemed to find this hilarious. Rebecca in particular almost spat out her drank before laughing uproariously.

Her amusement was curtailed as soon as she caught sight of Elliott. He raised his glass to her in salute, and for a few seconds she seemed unsure how to respond.

And then she took off.

Grabbing her bag, she slipped out of the booth and legged it. Elliott put his drink down on a nearby table and hurried after her, calling her name. She didn't stop. If anything, she increased her speed. Elliott picked up his own pace, ignoring the angry shouts of people as he barged past them.

'Rebecca!' he called. 'Please, I need to talk to you.'

She started heading to the entrance of the club, then suddenly changed her mind and went in the opposite direction. Elliott continued his pursuit, repeatedly calling after her.

Rebecca headed towards what looked like a fire door. She slammed her palms against the security bar and pushed the door open and dived outside. As Elliott raced for the door, he heard more shouting. A hand grabbed at his elbow and he shook it off before slipping through the doorway.

He found himself in a courtyard filled with metal beer kegs and empty beer-bottle crates. Rebecca was at a wooden door set into the wall, struggling vainly with the lock.

'Rebecca! Please don't run away from me. I need your help.'

She turned and looked at him, and for a brief moment he thought he detected some compassion in her eyes. But then his pursuers were on him. Burly security staff grabbed him, while the suited man who was at the booth came around in front of him, his expression containing little of the humour it had possessed earlier.

'What the fuck is going on?' the man asked.

'Ask her,' Elliott said. 'Ask Rebecca.'

The man looked over at her. 'Babe?'

Rebecca glanced at Elliott, then turned her gaze back on the man. 'This guy keeps following me, Matt. I don't know who he is but he just keeps turning up wherever I go.'

'That's not true!' Elliott said. 'She *does* know me. I helped her out when someone was stalking her, and now I need her to help me. Rebecca, tell them the truth. Please.'

Again Matt looked to her for a reply.

'He's obviously nuts,' she said. 'Listen to him. *He's* my stalker.'

She may as well have slapped him, for the sting her words carried. He couldn't believe that she was doing this to him again.

Matt took a couple of steps closer to Elliott. He exchanged

glances with the security men, who tightened their grip on Elliott's arms.

And then Matt punched him in the stomach.

It was the hardest punch Elliott had ever received. It seemed to drive right through to his spine, causing the air in his lungs to explode out of his mouth like the cork from a champagne bottle. The pain was excruciating.

The men allowed him to drop to his knees on a hard stone floor that was slick with spilt beer, and he thought he was going to die or at least pass out. He opened his mouth, praying that the contents of his stomach stayed where they were while he endeavoured to suck precious oxygen back into his system.

The next surprise was the kick in the ribs. It was like being whacked with a sledgehammer. He went all the way down, rolling onto his back as he tried to deal with the agony and the nausea and the inability to breathe.

Fingers clawed at his clothes. He tried to swat them away and received a sharp slap to the face for his trouble. A hand dipped into each of his pockets, emptying them of his possessions.

Elliott coughed, blinked, stared up at the man called Matt going through his wallet. Matt pulled out his money and let it flutter down, then did the same for each of his cards, stopping when he got to his driving licence.

'Elliott Whiston,' he read out. Then he dropped the wallet onto Elliott's face before squatting down next to him. 'Listen to me, Elliott Whiston,' he said quietly. 'This is my club you're in, okay? And that woman over there is my girl. I don't know what your little game is, but if I ever catch you here again, or if you bother Rebecca one more time, I will come for you, and I will not be so friendly. Understand?'

Elliott tried to speak, but somehow the words wouldn't form. Matt slapped him again.

'Do you understand?'

Elliott managed a nod and a croaky 'Yes'.

'Good. Now piss off.' He stood and turned to one of his henchmen. 'Escort this gentleman outside.'

While one of the bouncers dragged Elliott to his feet, the other started gathering up his belongings and stuffing them into one of Elliott's jacket pockets. Elliott watched as Rebecca went back into the club with Matt. When she cast one last look back at him, Elliott thought he saw sorrow in her eyes, but he could find no forgiveness.

The bouncers took an arm each, dragged him inside. Took him all the way through the dense crowds of people. He saw how the customers nudged each other and laughed. There was no sympathy here. They all thought he was a sad loser who needed to be thrown out before he spoilt their fun.

They reached the street and deposited him at the kerbside, telling him to 'Go home, man. And don't come back.'

And then, in front of all the staring punters waiting their turn to enter the nightclub, Elliott bent over and vomited noisily and copiously onto the pavement.

29

So close . . .

That was the thought going through Elliott's mind as he sat on his sofa, his hand alternately soothing his burning ribs and his throbbing abdomen.

He had come so close to Rebecca. Almost within touching distance. It was far more than he'd hoped for when he'd set off for the nightclub.

But close doesn't get you the big fat Cuban cigar, does it? No, it gets you beaten and threatened and humiliated.

He wished he'd taken karate lessons. Or kung fu. Anyway, one of those fancy martial arts so that he could have kicked some asses back there. But that wasn't real life. Real life sucked.

He'd let her down. Heidi, that is. He'd been handed Rebecca on a platter, so why hadn't he made more of the opportunity?

And then he told himself that it wouldn't have mattered anyway. Rebecca had washed her hands of him. Used him and thrown him away. Look at how she had lied to her new boyfriend. The beating Elliott took – that was down to her.

But why? What was she up to? Why did the truth need to be kept away from Matt?

And as for Heidi: how was he ever going to live with the knowledge that he could have done more to help her?

Because he *could* do more. It would be completely reckless, but he knew he had to do it. And he had to act now.

He left the house again, got into his car and drove back to the club.

He had no intention of going back inside. That would be foolhardy. Instead, he hunkered down in his seat and waited, his eyes on the front of the club. Adrenalin was the fuel that would keep him awake for as many hours as it took. He just prayed she hadn't already left.

Rebecca and the man called Matt exited the club at half past three in the morning. Even at that ungodly hour, Rebecca looked newly minted. Apparently insanely happy, she clung to the arm of her suitor, a taller and bestubbled version of Tom Cruise.

The pair crossed the street and climbed into a black Range Rover. Elliott fired up his engine and prepared to follow.

This time of night, the roads were quiet, and keeping the Range Rover in his sights wasn't hard. Elliott just hoped that he wasn't simultaneously in Matt's sights. He promised himself that if Matt suddenly jammed on his brakes and leapt out, then he was going to ram down the accelerator and drive hell for leather out of there. Bravery had its attractions but it could also be overrated.

He was thankful that the journey was a short one: barely ten minutes. The Range Rover turned onto the extensive driveway of a large modern property. Wooden panelling and acres of glass. Made Elliott's own house feel like a shed.

Elliott pulled over, then lowered his window and dowsed the lights before killing the engine. From here he could no longer see the Range Rover, but he heard the closing of its doors and then the tinkle of Rebecca's laughter before that, too, faded.

So now he knew how to find her. He didn't know if this was her permanent address, but he suspected that she spent a lot of time here.

Elliott took out his phone and typed a message to Heidi: *I've found Rebecca.*

He doubted that Darren would read it immediately. Might not even check Heidi's phone for the next few hours. But at some point this morning he would see it.

It would have to be good enough, because Elliott could do no more.

30

A second night tied to the post had been almost unbearable. Heidi felt so weak this morning, any energy she had possessed used up in trying to address her pain and discomfort. A third night would be impossible.

But then there wasn't going to be a third night, was there? If Elliott came through for her, then, according to Darren, she would be released. And if not, well . . .

To be honest, she didn't believe she would get out of here alive either way. Darren had dug himself a hole and he knew it. He couldn't allow her to go blabbing to the police.

Which meant only one thing: she would have to attempt to escape today. There was no alternative. If she failed, she would be no worse off. She had nothing to lose but her life.

Sunday is a good day to die, she told herself.

As if on cue, Darren arrived with breakfast. As usual, he untied her to allow a toilet break. These short trips had become almost routine – something on which Heidi was relying. She needed Darren to have stopped suspecting that she would somehow turn the opportunity to her advantage – which was, in fact, precisely what she was planning.

'Guess what?' Darren said to her as they munched on the pastries. He seemed unusually buoyant this morning.

'You've got news which is no news again, right?' she answered. She'd had enough of his games.

'I thought Elliott was your superhero.'

'He's not a superhero, Darren. He's just an ordinary guy whose life you've made a misery. His and mine and Rebecca's. I hope you're proud.'

Darren blinked. 'I'm the one who's had the love of his life taken away.'

'Whatever.'

They continued eating, and then Darren said, 'So, do you want to hear the news or not?'

'Thrill me.'

'He's found her.'

'Rebecca?'

'So he says.'

'How? Where is she?'

'My questions exactly. I think we should give him a ring, don't you?'

Heidi wolfed down her food and drink. She needed the calories if she was going to stay strong, but she was also desperate to know what Elliott had achieved. A spark of hope flickered inside her.

Darren tied her to the post again and made the call.

'Hey, Elliott,' he said. 'How are you this morning? Looking a little worse for wear there.'

Heidi had to agree. Elliott looked exhausted and in some discomfort.

'I'm fine,' Elliott said. 'Did you get my message?'

'I got it,' Darren said. 'Is it true? You found Rebecca?'

'Yeah. So now we make a deal, right?'

'A deal?'

'What we agreed. I find Rebecca and you let Heidi go.'

Darren nodded. 'That sounds fair. Put Rebecca on the phone.'

'I . . . She's not here.'

Heidi noticed how Darren suddenly tensed.

'She's not there? What is this, Elliott? Either you have Rebecca or you don't. Which is it?'

'I don't *have* her, but I know exactly where she is.'

Darren shook his head. 'No. That's not what we agreed. I told you that you have to bring Rebecca to me.'

'I have an address. I know where she's living. All you have to do is go there and—'

'Elliott, are you listening to me? I don't have to go anywhere. That's *your* job. If you know where she is, go and convince her to meet me.'

'It's not that simple.'

'Why not?'

'She's . . . she's living with someone else.'

'Who? Who's she living with?'

'A guy. Matt something. He owns a nightclub. I don't think he'd like it if—'

'Are you fucking with me? Do you see this knife? Do you see me pressing it into your girlfriend's face? I don't want to know about some fucking guy called Matt. Read my lips: *Not. My. Problem.* Go and get Rebecca. And don't call or message me again until you have her.'

He ended the call without waiting for a response, and then he jumped to his feet and punched angrily into the air.

'FUCK!'

'He found her,' Heidi said. 'That's got to count for something, Darren.'

He rounded on her. 'Shut up! It counts for nothing. He's trying to fob me off. Doesn't give a shit about me or you.' He paused and turned away from her again. 'Who the hell is this fucking nightclub guy?'

That was what was really bothering him. Not having Rebecca here with him was bad enough, but to know that she was in the company of another man, possibly even living with him . . .

'Maybe it's just her brother or something.'

'She doesn't have a brother. Try again.'

'Well . . . I don't know. The important thing is that Elliott found her. He's doing exactly what you've asked him to do.'

Darren paced up and down the garage for a while, then he sat on his stool at the bench. Tears were running down his cheeks.

'I gave up everything for that girl,' he said.

'I know. I understand. She means everything to you – I can see that. Why don't you just get her address from Elliott, and then go and see her yourself? Wouldn't that be easier than . . . than all this?'

Darren was toying with his knife again, gingerly sliding his finger along its honed edge, pressing a tad too hard, almost as though he wanted to bleed.

'No. Because I don't trust him. The police could be waiting for me at that address. And I don't trust you either, so stop pretending you give a shit. If Rebecca isn't here by midnight, you and Elliott can say goodbye to each other.'

31

Elliott threw his phone as hard as he could. It was his way of getting some of his frustration out, although it was tempered by the fact that he aimed it at a cushion to soften the impact and avoid damage.

He'd expected this, though. Underneath that surface layer of optimism in which he'd hoped that Darren would say something like, *An address for Rebecca? Well, that'll do nicely. Hand it over and we're all good*, was the knowledge that it wouldn't be enough.

Darren wasn't so stupid as to turn up at a house he knew nothing about, especially one containing another man.

Yeah, about that . . .

Elliott wondered whether it had been wise to mention Matt. In his defence, he'd been dog-tired and in agony when he took the call. His ribcage still felt as though it was in several more pieces than was normal. Should he have kept quiet about Rebecca? Had he put Heidi in even more danger?

On the other hand, if there was anything he had learnt from

recent experience, it was that he wasn't a very good liar. There had been a possibility that Darren already knew about Matt. Leaving him out and then getting caught out by Darren might have made things worse.

Elliott was starting to feel that anything he did was doomed. Someone had put a curse on him.

That wasn't an excuse to sit back and do nothing, though. He had to give it a try at the very least.

He left the house. Got in his car. Drove back to Matt's house.

The Range Rover was still parked on the drive, suggesting that Matt was in the house, and there was no way that Elliott was going to knock on the door while that maniac was around to beat the crap out of him again.

On which point, what was it about Rebecca's choice in men? Did she use a dating app specifically for psychopaths or something? Okay, she might not go for the Elliott Whistons of this world, but couldn't she at least date a guy with an ounce of decency, compassion and mental stability?

It baffled him. Rebecca had seemed such a lovely woman at first. But then what did he know about people? He had enough difficulty understanding the workings of his own mind. And what little he knew of Rebecca now suggested that she was just as deranged as the men she went out with.

He would never forget the image of her as she lied about who he was and then stood silently and watched as he was punched and kicked. Probably even wanted to dig her heels into him herself.

So now it would be a case of getting tough with her – inasmuch as 'tough' was in his vocabulary. No more listening to

242

her pleas of helping her to avoid problems with the men in her life. That was clearly all of her own doing, and none of his concern. All he was interested in now was getting Heidi out of Darren's clutches. His plan was to talk to her nicely at first, but to escalate to threats quickly if that didn't work.

That said, he wasn't entirely sure what kind of threats he could use. He had never threatened a woman before. Never threatened anyone, in fact. He also wasn't certain he could do so in a convincing way. Any attempt would probably be greeted with laughter.

He decided he'd cross that bridge when he came to it. The main thing was that he now knew where she was.

He just had to get in there and talk to her.

Which could take a long time.

Rebecca and Matt had arrived home in the early hours of the morning. They might not even have made it out of bed yet. And it was Sunday – what if they just stayed inside in their pyjamas all day? Today was all Elliott had. He had to get in there and talk to Rebecca, and then he had to persuade her to help the guy she had exploited to rescue his friend from the ex-boyfriend she wanted nothing to do with.

Should be a piece of cake.

When Darren returned at lunchtime, Heidi studied his face for signs of further news, good or bad.

She had to admit that Elliott had surprised her with his resourcefulness. Somehow, against all the odds, he had managed to find Rebecca. From there it was only a short hop to—

Well, she thought, let's not get too far ahead of ourselves.

Finding someone and then getting them to do what you want are two completely different things.

But still, it was possible. Elliott might come up with the goods.

Darren untied her and removed the tape from her mouth. 'I've brought sandwiches. You like tuna or ham and cheese?'

She ignored the question. 'Any news?' she asked.

'Yeah. I got sandwiches.'

'About Elliott. Has he been in touch again?'

'It's Sunday. He's probably watching a box set.'

'So he hasn't sent any messages? Have you checked my phone?'

Darren sighed. 'Yes, I've checked your phone, and no, he hasn't sent any messages.'

Heidi rubbed her wrists as she began to approach the work-bench, but her legs weren't working properly and she almost collapsed with the effort.

Despite Elliott's progress, she knew she couldn't put all her money on one horse. She was going to have to do something. Once again, she eyed up the items on the table, her attention flitting across the knife, the lamp, the scissors, the car keys. Escape was contained in those objects; she just needed to figure out how to bring them together and deploy them in the right way, and at the right time.

'What are you anyway?' Darren asked. 'Chinese or Japanese?'

Heidi wanted to roll her eyes. 'I'm English.'

'Yeah, but . . . originally?'

'Originally I was born in Liverpool. That makes me English.' She sighed. 'My grandfather came to England from Shanghai. He was a sailor.'

'Really? My grandfather was a sailor, too. Don't think he was Chinese, though. He was in the merchant navy.'

She wasn't really interested in Darren's ancestors, but she knew it was a good idea to get him talking about himself. If she knew what made him tick, she might find a way to make him stop ticking.

'What about your parents?' she asked. 'What do they do?'

'Not a lot. They're dead.'

'I'm sorry to hear that.'

'I'm not. We didn't exactly get on.'

Heidi didn't pursue it. She feared hearing a confession that he had been responsible for his own parents' death.

'Car crash on the motorway,' Darren continued nonetheless. 'Both wiped out in an instant. Funny the turns life takes sometimes.'

Heidi didn't think it was funny in the slightest. 'It's not all fate, though,' she said. 'Some things we can change if we want.'

Darren took a bite out of his sandwich and then spoke with his mouth full. 'There you go, getting all psychological.'

'More philosophical. We pilot our own ships. We can be good or we can be bad. We can be generous or selfish. We can—'

'Yeah, yeah, I get your point. We can also stand up for ourselves or we can let others walk all over us. You want to talk philosophy? What does your philosophy say about dealing with people who take our loved ones away from us?'

'Is that what's happened here, though? I mean really?'

'How else would you explain it? One minute everything's fine, and the next it's not. The person you planned to marry

245

suddenly disappears from your life and then turns up with another guy.'

'You mean Elliott? You don't really think that he—'

'Who knows? He won't give me answers unless I force him to. Funny how he keeps changing his story, though, don't you think?'

'Changes it how?'

'First of all he says he's her boyfriend and then he says he isn't. Then he says he doesn't know where she is, and then he wants to give me her address. You still surprised I don't trust him?'

'I just want to know how you think this is going to end, Darren.'

'How it'll end? With me and Rebecca together again.'

'And if that doesn't happen? I mean, what if Elliott can't convince her to come back to you?'

'That's his problem. And yours. Haven't I already made that clear?'

'You're really going to kill me if Elliott can't bring her to you? You'd really do that?'

Darren took a swig of water, then nodded. 'I'd really do that.'

'And what if he does get her here and she doesn't want to get back with you?'

'She will.'

'But what if she doesn't?'

'She will! She's confused. She made a mistake. I just need to explain it all to her.'

'You know her that well?'

'Like the back of my hand. She's not avoiding me because she wants to. Someone is making her.'

'Then why did you find this place and bring all this stuff here – the ropes and the tape and the water? It wasn't for my benefit. If you love Rebecca so much, why were you going to keep her here against her will?'

'Because . . . because sometimes you have to be cruel to be kind. It's like druggies, you know? They'll do anything for a fix. You have to lock them up, away from the drugs. Give them the cold turkey treatment. In the end, when they're better, they'll thank you for it. Rebecca is going to be so grateful to me when I've fixed her mind.'

Heidi decided not to challenge the delusion, knowing that doing so would only infuriate him.

'How did you meet her anyway?'

'Rebecca?'

'Yeah. What brought you two together?'

He eyed her with suspicion. 'Are you taking the piss?'

'No. I'm serious. I'm interested.'

He mulled it over. 'All right,' he said. 'I'll tell you.'

And he did. Took his time about it, too. Went through his whole relationship, from beginning to end, as if grateful for the opportunity to relate it.

Heidi listened, and this time it wasn't out of politeness. She was transfixed.

What she heard made everything suddenly much clearer in her mind. It all finally made sense.

Above all, it drove home the painful realisation that Elliott wasn't going to succeed in his mission to get her out of this mess.

32

Elliott looked down at his dashboard clock. Almost five o'clock. The February light was fading fast. The Range Rover hadn't moved from outside the house, which was a palace in comparison with Elliott's property. Matt probably had everything he needed in there, including Rebecca. He might have no reason to leave the place before midnight. And then Heidi would be dead.

He heard noises, and was convinced they were coming from the house. Despite the cold, Elliott had kept his window partially open so as not to miss anything.

He thought he heard a front door being closed, and then a car door. The Range Rover's engine roared into life, and the vehicle backed slowly down the driveway.

Elliott hunkered down in his seat, peering over the top of the steering wheel. He was convinced he could see only the figure of Matt within the other car. He waited for it to cruise down the street.

And then he took his chance, knowing that it might be the

only one he would ever get today.

He got out of his car and raced up to the house. At the top of the driveway he discovered another car – a Mercedes, presumably Rebecca's. He thumbed the doorbell. Deep, rich chimes sounded within.

Please answer, he thought.

The slab of pale oak swished open. There, in the doorway, was Rebecca, dressed in a figure-hugging white vest top and black shorts.

'Rebecca,' he said, and it was all he could manage to utter before she went to slam the door in his face. He leapt forward, shoving it open again and causing Rebecca to back-pedal into the vast hallway.

'Elliott! What the hell!'

'Please, Rebecca, we need to talk.'

'No! Get the fuck out!'

She came at him, arms raised to push him out of the house, but he grabbed her and tossed her away, surprised at his own forcefulness, before kicking the door closed.

'What are you doing?' she screamed. 'You can't be here. Matt will be back any second.'

'Rebecca, listen to me. You're my only hope. Darren has kidnapped my friend.'

She looked dumbfounded. 'What? What are you talking about?'

'Heidi. She's my best friend. My only friend. Darren has got her. He's taken her somewhere and he won't let her go unless you go to him.'

'You're making this up.'

'I'm not. He's crazy. You know he is. You knew how bad he was that first night we met. Why didn't you tell me what he would do to me?'

'I ... I didn't think he would do something like this. Kidnap? Are you sure?'

'I'm not making it up. You need to help me. I've only got till midnight, and then he's going to hurt Heidi.'

She shook her head. 'No. Not even Darren would do that.'

'He will. And if you don't help me, I'll have to go to the police. I'll have to bring them here.'

He saw how pale she went.

'You can't do that.'

'Why?'

'You just can't, all right? You don't know what you're doing.'

He thought at first that she was referring to his characteristic ineptitude – a charge he had heard so many times that he didn't usually question it. But this was different. There was a deeper meaning.

'What are you talking about?'

'Nothing. You have to go now.'

'I can't. I told you. You're my only hope. You have to come with me and talk to Darren. You're the only person he'll listen to.'

'I've tried talking to Darren a million times. He doesn't listen. He's fixated on me. Nothing I can say will stop him from wanting to be with me.'

'You have to try.'

'I don't *have* to do anything. Nobody tells me what to do, okay?'

'You owe me. I helped you, and you keep thanking me by spitting in my face. How could you lie to the police about me being your stalker? How could you just stand there last night and watch your boyfriend beat me up?'

For once, she actually looked regretful. 'I didn't want that to happen, Elliott. But you've only got yourself to blame. You put me on the spot. You were going to mess everything up.'

'Mess what up?'

She hesitated. 'Elliott, you don't even know what you're caught up in. I wish I hadn't come up to you on the street. I wish none of this had happened. If I could undo it all, I would. Please believe me.'

'Well, you *did* come to me. And now you need to undo the damage you've caused.'

'We're going around in circles here. If what you say is true, then I'm sorry about your friend. Call his bluff. I really don't think he will hurt her.'

'Call his bluff? What the fuck are you talking about? He's going to kill her!'

Elliott realised he'd just used the f-word. The first time in his life he recalled doing so. It actually felt good.

'You need to go now. Matt has only popped out for a bottle of wine. He'll be back any minute.'

'I'm not going anywhere. Not until you phone Darren.'

'I'm not going to phone him.'

'You don't have a choice. You call him right now and you arrange to meet him. I'm staying here until you do it.'

She stared at him open-mouthed. And then her eyes shifted away as something distracted her.

The low growl of the Range Rover arriving at the house.

Rebecca looked suddenly fearful. 'Matt's back. You need to go.'

Elliott stood his ground. 'Call Darren.'

Rebecca backed away into the kitchen. Elliott followed, saw that the room was as big as his whole ground floor. The centre of it was occupied by a massive island, and to the left was a glass-topped dining table that was long enough to be used for the Last Supper.

'Matt will kill you,' she said. 'You don't know what he's like.'

'I do. I've got the bruises. But I don't care, Rebecca. I'm desperate now. Call him.'

She flinched as the door chimes sounded. 'There's no time. You have to go.'

Elliott shook his head. 'I'll tell him everything. I'll make him understand. And if he doesn't ... well, he can hardly make things any worse, can he?'

Rebecca dashed to the bifold doors leading to the back garden and pulled them open.

'Go out this way. Please!'

The door chimes again.

'Go now, Elliott!'

'The phone call.'

'I'll do it.'

'You said that last time.'

'This time you've left me no choice. I promise I'll do it. As soon as I can without Matt hearing me.'

And now the sound of a key being inserted in the front door.

'He's coming. Please, Elliott. He'll rip you apart.'

'I've only got till midnight.'

'I know. I'll do it. Trust me.'

Trust me. He wanted to laugh at that.

'Rebecca!' An irritated shout from the hallway. 'Why didn't you answer the door? I'm carrying a case of wine and a box of beers here.'

'Go!' she urged, waving him through.

Elliott looked at her, glanced towards the hall, looked into the gloom outside.

'Fuck,' he said again.

And then he was through the door, his pupils struggling to adjust. He began to head towards the rear fencing, but then an outside security light flared on, blinding him, and he had to backtrack and duck behind a small shed-like structure containing logs for a wood burner.

He heard Matt's voice in the kitchen. 'Where the hell were you?'

'In the garden,' she said. 'I needed some fresh air.'

'Dressed like that? It's fucking freezing out there. Didn't you hear the doorbell?'

'Sorry, no.'

Elliott crouched down further as he heard heavy footsteps landing on the patio. Matt was clearly checking out her story.

And then Matt went back inside, pulling the door closed behind him and locking it. The voices remained in the kitchen, and Elliott knew that any attempt to escape would cause the lights to come on and attract Matt's attention.

Elliott waited, checking his watch. Time was evaporating

so quickly, and here he was, cowering in a garden while his best friend was within hours of losing her life.

Fuckity fucking fuck.

33

This is it, Heidi thought.

She listened to the familiar noises: the rattle of the chains on the gates, the car being driven through, the unlocking of the door and its steady rumble as it was drawn open.

Darren brought his car inside, put the lamp on, locked up the garage again. He opened the passenger door of his car, reached in and brought out some pizza boxes. As he took the food to the workbench, its aroma wafted across the garage, mingling with the ever-present odour of grease and oil.

This is it, she thought again.

She felt she was going to be sick. Her nerves were frayed. But it was now or never.

'You like pizza?' he asked.

She nodded, unable to speak through the tape over her mouth.

He came over to her, then removed the tape and untied her before heading back to the bench. Heidi followed, but then just stood there, staring down at the table, at each and every one of the items there, fixing their arrangement in her mind.

'What?' he said. 'You don't want any?'

She blinked. 'Have you . . . have you got any news?'

He stared at her. 'Sadly not. Looks like this could be your last meal.'

She looked down at her watch. Quarter to seven. Just over five hours left.

Elliott wasn't going to come through. He'd had all day. What more could he possibly do in the next few hours?

It was up to her now.

'I need the toilet.'

Darren had opened up one of the cardboard boxes and was inhaling the scent. He seemed irritated at the interruption.

'What, again? You must have a bladder the size of a peanut.'

'I've been here for hours. I had a lot to drink at lunchtime.'

Darren sighed and closed the lid again. 'Right.'

He picked up the lamp and the knife, then escorted her to the toilet. 'Here,' he said, handing her the lamp. 'Don't take for ever. My Quattro Stagioni is going cold. I got you a Margherita, by the way. Wasn't sure what you liked.'

She nodded and took the lamp. He stepped back immediately, as she knew he would. In running through the possible scenarios in her mind, she had considered this as one of the moments at which she might strike. A sudden dash at Darren, taking him by surprise.

The urge pulsed through her system now, then subsided. It didn't feel right.

She went into the tiny room, pushing the door closed behind her. She looked down into the toilet bowl, holding back the impulse to retch. On the other side of the door, Darren was humming a tune.

Now, she told herself. You have to do it now.

She screamed. As loud as she could.

The door burst open and Darren dived in, saying, 'What? What?' and she danced on the spot and pointed down at the floor behind the toilet bowl, and she continued to scream, and then she said, 'There! A thing. Right there!' and Darren closed the space between them, started to bend to get a better view . . .

NOW!

She brought her arm up and over and down again. Brought the lamp down with massive force onto the back of Darren's head. The lamp exploded, showering the room with glass fragments and plunging it into pitch blackness.

And then she ran.

She had spent her time in the garage wisely. Estimated its measurements in every direction. Mapped out everything it contained. Established a mental route through it and the number of strides she would have to take on each part of the journey.

All to be done while completely blind.

She ran through the toilet doorway first. Made a right turn. Several huge strides, then a jink left and another right. Straight ahead now. Just keep going straight ahead . . .

Her left shoulder struck something hard and unyielding, sending her spinning and crashing to the floor.

The concrete post. She had miscalculated.

She cried out with the pain and got to her feet again. But

now she was disoriented. She didn't know which way to go.

A moan from Darren. He was conscious. But at least it helped to restore her bearings.

She faced the direction she thought she needed and moved more cautiously now. She couldn't afford to run into something else – something that might knock her out.

A sharp jab into her hip, and she cried out again. But this was good. She knew what this was.

The corner of the workbench.

She put her hands down, felt the table's worn surface. Desperately she summoned up the image she had so recently tried to sear in her memory, tried to match what she could see in her mind with what she could feel below her. She found the drinks bottles, then the pizza boxes, and she knew that what she needed was just beyond them and a little to the left . . .

Where are they? Where the fuck are they?

A metallic jangle.

She had found her keys.

Another groan from Darren somewhere behind her, and then he was calling her name. 'Heidi? HEIDI?'

She grabbed the keys and continued to feel her way around. Darren's car was closest, and when devising her scheme she had considered going for the larger, more powerful car. But she had never driven one like that before, didn't know whether it had some fancy security feature that would scupper her plans, or whether she would just end up stalling it.

She thumbed the top button on her key fob. The flash of orange light as her car unlocked was brief, but enough to give her another snapshot of her surroundings.

She headed straight for her car door, felt the dirt and the familiar scratches on it.

'DON'T YOU DARE!'

She yanked the door open, jumped inside, then closed and locked the doors. She had to insert the ignition key by touch, which took longer than she'd hoped. She fired up the engine, turned on the headlights, flooding the garage with light. She could see again!

A bang. She screamed as something large and heavy landed on her bonnet.

Darren leered at her through the windscreen, his face drenched with his own blood.

She engaged reverse gear, took off the handbrake, stepped on the gas, came too quickly off the clutch. Darren lost purchase as the car leapt backwards. In her grand scheme, she had envisaged directing the vehicle towards the precise centre of the door behind her. But her aim was way off. There was a huge bang as the car slammed into the edge of the door and the brick wall alongside it.

Heidi checked her mirrors and realised how badly she had missed. She was going to have to try again.

She shifted into first, depressed the accelerator again.

The car didn't move. Its back end had somehow got caught up in the damaged brickwork behind.

Ahead, Darren rose up in front of the car. Bathed in the harsh light, he looked like a zombie.

She pushed harder on the accelerator pedal. The engine screamed until she thought it would burst into flames.

'*Move, you fucker! Move!*' she cried.

Darren was alongside her now, trying the door handle, pounding on the window.

'OPEN THE DOOR!'

Heidi gave out an almighty roar and then forced the pedal hard against the floor. There was a ripping of metal and plastic, the car seeming to tear itself in half before covering the whole length of the garage in a fraction of a second – too fast for her to react and stop what was coming.

The car rammed straight into the workbench, the thick wooden edge of the table concertinaing the car bonnet as if it were paper. Something exploded in Heidi's face, taking her head almost off her shoulders. She saw a million pinpoints of light and felt spears of pain in her neck and her nose and her jaw, and then there was the curious sensation of being surrounded by soft rubber that was trying to suffocate her.

It took her a while to realise that the car's airbags had been activated by the collision, pounding her face like a giant boxing glove. The engine had cut out, and one of the headlights had been smashed. Darren had already taken advantage of the situation, and was banging on the driver's window again.

Dazed, Heidi tried to start the car up again. The engine sputtered, but wouldn't catch, and now Darren was kicking against her window with the sole of his foot, and she began to panic, frantically turning the key and yelling at the damn car not to let her down.

Another explosion as the window gave way, showering her with glass fragments. A hand reached in and grabbed at her, and she batted it away, but it kept on clawing at her. She took hold of it and sank her teeth into it. Darren screamed and yanked his hand out of her mouth, but then it came back at her, much faster this time, balled in a fist that slammed into her cheekbone and then her jaw, opening up her lower lip. The world went into a spin again, and the next thing she knew was the sensation of her head being yanked with extreme force, as if to separate it from her neck, and she realised that Darren had managed to get hold of her ponytail and was using it to drag her out of the car. The pain was so unbearable that she thought her scalp might rip from her skull, and she had no choice but to follow the direction of travel. Even when her shoulders encountered the resistance of the window frame, Darren continued to tug with all his might. She pulled her shoulders in to squeeze through the tight gap, and then her back was scraping against what was left of the glass, breaking pieces of it away. Darren heaved again, and as her hips cleared the door she fell heavily to the concrete, jolts of further pain shooting through her bones. Ignoring her yells, Darren maintained his grip on her hair and dragged her along the floor. And then he was on her, straddling her, raising his fist, but she had no energy left to fight. She knew she was about to die.

34

Elliott remained crouching in the shadows for almost an hour. He sat shivering on the cold stone tiles, nestled between the log store and another wooden structure housing the wheelie bins, feeling the bite of the wind as it built in intensity.

A couple of metres past the bins was a pair of wooden gates barring entry to the front of the house, but they were tall and sheer, impossible to climb. His only possible escape route was his original choice: over the rear fencing. The problem was that Rebecca and Matt had not left the dining area. He could hear their voices above a steady stream of R&B music, and a rectangle of light from that room still jutted out across the garden.

So he stayed where he was. And he waited, praying that Matt didn't need to empty anything into one of the wheelie bins.

When the voices faded and the music stopped, he counted to twenty, then made his move. His bones creaked as he stood up and made his way to the rear corner of the house. He kept his back to the wall as he crept along the patio, and then he risked a quick peek through the bifold doors. The light was still on, but nobody was in there. Further along was another set of doors, but blinds had been drawn across those. His hope was that Matt and Rebecca had relocated to that room, and not to an upstairs viewpoint where they could still catch sight of him.

He took a few deep breaths.

And then he ran.

As soon as he began sprinting across the lawn, the security lights came on full beam, and he felt like he was in one of those old war films, trying to escape from Stalag 17 or wherever while the Germans shone their spotlights down at him as they prepared to rip him open with machine-gun fire. He expected shouts for him to halt, and he knew that even if they came he would have to press on; he was committed now, even though his unfit lungs were already urgently impressing upon him their desire to surrender.

He reached the back fence, and it was only then that he realised how tall the panels were – almost as tall as the front gates – and he wasn't sure he was capable of scaling them. But there was a tree here, and he had no idea what kind of tree it was, but it looked sturdy and it radiated stout branches and he had vague memories of having climbed trees as a child, and so that would have to be his salvation.

He launched himself upwards. Found footholds and hand-holds without consciously seeking them out, driven by sheer fear.

And then he was swinging himself over the fence, dropping

into blackness again, the drop seeming to go on for ever, as if he were falling down a well. When he landed with a thud, it was on a maliciously uneven surface that twisted his ankle and drove spikes of pain up his leg. He grunted and bit his lip to stifle a scream, then limped across the neighbouring garden, hoping that he hadn't just jumped from the proverbial frying pan.

But the neighbour's lights stayed off. The house ahead looked empty. Elliott took a glance behind him, but there was no sign of anyone following. He made his way along the side of the house and found a gate that, mercifully, was easier to climb.

And then he was out on the road, hobbling back to his car, praying that he'd done enough to save Heidi.

He had come so close to killing her.

Rage had been pulsing through his whole body. He had so wanted to pummel the life out of that evil little bitch.

He looked over at her, tied to the post, snivelling.

Why had she tried to escape like that? Why was everyone trying to stand in the way of his love for Rebecca?

His head hurt more than ever. Twice now he'd had glass smashed across it – both times by women. They were a dangerous species.

He had lost track of how long he had been sitting on this stool. The only time he had moved was when he had ventured outside to check that nobody had been attracted by the noise. The girl had done a lot of damage to the wall and the door of the garage.

He looked down at the remains of the bench, now melded with the front of Heidi's car. The items it had supported were still scattered across the floor; he had no energy to gather them up. One of Heidi's car headlights was out, but its other lights were enough to see by. Not always, though: his vision kept swimming in and out. It was making him nauseous.

He brought a hand to his head, felt the sticky wetness. He hoped his scalp had stopped bleeding. His fingers explored further and found a piece of glass embedded in his skin. He pulled it out and let it drop to the floor. His vision blurred again.

He blinked several times, then checked his watch. Only a few hours left. With any luck he would be with Rebecca again soon. Couldn't discuss things looking like this, though. Gotta make a bit of an effort to look presentable.

He slid off the stool, stood wavering like a drunk. The room began spinning slowly. Water, he thought. I need to clean myself up.

There were bottles of water near his feet, and also napkins that had come with the pizzas. He bent down to retrieve them.

His stomach had other ideas. Darren whirled, turning to face the wall as a stream of vomit ejected from his mouth and splashed loudly against the whitewashed bricks.

When the retching eventually stopped, Darren remained stooped, his hands clutching the stool for support. He groaned.

'Are you okay?'

This from Heidi. He turned slowly towards her. 'What the fuck do you care? You tried to kill me.'

'I didn't. I just wanted to—'

'Shut up! Don't talk to me. I have to get ready. For Rebecca.'

He picked up a bottle of water and the napkins, then crouched in front of the wing mirror of his own car. The image that jumped out at him was terrifying – a ghostly face streaked with blood.

He opened the bottle, dribbled some of its contents onto a couple of napkins, and began dabbing at his face. After a couple of minutes of effort he persuaded himself that his appearance was drastically improved, although it still looked as though he'd just survived a train crash. He considered going back to his hotel to wash and change, but he could imagine the attention he would get when he walked through the lobby. He also wasn't convinced he was capable of driving safely just yet.

And besides, he had unfinished business with Heidi.

He got down on his hands and knees. In the weak light, it took him a while to find his car keys. When he did, he unlocked the boot of his car, then fumbled around until he found his large, rubber-encased torch. Switching it on, he made his way back to the toilet, weaving on legs that seemed to want to take him in different directions.

In the washroom, he trained the torch on the floor. Shards of glass glinted back at him, but so did something else.

His knife.

He had dropped it when Heidi attacked him.

He picked it up, hefted it in his hand. It felt good to have it with him again.

When he was a bit more in control of himself, he was going to need this knife.

35

Matt Blaine believed he was an excellent judge of people. It was that keen instinct that had got him to this point in life. You didn't get to be this successful if you couldn't read people.

He knew when to trust and when to call out bullshit. He also knew that you have to act decisively when others are trying to take advantage. Put them in their place. Sometimes that meant getting physical.

Matt didn't mind inflicting a little violence when necessary; in fact, he quite enjoyed it. Often it was the quickest and most effective way of driving a message home. He remembered fondly how he caught one of his accountants ripping him off. Guy kept denying it, but Matt trusted his instincts more than he trusted the accountant. And so he persisted. Applied a little pain. Eventually the accountant confessed. Another victory for Matt's intuition. So he broke both the accountant's legs. He could still hear that lovely snapping sound.

His true friends were few in number; he was happy to accept that. Others in his position would delude themselves.

All those people at the club who spent their time stroking his ego – they were just hangers-on. Parasites. They didn't like him for what he was; they liked his money and his power and his influence.

He would be opening a new club soon, down in London. That was going to be huge. It would be very upmarket. Attract the celebs. Put him in touch with the movers and shakers of this world. He was going places.

He had wanted Rebecca to go there with him.

Now he wasn't so sure.

Something weird was happening with her. She was keeping something from him. His gut kept telling him so, and his gut was rarely wrong. Actually, it had been nagging at him for a while now, but he had allowed her beauty to distract him.

It began when she moved in with him last Wednesday. Turned up at his door with a bag of clothes, telling him she was sick of spending so much time on her own. It had come as a huge compliment, and why wouldn't he want a woman like that constantly at his side or in his bed?

But even then there had been doubts trying to bubble their way to the surface. Rebecca had always come across as some-one who loved her independence, her own company. What had changed? Why was she so reluctant even to go back to her house to collect more of her things?

And then there was that freak in the club last night. What was that all about?

He'd asked her. Of course he had. She told him that the guy had seen her in the gym and kept trying to chat her up. Matt then asked her if that was the reason she'd moved in with him, to escape from the weirdo, and she said no, he didn't know where she lived. He also demanded to know why she'd never bothered to tell him about this stalker making her life a misery, and she'd told him that she knew he would overreact.

But it wouldn't have been an overreaction. You can't pussy-foot around with sad twats like that. You have to stamp on them, hard, so that they never bother you again.

He would have done that for her. That's how much he had fallen for her. And he still would. All she had to do was ask.

But still he felt there was something not quite right about her story. Couldn't put his finger on it, but there was something . . .

He watched her now as she checked her watch and suddenly stood up.

'What's up?' he asked.

'I'm supposed to be at Kirsten's in half an hour.'

This wasn't a lie. Kirsten worked at the club, and had become a good friend of Rebecca's. They had arranged this meet-up a week ago. And if Rebecca went out but didn't actually go to it, Kirsten would let him know.

'Okay,' he said. Then he added, 'Is everything okay?'

He thought her smile looked forced. 'Yeah, of course,' she said. 'Why wouldn't it be?'

'I dunno. You seem a little stressed lately.'

'Do I?' She laughed. 'I'm always like that. Too much of a thinker.'

'What is it you think about?'

'Oh . . . everything. Life, I suppose.'

It was a non-answer.

273

'Come here,' he said.

She glanced at her watch. 'Matt, I've got to go. Kirsten will—'

'Kirsten works for me. Don't worry about her. Just come over here.'

She crossed the thick carpet in her bare feet. Stood in front of him. Her very closeness made him want her again. He opened his arms, beckoning her in. She climbed onto the plush leather sofa and curled up against him like a pet. God, she was beautiful. She could ask for anything from him and he would give it.

And maybe that was the problem.

He looked deep into her eyes.

'You'd tell me, wouldn't you?' he asked. 'If there was anything wrong, you'd tell me?'

She nodded, but it was as if there was a curtain behind her pupils, preventing him from seeing the truth.

'Of course I would,' she answered. 'You know that.'

He moved one of his hands up to cup her chin. His fingers caressed her cheeks, and she closed her eyes.

She opened them again when he squeezed harder, digging into her flesh and contorting her features, making them ugly.

'You'd tell me, right?' he asked.

She tried to speak, but couldn't get her mouth open, so she nodded instead.

He released his grip, then pushed her off him. She rubbed at the pink marks he had left on her face.

'What was that about?'

He stared at her. 'Don't let me down, Rebecca.'

'I won't. I promise.'

He nodded, then let it go. This didn't need to become a full-blown argument. He had already told Kirsten to do a little probing. Maybe Rebecca would open up to another woman.

He watched her head towards the door, wondering if she had taken the hint and would turn around and tell him everything. One of the reasons he had fallen for Rebecca was that she was a woman of mystery. Hidden depths and all that. Now he decided that he didn't like secrets. He preferred women who didn't think too much, who weren't bright enough to scheme.

Clever people could be dangerous.

But she didn't turn. She left the room, left him to his thoughts.

He didn't move from the sofa while she got ready. And when she returned, in make-up and a figure-hugging dress, he was almost willing to fling all his reservations aside. How could he doubt someone who looked like this?

And then she kissed him – a deep, passionate kiss that promised much for when she returned later – and he felt her power, her ability to hypnotise and draw him in.

She said goodbye and slinked out of the room, and for a full five minutes afterwards he stared at the space she had occupied.

And then he got up from the sofa, left the room and walked across the hallway to his study. He spent a lot of time in his study, drawing up plans, making business calls, deciding how best to spend his money.

He heard the slight sigh of air from the cushioning of his luxurious office chair as he lowered himself onto it, then he nudged the mouse in front of him and the computer came to life. He double-clicked on an application. An array of images was presented to him. He selected one and blew it up to the size of the screen.

He was looking at footage from the camera situated on the rear wall of his house, overlooking the garden.

Using the mouse, he dragged a slider back to indicate the approximate time that he had come home with the wine and beer, then allowed the video recording to run.

He stared into shadows for a while. When the security light suddenly flooded the garden, he leant forward to get a better view. He watched intently for movement, but saw nothing, and shortly afterwards the light extinguished itself again.

He rewound the recording. At the moment the light came on, he pressed the pause button. Something had intruded slightly into the bottom edge of the camera's field of view. He zoomed in, but it was indistinct. Rebecca? Or something else?

He moved forward frame by frame, but the blurry object or person dodged out of shot again.

Matt sat back in his chair, still thoughtful. Rebecca had told him she had just wanted some fresh air. Maybe that was true. Maybe that's all this was. He certainly had nothing here to disprove it.

He grabbed the mouse again and began dragging the time-line forward to the present. Frame after frame of darkness flashed past on the screen.

And then it changed.

The rear light had come back on. The garden was almost as clear as it was in the daytime.

He clicked the play button.

And he saw him.

A man was running up the garden, away from the house. He could be seen scrambling up the tree as if his very life depended on it, then dropping over the fence onto the neighbour's land.

Matt rewound, zoomed in, watched it again.

There was no doubt about it. A man had been hiding in his garden.

And Matt knew exactly who it was.

It was the guy who had come after Rebecca last night. Her so-called stalker.

What the hell had he been doing here? And did Rebecca know he was in the garden? Could he even have been inside the house?

It was possible, Matt told himself, that Rebecca knew nothing about it. Maybe she just heard a noise and opened the back door to investigate, not realising that her stalker had been observing her.

That would be the preferable explanation. That's what Matt desperately wanted to believe.

He would put it to her later, get her to give her side of the story.

Right now, though, there was somebody else he needed to talk to.

Matt was grateful that he was not only a good judge of character. He was also blessed with an excellent memory.

Last night, Matt had taken a good look at the weirdo's driving licence. The guy's name – Elliott Whiston – was seared on his brain.

As was the guy's address.

36

He kept staring at her.

Every time Heidi looked his way, Darren's eyes were on her. It wasn't simply a malicious glare because of what she'd done to him. No, he was contemplating something, building himself up.

She wondered if he was mentally preparing himself to kill her.

She was almost afraid to speak, in case it tipped him over a precipice.

The knife was in his hand. Even though the blow to his head seemed to have done some damage, he'd gone to the effort of dragging himself to the toilet just to get that knife back. He had sat on the stool ever since, knife in his grasp, eyes on his captive.

She kept hoping that he'd keel over, that she'd battered his brain enough to make him have a stroke or something.

Go on, she thought. Die in front of me, you sick fuck.

But he just kept on staring.

Even without the duct tape over her mouth, she was finding it difficult to breathe. Her nostrils were blocked, blood had run into her mouth, and the front part of her face felt on fire. She was convinced that the airbag had broken her nose.

The light wasn't helping her anxiety either. Darren had added to the meagre illumination from her car by setting his torch on its base on the floor. Its upward beam was casting weird shadows on the ceiling, giving her the sensation of dark figures waiting to drop on her from above.

When Darren finally broke the silence, his words seemed somewhat slurred, as though he was intoxicated.

'You shouldn't have done that,' he said. 'I treated you well.'

Anger and incredulity elbowed aside any desire to be circumspect. 'What the fuck are you talking about? You kidnapped me. You tied me up. You leave me here alone with the rats at night. You threaten to kill me. And you call that treating me well?'

Darren brought a hand to his head, winced. 'You hurt me.'

'Yeah, well, what did you expect, Darren? I mean, seriously, what did you fucking expect? Do you even realise how serious this is?'

'I know exactly how serious this is. Rebecca needs to understand it too. I'm doing this all for her. I have to see her, to—'

'SHE'S NOT COMING BACK, DARREN! Don't you get that? She doesn't want you anymore!'

'I have no life without Rebecca. If I can't get her back, I'm ... I'm going to kill myself.'

'Fine. Kill yourself then. There's no way that Elliott will be able to bring her to you. You know that. You might as well finish yourself off now. Untie me, let me go, and then do what you have to do.'

He continued to observe her, and in a brief moment of optimism she thought he might actually take her advice.

But then he checked his watch. 'It's eight thirty. Still three and a half hours left.'

Heidi sighed. 'Darren, she's not coming. I don't see what can change between now and midnight. Do you?'

'I can make it change.'

'How? How the hell can you possibly do that from here?'

'Elliott needs a little push, that's all. He needs a reminder of what will happen if he doesn't get Rebecca for me.'

Heidi didn't like the sound of this. And there was a distinct glint in Darren's eye – a promise of something extremely unpleasant.

Darren got up from his stool. For a brief moment he closed his eyes, as if in pain.

And then he started walking towards Heidi, his knife at the ready.

'Darren,' she said. 'What are you doing?'

'Nobody is taking this seriously. You're all trying to stand in our way.'

'No. We're not. Think about this. Think about what I said. Rebecca wouldn't want this.'

'Rebecca needs to be with me. She just doesn't know it at the moment. She's confused. I need to fix that.'

He continued advancing. Slow, unsteady steps. His elongated shadow shifting menacingly as he approached.

'Please. You don't have to do this. Maybe you're right.

Maybe Elliott has nearly done what you asked. He might be going to phone you any minute now.'

'Or he might not. Don't worry, I'm not going to kill you. I just need to give him something to make him realise how important you are to him.'

Crouching in front of her. Holding up the knife. Twisting it in the air to give her a good look at the razor-sharp toughened steel.

'Please, Darren. Please don't.'

And then his hand shot out and he grabbed her head while the other hand wielded the knife, cutting, cutting, and she gave up pleading and began to scream.

37

Nine o'clock.

Elliott decided he couldn't leave it much longer. He couldn't just sit here at home till midnight and watch the clock while it ticked away Heidi's final minutes.

He had done everything in his power. Exceeded his own expectations, in fact. He had found Rebecca, had told her how important it was that she acted immediately. Short of going back again and physically dragging her out the house, what more could he achieve alone?

Not that Matt would allow him to do any dragging. Elliott got the impression that he would only have to show his face at Matt's door in order to get beaten to a bloody pulp. Attempting to get physical with his girlfriend would undoubtedly call for capital punishment.

He had come away from there hoping that his begging had been enough. She had promised faithfully that she would call Darren. She had made promises before, of course, and then broken them, but this time he had really wanted to believe that she possessed enough humanity to keep her word.

So where were the messages from Darren? Why was he still not responding to Elliott's own messages? Why wasn't this nightmare finally over?

He knew why. Rebecca had failed him again. It was what she did, what she was. A taker, not a giver.

Elliott realised he had only one option remaining.

The police.

Maybe it wouldn't help in the slightest. It was highly probable that they wouldn't be able to find Darren and Heidi before midnight, in which case Elliott would forever regret that he hadn't gone to them sooner.

On the other find, they might find them and provoke Darren into killing Heidi, in which case Elliott would forever regret that he'd gone to the police at all.

He could be damned either way, but what other choice did he have?

He looked down at Bill, stared into those Jaffa Cake eyes. 'What would you do, boy?'

Receiving no words of wisdom, Elliott got up and left the house.

Five minutes after Elliott drove away, a Range Rover pulled up on the street. Behind its wheel, Matt Blaine looked across at the house.

It looked a dump. Exactly the sort of place that a creepy stalker would live in.

It hit him that he had been born and brought up in a house like this himself, and he felt the rush of anger that often washed over him when he thought about his childhood. There was no excuse for being poor and living in a shithole. You have to get off your arse and do something about it, just as he had done. His parents had been weak, lacking in drive and ambition. The silver lining was that it had made him determined that he was never going to be like them. It had also taught him that if you really want something, you have to be prepared to fight for it.

This guy Elliott Whiston wouldn't understand that. He was a bottom-feeder. The sort of worm who goes skulking around in other people's gardens.

He needed to be taught an important lesson, and Matt was exactly the person to teach him.

He left the car and strolled over to the house. It was in darkness, and there was no car outside it.

Probably can't afford a car, Matt thought. Probably goes to bed at six o'clock, too. Lies in his bed jerking off while he fantasises about my Rebecca.

He thumbed the doorbell angrily. While he waited for a response, he took out a set of brass knuckledusters and slipped them on. A good couple of whacks with those babies would give anyone food for thought.

No answer.

He tried the bell again, then knocked.

Still nothing.

He walked up the side path to the rear of the house, looking through each of the windows as he went. No signs of life. He tried the handle of the back door and found it locked, but he really didn't want to leave it at that after coming all the way over here.

No problem.

He returned to the car, fetched what he needed and came back. A bit of elbow grease and judicious application of a crowbar, and he soon had the flimsy rear door open.

Once inside, he closed the door and used the torch on his phone to look around. He was in a kitchen that smelt of damp and animal food. He checked out the other ground-floor rooms, and then upstairs. In the first bedroom he entered, he had to stifle a yell as a dark shape jumped off the bed and shot towards him. He thought he was about to be attacked, only realising it was a frightened cat as it scooted past him and practically fell down the stairs.

He completed his search and confirmed the house was empty.

Got to be back soon, he thought. It's way past Elliott's bedtime.

Matt retraced his steps to the living room, where he settled into an armchair and waited.

38

Elliott sat in his car, debating his next move. This was a matter of life and death. What he said or did now could save Heidi or condemn her.

He continued watching the police station. He saw people enter and he saw people leave, and he told himself, See, that's all you have to do. You go up those steps and you speak to whoever is on the desk and you tell them that your best friend has been kidnapped and is about to be murdered, and please could something be done about it?

It sounded so easy. And yet still he was racked with the fear that such a simple action could also set in motion a sequence of events that would kill Heidi.

You never know, he thought. Rebecca might stick to her promise. Or maybe Darren's threat is an empty one. Maybe he never had any intention of harming Rebecca. The wisest move might be simply to call his bluff.

But then his thoughts swung the other way again. This was way too big for him. If he could agonise over which flavour of cat food he should give Bill, what chance did he have with a decision of this enormity? Somebody else would have to call the shots. Someone who knew what they were doing.

He got out of the car. Began walking towards the police station.

It's the right decision, he told himself. Go with your gut.

The wind was much fiercer now, and starting to throw drops of rain at him. He reached the building. The doors opened and two massive policemen came down the steps. One of them said 'Evening' to him, and he flashed them a weak smile in return. He watched their backs as they walked away, laughing and joking about something, and he wondered if they really were capable of finding and rescuing Heidi. They brought to mind the two officers who had visited him at his house – both sceptical about his claims to the point of seeming antagonistic.

Could he trust them with this most important mission?

He climbed onto the first step. Five more steps and he would be inside. He could hand over total responsibility. What a temptation it was to be freed from this dilemma.

He took another step upwards.

No time like the present. You're nearly there. Just get it over with.

He raised his foot . . .

And then his phone rang.

He took out his mobile and glanced at the screen. It was Heidi's number. No video this time – just a normal phone call.

He dropped back down to the pavement as he answered the call.

'Hello?'

'Hello, Elliott. How's it going with Rebecca?'

It was definitely Darren's voice, but it sounded different. Slower and less assured.

'I . . . I've seen her. I've spoken to her. It's up to her now. I've done all I can.'

'Do you know how pathetic that sounds?'

'I don't know what else you want me to say. She told me she was going to contact you.'

'For all I know, you could be making this up just to save your friend.'

'I'm not. I swear. She looked me right in the eye and told me—'

'Well, she hasn't contacted me, okay? It's not good enough. You're not trying.'

'I *am* trying. I found her, didn't I? How can you say that's not trying?'

'She's not here. That's all I care about.'

'There's still time, right? She's got a couple of hours yet.'

'I think you mean that *you've* got a couple more hours, Elliott. I'm hoping for one last big push.'

'Meaning what?'

'Meaning I need to give you a bit more incentive.'

Elliott felt a tingling on the nape of his neck. 'I don't need any more incentive.'

'I think you do. I thought that your little Chinese friend being here with me would be enough, but it looks like I was wrong.'

Something was coming. Something very bad.

'Darren, why aren't we on video?'

A snigger. 'I didn't want to spoil the surprise.'

'What surprise? Darren, what have you done? Let me speak to Heidi.'

'She can't come to the phone right now. She's . . . indisposed.'

'What have you done to her? If you've hurt her in any way—'

'Don't start being all macho now, Elliott. It's not your style. Your friend got a bit frisky earlier, so I had to put her in her place. But she still has her uses.'

'Darren, please tell me what you've done to her.'

'Let's just say there's a bit less of her than there was before. She'll survive, but only if you get a move on.'

Elliott found himself walking away from the police station, tears in his eyes.

'Please. You don't have to hurt her. Let her go.'

'All in good time. Right now, I want you to run an errand.'

'What kind of errand?'

'You want to know what's happened to Heidi, don't you?'

'Yes. Please.'

'Then go to your little cat shop. You'll find the answers there. Maybe it'll give you the motivation you need. And remember: no police.'

The call was ended, and it suddenly felt to Elliott that he was being watched, that Darren somehow knew exactly where he was right now.

He turned to take another look at the police station.

And then he ran back to his car.

*

When he pulled up opposite the charity shop, it looked the same as always. Like every other shop along here at this time on a Sunday, its lights were off. Nobody was walking the wet pavements. The street felt abandoned.

Elliott got out of his car with some trepidation. He wondered if this was some kind of a trap. Some malicious game devised in Darren's warped mind. He scanned the street for anything out of place. He found nothing.

As he began to cross the road, a car whizzed around the corner and came straight towards him. He prepared to take evasive action, but the car just went straight on past. Just a random driver, but Elliott's nerves were on edge.

He went up to the shop window and peered through the glass. No signs of light or movement inside.

He went to the door, tried the handle. It was locked.

And then he saw the note stuck to the door with what looked like a piece of duct tape.

It said simply: 'Pizza delivery!'

Elliott was mystified. He looked left and right for more clues, and found nothing. Could Darren possibly have got into the shop and left something there?

Elliott started to fumble in his pockets for the shop keys. As he did so, he turned around to check that nobody was behind him.

That's when his eyes alighted on the bin.

It was a black council bin. Stuffed into the top of it was a pizza box.

Elliott put his keys back into his pocket and approached the bin cautiously. He checked his surroundings again, then took hold of the box. He tugged at it gently, sliding it towards him. He almost expected an explosion.

A young couple came around the corner, fighting with an umbrella against the wind. They looked at him standing there eyeing the pizza box as if he was in a catatonic trance, then they chuckled and walked on.

Elliott wanted to know what was in the box. At the same time, he didn't want to know. His stomach was in knots at the thought of what it might contain.

He carried it back to his car, got in, closed the door. He didn't want his reaction, whatever that might be, to be observed.

He took several deep breaths. Then, in one swift motion, he grabbed the lid and lifted it.

At first, he wasn't sure what he was looking at. When he realised, tears flooded down his cheeks.

They were tears of relief. Heidi had been damaged, but not beyond repair.

Inside the pizza box was her severed ponytail.

He picked it up. Below it was another note. 'Next time it will be her face.'

39

Matt was starting to get fed up. He had never been a patient man. He liked results to be quick, preferably instant. It was one of the things he made crystal clear to everyone he employed: *If I ask you to do something, you do it immediately. If not, you're gone.*

If he made an appointment with you to take place on the hour, you'd better be there at that time. Slightly early was okay, commendable even. Lateness told Matt that you thought your time was more important than his, and that was unforgivable.

He'd once set up a meeting with a millionaire who was looking to invest in his nightclub business. Matt had turned up ten minutes before the appointed time, wearing his best suit and prepared to be so ingratiating it made him sick. The millionaire appeared half an hour late, so Matt told him he could stick his money up his arse. He wasn't going to kow-tow to anyone who treated him with contempt like that.

And now there was Elliott. Even though he didn't have an appointment with the nerd, Matt still felt his time was being wasted. He was getting more irritated by the minute, which meant that the severity of the beating he was about to administer was also increasing.

He was tempted to go away and come back later, maybe in the middle of the night. Pummel the shit out of the guy while he was still in his Thomas the Tank Engine pyjamas, or whatever dorks like him wore. Problem was, Elliott would soon see that his back door had already been forced open. He might even call the police.

So, he'd have to wait. Have to let his anger build to boiling point.

Rebecca was more fuel on the fire. It still puzzled him why she hadn't said anything about being stalked. He liked to think that she saw him as her protector. He had certainly always done his best to fulfil that role. When guys came on to her at the club, he let them know in no uncertain terms that they were in danger of losing the use of one or more of their limbs for a lengthy period. Rebecca could easily have asked him to get Elliott off her back ages ago, and then he wouldn't be sitting in this fleapit.

The biggest mystery was why Elliott had turned up in Matt's back garden. What was he hoping to achieve? Did Rebecca know about it, and if so, why did she cover it up?

He hoped that Elliott would be able to provide some answers. He further hoped that those answers did not implicate Rebecca. He didn't appreciate being taken for a fool. He recalled how one of his bartenders had been caught taking money from the till. Wanting the punishment to fit the crime, Matt got two of his bouncers to hold the bartender's fingers in the till drawer while he slammed it shut again and again. The guy had to give up playing guitar after that.

He wondered what the most appropriate punishment for Elliott might be. How do you punish a stalker in a way that makes them never want to do it again? The eyes? Difficult to stalk someone if you can't see them. Or maybe the sex drive. He could crush Elliott's scrotum with a hammer – that should do the trick.

It was while Matt was considering this panoply of suitable acts of violence that he heard a noise.

A key being slipped into the lock of the front door.

Matt got up from the chair and went to stand near the door. He slipped the brass knuckledusters on again, then flexed his shoulders and arms. He was going to enjoy this.

He heard footsteps in the hallway, then a voice saying 'pss-pss-pss', presumably to summon the cat.

The steps got closer. The door was pushed open. The switch on the wall was flicked, flooding the room with light.

Matt was face to face with Elliott.

Except . . .

This wasn't Elliott.

He didn't know who the fuck this was.

40

Darren was immensely proud of his little plan.

Even though his head felt like it was being crushed in a vice, and his thinking was muzzy, he believed he had still managed to come up with an ingenious scheme.

The train of thought had begun with notions of all the things he might do to Heidi, but his heart wasn't in torturing her. He wasn't a monster. The ponytail was a good start. It sent a message. It frightened Heidi out of her wits, making her more compliant and therefore less likely to crack his skull again, but it also said something to Elliott. It told him that Darren would have no hesitation in using a knife to ruin the looks of his pretty Chinese friend.

But Darren worried that it might not be enough. It concerned him that Elliott's thinking might be, *Hair? You cut her hair? You could send me a finger or an ear and you give me her hair? What kind of pathetic kidnapper are you?*

Hence the second part of his plan.

He really didn't want to start slicing pieces off Heidi unless he had to.

But he had no such qualms about an animal.

To be specific: Elliott's cat.

He hated that stupid moggie anyway. Hated the way it looked at him in that supercilious manner. It would be a pleasure to cut off its hide and leave it on display for Elliott to find when he came home. Elliott couldn't possibly fail to get how serious this was once he saw that.

Darren had remembered Heidi telling him that she often came into Elliott's house to feed the cat when he was away. His house key was among her other keys now in Darren's possession. All he had to do was make sure that Elliott wasn't at home while he carried out his butchery. The ponytail ruse accomplished that.

And so here he was, ready to divest the cat of its nine lives and its fur coat.

What he found in Elliott's living room was an animal of a very different kind, and presenting much more of a threat.

Darren's first thought was that this was clearly a trap. The guy had been sitting in the dark waiting for him. Darren didn't know how, but Elliott had obviously been expecting a move like this and had prepared for it. He'd brought in backup.

And this guy meant business. He was stocky, athletic-looking. A meanness in his eyes and on his lips. He was also wearing brass knuckledusters. Not exactly welcoming.

Darren had learnt a long time ago that, faced with a more formidable opponent, the best advantage you have is to make the first move.

He charged. Went at the guy like a missile, fists flying,

screaming like a banshee. He landed a punch on the man's chin, then another on his cheek, and he thought, I'm winning here, I can beat this fucker, take that, you bastard. But then suddenly his hands were being swatted away like they were bluebottles, and try as he might to prevent it, the tide was turning, and his hands changed from weapons to shields, struggling to ward off the blows now coming his way. When one particularly mighty punch sneaked through his defences and crashed the knuckledusters into his jaw, he went staggering backwards. He slammed into a set of shelves and one of them came away from its fixings, showering him with books.

And then he remembered his knife. The knife he had used on Heidi's hair. The knife that he'd been planning to use on the cat.

He pulled the weapon from his waistband, thinking, You asked for it, mate.

But he was too slow. The stranger was already on him, slapping the knife out of his hand. Darren heard it clatter against a radiator, and then the man's voice saying, 'A knife? You want to use a fucking knife on me?' And then there were more blows to his head – a head that had received more battering in the past few days than a head should be able to take without collapsing in on itself – and he felt himself being grabbed and spun around and flung across the room.

He crashed into a small table, upending it. His vision blurred again. The world stopped making sense. But he knew that to stay on the floor would be fatal; he had to get back on his feet. He tried to push himself up, but received a kick to the ribs for his efforts. He rolled away, gained a little distance

– enough to give him time to get up again. His first-strike philosophy hadn't paid off; pulling the knife had only made things worse. He was going to die.

He blinked, saw the menacing shape advancing on him, probably for the very last time. Darren was spent, his energy for fighting gone, his fogged brain pulsing in agony.

He lashed out, one final attempt to stave off the inevitable.

The sound was unexpected. Not the slapping noise he expected. More of a thud combined with a crack. Like a hammer hitting wood.

Darren blinked more furiously, sharpening the image. The man was acting weirdly, like a malfunctioning robot. He was just standing there, head bowed, hands coming up slowly to cradle it, his mouth opening and closing, but emitting non-sensical sounds.

And then Darren realised how heavy his own hand was, and he glanced down and saw that it was no longer empty. A stone paperweight had fallen from the table and he had picked it up – he wasn't even aware that he had done so.

Darren drew his arm back wide and then swung it once more at the man's head. He heard that curiously satisfying noise again, but it contained more of the higher tones – like finally breaking an egg after the first few taps of a spoon.

The man's legs gave way beneath him and he collapsed to the floor in a heap, still babbling.

Darren dropped to his knees, grateful to be spared the effort of holding himself upright. He stared down at the gibbering wreck next to him.

'Who are you?' he asked.

The man continued to garble.

'Did Elliott tell you to hurt me? Did he want you to kill me?'

Still no answers that made any sense.

They're all against me, Darren thought. All of them. But they can't stop us. They won't keep me and my beautiful Rebecca apart.

He raised the paperweight, brought it down, again and again, until the man stopped speaking and breathing and living.

41

When Elliott got home, he carried the pizza box almost reverently to his front door. He wasn't sure why he'd kept it, or even its contents – the ponytail could hardly be stuck back on again – but somehow it felt wrong to dump everything back in the bin.

He pushed back hard on the thought that the reason he was keeping it was that this might be the only part of her he would ever see again.

He put the key into the lock, turned it, entered, put the hall light on, opened the door to the living room, switched on the light there ...

... and let the pizza box drop to the floor.

The room was chaos. It was like a tornado had swept through it. Furniture moved and overturned. Possessions scattered across the carpet.

Oh, and not to mention the body.

What the hell ...?

Elliott moved tentatively towards the prone figure. Was he alive? Could anyone who was simply unconscious lie as still as that?

Elliott moved closer. When he saw the misshapen head, he had to turn away and retch.

'Oh, Jesus,' he said.

He risked another glance through half-closed eyes. It wasn't a dream. There was definitely a dead man in his living room. A fucking dead man!

'Oh, God,' he said.

He forced himself to take another, longer look.

And that's when he realised that he'd seen this man before. Despite the figure's bloody mask, he knew that it was Matt, the guy who, up until a few hours ago, had been cohabiting with Rebecca.

Confusion reigned in his mind. Why was Matt here? More to the point, why was he dead here?

It had to be something to do with Darren. Had to be. Someone had clubbed this man to death in Elliott's house, and the only person who had anything more than a vague connection to the pair of them was Darren. Well, there was Rebecca, but it seemed unlikely that this could be her handiwork. Not unless she was even more full of surprises than he'd ever imagined.

But why? What was going on? How had the two of them come together, and here of all places?

Something brushed against Elliott's leg. He yelled and whirled.

Bill backed away at the unexpected reception.

'Sorry, boy,' Elliott said. 'Sorry.'

He stared at the body yet again. He'd never seen a corpse before. He'd certainly never expected one to turn up in his home.

Bill moved towards the body and sniffed it. Elliott wished the cat could talk. Wished he could relate in detail the sequence of events that had led to this sickeningly absurd scene.

He found himself reaching for his phone, almost on auto-pilot. There was no alternative now: he had to call the police. You come across a man battered to death on your property, you call the police. You don't have to think twice.

And then he thought twice.

The police already had suspicions that he was a stalker, thanks to Rebecca. There were also witnesses to him turning up at Matt's club last night, seemingly intent on causing trouble, and being forcibly ejected. Rebecca might even confirm that he followed her to Matt's house and forced his way in. And now the man who she was going out with is found dead on Elliott's living-room floor, the side of his head caved in in an act that seemed to have an extreme level of hatred behind it – like, say, a deranged stalker might have for a competitor.

Doesn't look good, does it?

It'll be okay, he told himself. They have forensics and stuff. They'll be able to work out what happened.

He went to dial 999.

Paused again.

What if there were no forensics? This looked to have been staged by Darren. He must have planned it carefully. Would he have been so stupid as to leave any evidence pointing to him as the culprit?

Shit.

So what to do now? He couldn't throw a rug over the body and act like it wasn't there. A corpse on your floor is one of the things that requires urgent action. He just couldn't work out what the action should be. Every scenario running through his mind ended up with him in a prison cell and Heidi dead.

He practically crapped himself when the phone jangled in his hand.

42

It was Heidi's number. On video this time.

Elliott braced himself, glancing at the body in front of him. He still got the shock of his life when he saw Darren and Heidi on his screen. Neither looked much better than Matt. Heidi's face was caked in blood, her nose squashed flat, her eyes swollen. What remained of her hair stuck out in wild tufts. A blood-stained piece of duct tape was plastered across her mouth. There was blood on Darren's face too, but it looked as though he'd made an attempt to clean himself up, leaving dried smears across his cheek and chin. He'd clearly had a battering, though: his face was covered with lumps and bumps. What was more alarming was that he seemed drunk; his eyes were unfocused and his head was constantly bobbing as though he'd lost control of his neck muscles. The phone was also wavering wildly as Darren seemed to struggle to hold it still. Elliott had no sympathy, but he dreaded what Darren might do if not in mental control of himself, especially now that Darren had his knife at Heidi's throat again and an insane look in his eyes.

There were a million questions on Elliott's lips, but Darren got his in first.

'What the fuck are you playing at, Elliott? Give me one reason, one really good reason, why I shouldn't slit this bitch's throat right now.'

Elliott was almost stumped for words. He had expected Darren to be a lot more rational, outlining what he expected of Elliott now that he had put whatever cunning plan this was into effect.

'I don't understand,' he said. 'Please don't hurt Heidi. I don't know what's happening anymore.'

'You tried to trap me. You tried to get me killed. But it didn't work, did it? I ruined your little game.'

He sounded truly unhinged, and his words were slurred again. Heidi's eyes were wide and darting. She looked like a captive wounded animal, on the verge of dying from a heart attack provoked by her sheer terror.

'I don't know what game you're talking about. Please don't—'

'The man, Elliott. The muscle. Thought you had me there, didn't you? I may not look much to you, but I can fight. I told you never to underestimate me; didn't I tell you that? Now you'll have to pay the price.'

'Wait. No. You talking about Matt?'

'Who's Matt?'

'The guy on my floor. The guy you killed. It's Matt.'

'Why do you keep telling me his name? So it's Matt. I don't fucking care. Whoever he is, he—'

'No, I mean it's *Matt*. The man who Rebecca has been staying with. I told you. Didn't I tell you about him?'

Darren paused for a moment, his eyes roving as he tried to remember. Elliott could see that he was breathing heavily.

'So you ganged up on me?' Darren said. 'The pair of you, trying to keep me from Rebecca; you ganged up on me, tried to kill me.'

'No. It's not like that at all. Matt hated me. I was just trying to do what you asked, but he didn't like it. He wanted to keep me away from Rebecca. He must have come here to hurt me when I wouldn't leave her alone.'

It was starting to make sense to Elliott now. It was all about timing. Both Matt and Darren had come to Elliott's house at about the same time, intent on doing him harm. Fortunately for Elliott, he had been out of the house when they arrived. It hadn't been so fortunate for the other two, though, one of whom ended up dead while the other looked as though he had one foot in his coffin.

Darren wasn't convinced.

'Bullshit,' he said. 'You've made this up on the off-chance things went pear-shaped. You've only got yourself to blame for this.'

He pressed the tip of the knife into Heidi's neck. A bead of blood swelled and then trickled down to her collarbone.

'NO! No. Please. Listen to me. How could I have known you would come to my house? Think about it. How could I possibly have set up a trap for you when I didn't even know you were coming here?'

Darren thought about it. 'You . . . you didn't have to know. He could have been there for ages, as a precaution.'

'What, just sitting here in the house all day, in case you

309

happened to show up? Why would he agree to that? And why would I ask him to do it?'

'Maybe you paid him. Hired him to protect you.'

'My own personal bodyguard? Have you any idea how little I earn? Please listen to yourself, Darren. Listen to how . . . how far-fetched it sounds.' He'd wanted to use the word *crazy*, and had to restrain himself.

When he noticed Darren relax the pressure on the knife, Elliott pressed home his advantage. 'It was just bad luck, Darren. But it was nothing to do with me. I can see how much he hurt you, but it—'

Darren interrupted him with a bark of laughter. 'Not him. No, not him. He was nothing. You saw what I did to him.' He laughed again, then pointed his knife at Heidi. 'Your friend here, now she's something else. She really hurt me. Women, they do that, you know? They hurt us. They cut us deep. They mess with our heads. They . . .'

He started crying. Full-blown sobbing. Shoulders heaving.

'Darren, I—'

And then Darren let out a shriek of pain. He brought one hand up to his head, and then the picture went haywire. Elliott heard a bang and found himself staring at an image of a ceiling. He realised that Darren had dropped the phone.

'Darren! Pick up the phone, Darren.' He was terrified that Darren, in combating whatever mental torture was afflicting him, might lash out at Heidi. All he could hear was Darren's high-pitched moans, and he hated that an already precarious situation had suddenly become so much more unpredictable and dangerous. 'Darren, can you hear me? Please pick up the phone. Talk to me, man.'

Elliott continued to yell into his phone, seemingly to no avail.

But then the moaning subsided, became sobbing again. Elliott heard muffled noises and then saw the camera image move and spin until it was focused on Darren and Heidi again. Tears were streaming down Heidi's face and over the duct tape.

Darren said, 'It's over, isn't it?'

Elliott didn't know how to interpret the words. Was this the beginning of a surrender, of Darren delivering himself into the hands of the law? Or was it the start of a suicide note?

'I think it's time to let Heidi go, if that's what you mean. She has nothing to do with any of this.'

Darren seemed not to have heard him. 'It's a mess. It can't go on any longer. I know that now. Rebecca and me, we're not going to get back together. There's been too much pain. Too many deaths.'

Elliott wondered what he meant. He knew only of Matt's demise. Yes, one death was too many, but Darren seemed to be suggesting there had been more.

'Tell me where you are, Darren. I'll come and get you.'

A mirthless laugh broke through the tears. 'Too late. It's all too late. What's the point of living if I can't have Rebecca?'

'Nobody else has to die. It could stop right now, if that's what you want. Where are you?'

Darren stared into the camera. 'I should have known you wouldn't be up to it. But I had nobody else, you see. You were my only hope.'

'I still can be. I'll find you the help you need.'

'I think I'm beyond help. But thank you, anyway.' He paused. 'Would you like to say goodbye to Heidi now?'

Elliott saw how Heidi's breathing suddenly became heavier, her eyes even wider. She grunted noises through the tape over her mouth.

'Darren, no. Please don't do this. If you have to hurt anyone, hurt me. I'll come to you right now, and you can swap me for Heidi. How does that sound?'

He saw Heidi shake her head vigorously: *Please stop!*

'What do you know?' Darren said. 'You've got some balls after all.'

'So you'll do it? You'll take me instead of Heidi?'

Darren licked his lips. He seemed to be warming to the idea.

And then he said, 'What would be the point? It still wouldn't get Rebecca back. Goodbye, Elliott.'

'NOOO!'

The screen went spinning again. A clatter as the phone hit the floor. A view of the ceiling, any second now to be obliterated by a spurt of fresh blood. Heidi's muffled protestations.

What to do? What to do? What to do?

'WAIT! Darren! A message from Rebecca. I've just had a message on my phone from Rebecca. She's agreeing to meet you. Darren! DARREN!'

Silence.

'DARREN!'

More silence.

And then . . .

Sounds. Movement. The phone being picked up. Two faces, both very much alive.

'What?' Darren asked.

'I've just been messaged by Rebecca. She's going to ring me in ten minutes. She wants to arrange a meeting with you.'

'You're lying.'

'What would I gain by lying? Ten minutes, that's all I ask. Let me speak to her, find out what she's proposing. Isn't that worth another ten fucking minutes?'

Darren stared.

Take the bait, Elliott willed. Take it, you fucking son of a bitch.

'Ten minutes. I'll ring you back in fifteen. If you don't answer, it's over. If I don't like what you tell me about your conversation with her, it's over.'

'I understand. Give her this chance, Darren. This could be it. This could be what you've been waiting for.'

Darren remained impassive.

And then he terminated the call.

Elliott checked the time on his phone. 10.07. Fifteen minutes from now would be 10.22.

Fifteen minutes to save a life. It wasn't a lot. Why hadn't he asked for more time? Why hadn't he said that Rebecca would call at 10.30 or even 11.00?

He knew the answer. It was because Darren wouldn't have gone for it. He wouldn't have been willing to wait that long.

Fifteen minutes, he reminded himself. Better get working – harder than you've ever done in your life.

And you'd better come up with something pretty damn good.

43

Elliott needed to get hold of Rebecca fast. But there was no chance she would answer a call from him.

There was only one solution: get Matt to call her.

Trying not to throw up, Elliott searched the body. He found Matt's phone in his inside pocket. Grimacing, he pushed Matt's eyes open and then pointed the phone at Matt's face, angling it slightly to avoid catching the massive dent in the side of his head.

The facial recognition didn't work, the phone remaining locked.

'Shit.'

Elliott ran into the bathroom. He soaked a flannel, took it back into the living room and wiped the blood and gore away from Matt's face. When he thought the corpse looked vaguely presentable, he tried again.

The phone unlocked.

Elliott quickly opened up the contacts and found Rebecca. He called her.

She answered almost immediately. 'Hi, babe. You okay?'

'Rebecca, please don't hang up.'

A silence. And then: 'Who is this?'

'It's me. Elliott. Please don't hang up.'

'Elliott? What . . . what's going on? My phone says this is Matt.'

'It is. I mean, it's Matt's phone. He . . . lent it to me so you'd answer.'

'He lent it to you? Elliott, what kind of sick joke is this?'

'It's not a joke. It's deadly serious. We have to talk – right now.'

'I can't. I'm at a friend's house.'

'Then you need to leave.'

'Leave? Why would I leave?'

'Because nobody else can know about this. You need to hear what I have to say.'

Another pause. 'I'm hanging up now. I don't know how you managed to hack Matt's phone, but—'

'I didn't hack it! Matt is here with me now.'

'Really? Then put him on.'

'I haven't got time. Please, do what I say, and I'll explain everything. Is your car at your friend's house?'

'Yes.'

'Then make your excuses and go out to it. Call Matt's phone when you're there. Okay?'

'Elliott, if this is about trying to get me to talk to Darren again—'

'JUST FUCKING DO IT, WILL YOU?' he yelled, then realised it probably wasn't productive. 'I'm sorry. Please, do this one thing.'

He had to wait an age for an answer. 'All right,' she said. 'But this better be good. Give me a few minutes.'

'I haven't got a few minutes. Please hurry.'

The line suddenly went dead. Gripping the phone tightly, Elliott paced the room. He kept glancing at the time, watching the precious seconds tick away.

The phone rang. Rebecca's number.

'Are you in your car?'

'Yes. I'm driving home.'

'Pull the car over.'

'What?'

'Please. Pull in somewhere.'

More time elapsed.

'Okay. I've parked up. What's this about, Elliott? Why is Matt with you, and why have you got his phone?'

'Matt's dead, Rebecca.'

'What are you talking about?'

'He's dead. Darren killed him.'

'Darren? You're not making any sense.'

'None of this makes any sense to me either, but right now I'm standing here in my living room, looking down at the dead body of your boyfriend.'

'Matt was still at home when I left the house. Why would he be at your place?'

'I think . . . I think he probably came here to have a quiet word in my ear about you. I wasn't here when he arrived, but Darren must have paid me a visit at the same time. They didn't hit it off.'

'No. You're making this up. Matt can't be dead.'

'Is there a landline at his house? Call it. I guarantee he won't answer. Better still, we can turn this into a video call and I can show you his body. I warn you, though: it's not a pretty sight.'

The line went quiet once more.

'Rebecca, are you still there?'

'He's . . . he's really dead?'

'Yes, he is. I'm sorry. Now do you finally understand what I've been trying to tell you about Darren? He is fucking insane.'

'I . . .'

'Yes?'

He suspected she was overcome with sadness, unable to get the words out through her tears.

'You've ruined everything, Elliott.'

Not the reaction he expected.

'What?'

'You've ruined everything. You don't even know how much you've messed up my life. Jesus!'

'Why are you angry with *me*?'

'Because . . . You know what? I'm not explaining this to you. I have to go now. Thanks to you, I've got things to sort out.'

'Wait! This has nothing to do with me. This is about Darren. He's crazy. He killed Matt, and in less than two hours he's going to kill my best friend. You have to help me stop him.'

'I don't have to do anything, Elliott. I've got other priorities.'

'Other priorities? More important than saving a woman's life?'

'What exactly are you expecting me to do about that?'

'Darren wants to meet you. That's all he wants. It's the only thing he's ever asked for. Please, come with me. Meet him. Save my friend. You owe me that much.'

'Can you hear yourself? You've just told me that Darren is a murderer!'

'He won't hurt you. He loves you. He would do anything for you.'

Rebecca lowered her voice. 'Darren doesn't love me. He's infatuated with me. He doesn't just want a meeting, he wants me to come back to him. Nothing else will do. I can't give him that. If I meet him and tell him that, he'll kill me.'

Elliott didn't know how to counter this. If what Rebecca said was true, how could he possibly expect her to put her neck on the line?

'Rebecca, if you don't help me, Heidi dies. I don't know where she is. The police won't be able to find them in time, either. Darren told me that he'll kill Heidi at midnight unless I bring you to him. I've got a dead body here that says he will. You're my only hope.'

'Elliott, I'm not . . . I'm not the nice person you seem to think I am. There are things going on in my life that you couldn't possibly know anything about. I'm a mess. You were kind enough to help me, and I wish I could return the favour, but I can't. All I can do is what I always do.'

'What's that?'

'I run away.'

'Where will you go?'

'I don't know. But I won't be answering any more calls. And don't go to Matt's house, because I won't be there either.'

She paused again, and he got the impression she was crying.

He started crying too, but they were tears for Heidi.

'You're leaving me to deal with this alone,' he said.

'I'm so sorry.'

He knew she was on the verge of ending contact permanently.

'Wait! Give me one thing. If you won't come with me, just tell me one thing that could help me.'

'I don't understand. What is it you want to know?'

'When you and Darren were together, you must have had some happy times, right?'

'I suppose so.'

'Was there a place that was special? Somewhere you would go to be alone. A beauty spot or something?'

'I . . . I can't think.'

'Please try. Somewhere quiet. Just you and him.'

'Well . . . there was this one place . . .'

'Where?'

'It's not that close, but it's all I can think of.'

'How close?'

'About a thirty-minute drive. Cromley Point on the coast. There's a tiny car park there where you can watch the sunset. Can't imagine anyone will be there on a night like this, though.'

Elliott made a mental note. He had a rough idea of the location. He had hoped for something a little closer to home.

'Thank you,' he said.

'I don't know how that helps.'

'Me neither. Maybe it won't, but it's all I have.'

'I wish I could give you more. And I wish I could have got to know you better.'

'Yeah,' Elliott said, but he didn't mean it. He didn't want anything more to do with this woman. Wished she had never come into his life in the first place.

'Goodbye, Elliott. And good luck.'

'Goodbye, Rebecca.'

The call ended. Elliott dropped the phone onto the carpet next to Matt's body. Neither of them would be needing it now.

He watched the clock on the wall, his mind and his heart ticking along at a much faster pace. At precisely the moment marking the end of his allotted fifteen minutes, Elliott's own phone rang.

'Hello, Darren.'

'Hello, Elliott. So go ahead. Disappoint me, like you always do.'

'Rebecca rang me, just like she said she would.'

'Go on. Just remember I'm holding a knife at your friend's throat here.'

'She . . .' He took a deep breath. This was the biggest decision of his life. And of Heidi's. 'She wants to meet.'

44

Darren's tone was naturally sceptical. 'Why do I always think you're lying when you raise my hopes?'

Elliott considered his answer carefully. He was committed now, and he knew he was going to have to get every step of this right. He was also going to need a huge dollop of luck.

'What can I tell you? She rang, she wants to meet. If she doesn't turn up, you still hold all the cards.'

'How do I know it's not a trap?'

'You don't. Look, Darren, at some point you're going to have to start trusting people. You're going to have to come out of your hole and actually speak to Rebecca.'

'That's assuming *you* actually spoke to her.'

'Well, that's for you to decide.' He allowed anger to creep into his voice – it felt alien to him. 'I've done everything you asked. I found Rebecca, I spoke to her several times, and I got a good kicking in the process. And now I've arranged the meeting you have been so desperate for. You, on the other hand, have persecuted me, kidnapped and hurt my best friend, and killed a man in my house. Which of us does that make the most trustworthy?'

Darren gave a low chuckle. 'Well, when you put it like that . . . So how do we organise this meeting?'

Elliott thought this was interesting. It seemed that Darren was stumped – as though he hadn't thought his plans would work.

'I don't care. All I want is to see Heidi again. The rest is for you and Rebecca to work out.'

Elliott bit his lip. He wanted it to sound as if he was just an outsider here, that he was not involved in the fine detail. But he worried he might be pushing it too far.

'And how the fuck is that supposed to happen if she won't even speak to me?'

'She gave me a time and a place to pass on to you.'

'Are you going to tell me?'

'That depends.'

'On what?'

'On you releasing Heidi. Then I'll tell you.'

There was a long silence. And then . . . laughter.

'That's a good one. You had me going there.'

'I'm not kidding.'

'You'd better be. You think I'm really going to tear up my insurance policy? Little Heidi here is the only guarantee I have that you won't try to shaft me. Think again, genius.'

Worth a try, Elliott thought. And the reaction was hardly surprising.

'Then I don't know how we move forward. You've got Heidi,

I can give you Rebecca. Somehow we need to do a trade.'

'I'm not letting Heidi walk out the door, just like that. The first thing she'll do is go straight to the police.'

'What if we give you our word that she won't do that?'

'Forget it. You'll have to come to the meeting.'

'What?' Elliott feigned surprise as best he could, but he'd been expecting this all along.

'You heard me. You come with Rebecca, and I'll bring Heidi. We do a swap. Like in a spy film.'

'But I don't even know where your meeting's going to take place.'

'I thought Rebecca told you where?'

'All she said was, "Tell Darren to meet me at midnight at our sunset place." I don't know what that means.'

Elliott chewed his lip again while he awaited a response.

'Our sunset place?'

'That's what she said.'

'I know where that is.' There was noticeable excitement in his voice now. 'Cromley Point.'

'What?'

'Cromley Point. We used to go there to watch the sun go down. She wants to meet me there?'

'If that's your sunset place, then I guess so.'

'At midnight?'

'That was the deadline you gave me. She agreed.'

'All right. Okay. Let's do this.' Darren sounded like a little kid at Christmas now. 'Do you know where Cromley Point is?'

'I can look it up.'

'It's about a half-hour drive. Be there at midnight.'

'Well, wait a minute, Darren.'

'What?'

'I'll need to clear this with Rebecca first. She thinks it's just going to be you and her. She doesn't know anything about Heidi.'

'You haven't told her?'

'Of course not. Don't you think she might be put off a little if she knew you'd kidnapped someone?'

'Yeah. That could be a problem. Okay, so what if I have the meeting and then tell you where Heidi is?'

'No way. If I did that, I'd be tearing up my own insurance policy.'

'You don't have one anymore. I already know where and when to meet Rebecca.'

'Don't play games, Darren. One more phone call from me to Rebecca is all it would take to call this off. I'll tell her about Heidi and I'll tell her about what you did to Matt, and then she'll never dare to meet you – not now, not ever.'

Elliott screwed his face up. The risk was that Darren would threaten Heidi again if things weren't done his way.

Instead, to his immense relief, he heard another low chuckle.

'You're a man after my own heart, Elliott. So what do you suggest?'

Elliott blew out air while he pretended to think about it. 'Okay, what if I tell Rebecca that you suggested I come along as a chaperone, to make her feel safer? Tell Heidi to keep low on the back seat of your car so that Rebecca doesn't see her. Then we do the swap. You stay with Rebecca. Heidi and I will leave you to it.'

'Rebecca will see Heidi eventually.'

'Yes, she will. Will it matter by that point?'

He knew it wouldn't. It had become obvious in recent hours that Darren's envisaged future for Rebecca did not have a happy ending.

'No,' Darren confirmed. 'That . . . that sounds like a plan.'

'Okay. Good. Cromley Point, you said, right?'

'Yes. Cromley Point.'

'Right. I'll find it. But Heidi better be there, and she'd better be in one piece. If not, Rebecca and I will turn the car around and drive away for ever.'

'Same goes for you, Elliott. I want to see just you and Rebecca at that meeting. Anyone else turns up, and Heidi dies.'

Elliott swallowed hard. 'I think we understand each other.'

'Good. Then I'll see you both at midnight.'

Elliott hung up. He had no idea what he'd just landed himself in. The only thing he knew for certain was that he wasn't going to be able to pull this off without Rebecca.

45

Darren stood up, then sat down again. He wasn't sure what to do with himself.

Rebecca. He was finally going to be with Rebecca again. It was hard to believe.

Too hard?

Was this a trick? A trap?

But then how could it be? Elliott wouldn't have known anything about Cromley Point. That had to have come from Rebecca.

And why would Elliott not be telling the truth? What would he gain? If the police were brought in, or Rebecca wasn't there, then Darren would simply kill Heidi. Elliott was at this moment standing right next to the body of a man who had dared to go up against Darren. He would be fully aware that Darren was not afraid to carry out his threats.

So it had to be true.

Darren smiled. He found it warming that Rebecca should

have suggested their sunset place for a reunion. It held such memories – clearly as much for her as it did for him. Maybe this would work out well after all. Maybe she really would see the sense of coming back to him once they'd talked things over.

And if not? Well, things would have to end differently. Tragically. Like Romeo and Juliet. There was a certain beauty in that. A certain satisfaction in finishing their tale at the spot they found so romantic.

His head hurt.

Waves of pain kept crashing in, and they were becoming more frequent. He knew he needed medical attention, but that couldn't happen yet. He just hoped he could live long enough to see this through. If he was to die, let it be in the arms of his beloved Rebecca.

He realised he was getting all poetical. Tears kept jumping to his eyes. He was turning into a bigger wuss than Elliott. That's what Rebecca could do to him.

Focus.

He jumped off the stool, went across to Heidi. Ripped the duct tape away in one savage motion.

'Did you catch any of that?' he asked.

'Some of it.'

'It worked. I'm going to see Rebecca again. Your boy Elliott somehow managed to convince her.'

'It doesn't surprise me. People underestimate him.'

Darren smiled again. 'Of course, you helped. If you hadn't followed me, I wouldn't have had leverage.'

'Yay for me. So what happens now? You letting me go?'

'I'd love to. But there's one more thing we need to do together.'

'And what's that?'

'We're going for a drive. We'll use my car, if you don't mind. I don't think yours would get very far. You can't drive for shit.'

'And where are we going?'

'Somewhere nice. Weather's not so good right now, but you can't have everything.'

'Well, I could do with a change of scenery. We taking a picnic?'

Darren laughed at her display of bravado, but then had to screw his eyes shut with the pain.

'You . . . you haven't met Rebecca yet, have you?'

'No, but I've heard a lot about her. She sounds quite a character.'

'You'll like her. Everybody does.'

'I'm looking forward to it.'

What the fuck, Elliott? What the actual fuck?

Heidi was convinced Elliott had lost his mind. This was certainly not going to be a picnic. She had heard Darren mention Cromley Point on the phone. She knew where it was. Knew that it was in the middle of fucking nowhere. There would be no witnesses.

Darren had reached breaking point. Since that last knock on the head he had gone haywire. He didn't care anymore. The only thought occupying his screwed-up brain was being with Rebecca for ever, and it didn't matter to him whether that was alive or dead. In fact, she was pretty sure that he'd already opted for the latter.

But even getting that far required Rebecca actually turning up, and it seemed extremely unlikely that Elliott would achieve that. Managers of cat charity shops do not superheroes make. Without Rebecca on his arm, he would undoubtedly be walking into a deadly situation, both for himself and for Heidi.

What the hell are you doing, Elliott?

46

Elliott wondered what the hell he was doing.

There were so many ways this could go wrong. Probably only one way it could go in his favour. And the latter would require the alignment of so many chance elements as to make a desirable outcome virtually impossible.

This was insane.

Even the weather seemed to be trying to warn him against his foolhardy mission. Fierce gusts of wind buffeted his car as he drove, while the rain came down in steady sheets across his windscreen, blurring his view.

But still he pressed on. He felt he had no choice.

Maybe he would die tonight. Weirdly, the notion didn't upset him, didn't tempt him to turn back. What he knew in every fibre of his body was that this was right. It was what he had to do.

He turned to his passenger. 'You okay about this, Rebecca?'

She remained silent, her gaze fixed on the route ahead.

*

Darren drove up the narrow country lane, his headlights on full beam to cut through the blackness. Tall hedgerows bordered him on either side. A minute or so later, the hedgerows suddenly ended, the view opening up. Ahead was a small car park. Beyond that, Darren knew there was a sheer cliff edge that, in good weather, offered breathtaking views across the sea. Right now, it felt like the end of the world.

He reversed his Audi into a bay, so as to be face-on to any approaching vehicle. The car park was otherwise empty – all sensible people tucked up in bed. He checked the time. Three minutes to midnight. Three minutes to being with Rebecca.

He turned off the engine and doused the headlights, but kept the car's sidelights on. The wipers came to a halt. Rain pounded down, dissolving his view, but he would see the other car's lights when it approached. The Audi rocked as the roaring wind thumped at it.

Darren turned to look behind him at Heidi, lying across the back seat. To be on the safe side, he had bound her legs and arms before dragging her into the car. The girl could be impetuous, and he didn't want her attacking him from behind while he was driving.

'We're here. It'll all be over in a few minutes.'

'And then you'll let me go?'

'I promised, didn't I? But Elliott has to come through first. Otherwise, all bets are off.'

Elliott had never been here before. It seemed so remote from civilisation, so distant from anyone who might come to his aid.

He drove up the lane, squinting to see through the squally weather. A minute later he found himself in the car park. There was only one other car here, its sidelights staring back at him.

He parked facing it. Keeping his headlights on full beam, he could make out the head and shoulders of Darren in the driver's seat of the Audi. There was no sign of Heidi.

Darren's pulse quickened. The rush of blood through his head was like a stream of hammer blows. The intense light shining into his eyes from Elliott's car didn't help matters.

He turned on his own headlights and the windscreen wipers, then he picked up his phone and called Elliott.

'I'm here,' Elliott said as he answered.

'Turn off your headlights,' Darren ordered.

The lights ahead went out. Darren leant forward to peer through the rain.

She was there! Sitting beside Elliott. Rebecca was there!

'You brought Rebecca?'

'I said I would, didn't I?'

'Put her on the phone.'

'Not so fast. Where's Heidi? I don't see her.'

Darren twisted around. 'Sit up,' he told Heidi. It no longer mattered that she would be in plain sight. It was too late for Rebecca to do anything about it now.

'She's behind me,' Darren said. 'Can you see her?'

They swapped illumination, Darren dousing his lights while Elliott put his back on. A few seconds later, they swapped back.

'Okay,' Elliott said. 'Then we're good to go.'

'Let me talk to Rebecca first,' Darren asked again.

Ahead, he thought he could see Elliott turning and leaning towards his passenger. Elliott's lowered voice was still audible: 'He wants to talk to you.'

And then a quiet reply: 'I'm not going to discuss it over the phone.'

'What was that?' Elliott asked.

Again, louder this time: 'I'm not going to discuss it over the phone.'

Elliott said into the phone, 'Did you hear that? She said she—'

'Yes, yes. I heard.'

But Darren didn't care. What he'd just heard was, without a shadow of a doubt, Rebecca's voice. She was there, just a short distance away. He could hardly contain his excitement.

'We need to do the trade,' he said. 'Send Rebecca across, and I'll send Heidi.'

'Okay,' Elliott said. And then, 'Hang on.'

Darren heard Rebecca's voice cutting in. Heard her say, 'I don't think it would be a good idea for me to go there.'

Elliott started to relay it. 'Rebecca says she—'

'Yes, I heard. Fine. Tell her I'll come over to her. You come over to Heidi. We'll do it that way.'

'Okay,' Elliott said. Darren heard him pass the message to Rebecca, and then her saying, 'All right.'

Darren turned to Heidi again. 'You hear that? Elliott's coming over. You can get all lovey-dovey with him while I talk to Rebecca.'

And then Darren opened his car door, struggling to keep

the wind from whipping it out of his hand, and stepped into the fierce rain.

From the back seat, Heidi watched him leave. She still didn't understand what was happening. How the hell had Elliott managed to persuade Rebecca to come with him? Surely she would know she was in danger?

Frantically, Heidi tried to work on the rope binding her wrists behind her. She had a terrible feeling this was a long way from being over.

As Darren emerged from his car, Elliott looked to his left again.

'It's all up to you now, Rebecca,' he said. 'Don't let me down.'

He opened his own door, heaved it against the wind coming in from the sea. As soon as he stepped out onto the tarmac, the rain slanted straight through his clothes, soaking him.

He started walking.

Darren came towards him.

They crossed paths at the mid-point. On Darren's face was a twisted smile. Elliott tried to put it out of his mind. He needed to concentrate on the task at hand.

A bit more time, he thought. Just give me enough time.

He wanted to start sprinting to the Audi, but knew he couldn't because it would arouse suspicion.

A steady pace, he told himself. Just keep walking. Nearly there.

He could see Heidi bobbing around on the back seat.

I'm coming. Stay strong.

His plan, such as it was, was to get Heidi out of the car and then for the pair of them to just start running. Get the hell out of there. Forget about Darren and whatever it was he was up to. Just run. Find a hiding place if possible. If not, then take him on if needed. Two against one was much better odds.

Nearly there...

Darren approached the car. Rebecca was just sitting there, making no move to get out or open the window.

He wondered what he should say, what his opening line should be. But there was no rush. They had all the time in the world now. Time to fix everything.

He could see her long blonde hair now, her pale features. She was almost shining.

And then the oddness of it all struck him, and he turned and saw Elliott reaching for the rear door of the Audi...

Elliott went to grab the door handle...

And then amber lights flashed and there was a brief blip of noise, and Elliott realised that all the doors had just been remotely locked.

He turned. Saw Darren looking at him, the Audi key fob in his hand.

He knows!
I'm too late.

Darren yanked open the passenger door of Elliott's car and stared in at the occupant.

She didn't turn towards him, didn't say anything. Didn't react at all.

Shop mannequins don't do much of that.

Myrtle was now in a long blonde wig. On her stiff thighs rested a laptop.

Darren realised he'd been had. Rage took hold of him.

It was time to kill.

47

Elliott tried the handle of the Audi. When that didn't work, he pounded on the window.

'Open the door!' he implored.

'I'm tied up,' Heidi screamed back at him. 'I can't.'

Elliott hadn't factored this into his plan. *Stupid!*

He looked back towards his own car. Darren was striding towards him, his expression murderous.

Elliott thumped the window again. He looked around on the ground for a rock or something that he could use to break the glass.

'RUN!' Heidi yelled. 'Get out of here!'

'I'm not leaving you!' Elliott screamed.

He took a step back and kicked the window, but his foot simply bounced off.

And then Darren was on him, his head down and shoulders bent, bulleting into Elliott's midriff.

Elliott felt the air explode out of him as his feet left the ground. He crash-landed on the tarmac, tried to breathe again through the freezing rain that seemed intent on drowning him.

'You bastard!' Darren yelled. 'What have you done?'

Elliott started to get to his feet. He saw Darren glaring murderously at him, his body swaying drunkenly and his arms swinging before him like a gorilla.

'It's over, Darren. It's all over now.'

Darren moved closer. 'No. Not yet. I'm still alive and Rebecca is still alive. There's still a chance for us. Not for you, though. You fucked up, Elliott.'

Even though he knew what was coming, Elliott kept himself between his opponent and the car containing Heidi, hoping to act as some kind of human shield.

And then the first punch landed, and he knew that he was going to have to think again.

It hit Elliott squarely on the cheek, catapulting his head backwards, and he felt himself crash against the car, and for a couple of seconds he could see nothing. When the world began to make sense again, it was only to catch a glimpse of another fist rocketing towards his face. This one collided with his mouth, and it felt to him that his lips exploded.

He staggered away from the car, blood spurting from his mouth, his tongue frantically checking that his teeth were still intact, but Darren continued to pursue him, the blows now raining down like the elements, penetrating their way through Elliott's meagre defence of his raised arms. They found their targets unerringly, smashing into his jaw, his nose, his cheek; and as if just for a little variety, there was the occasional foray into his lower body, each sledgehammer into his solar plexus driving home that he was about to die.

Then came a missile of a punch that zoomed right in on the point of his chin, and Elliott lost consciousness.

Heidi watched in horror. It was a complete mismatch of fighting spirit and ability. It was going to be a bloodbath, a massacre.

She had no idea how to control the door locks from within the vehicle – didn't even know whether it was technically possible to open the doors from inside once they had been remotely locked. But with her ankles tied together and her hands bounds behind her, experimenting with the various switches in the car wasn't an option.

In desperation, she threw herself onto her back across the rear seats. She raised her legs, kicked the soles of her feet against the window. Once … twice … deep breath and a yell … three times …

The glass exploded into the night.

Darren whirled at the noise behind him.

He saw a head protrude from the rear window of his car. It was quickly followed by shoulders, a torso, squirming out of the hole like a fat juicy maggot …

And then Heidi's whole body slipped out of the car and landed face first on the rain-soaked tarmac.

Darren looked again at the prone body at his feet. Elliott could wait. There was more fun to be had right now.

'That's gotta hurt,' he called to Heidi.

And then he went over to her, and he looked down at her.

The rain carried away the blood streaming from her face, and the wind whipped away her cries, but he could see how much pain she was in, how much distress.

He laughed hysterically as he administered the first kick into her ribs.

Consciousness took a gamble and returned.

Elliott raised his head, wondered for a second what hell he'd landed in, why the skies were so dark and furious, why his whole body was on fire.

He turned his head and spat out blood mixed with rainwater, then he gasped for air and remembered where he was.

He pushed himself up, blinked the rain away.

Two figures caught in the headlights, one on the ground, the other getting the shit kicked out of it.

Heidi.

Elliott scrambled to his feet. He had no thought for himself, no thought for the additional beating he was going to receive. He knew only that he had to put a stop to the merciless punishment of his friend.

He sprinted through the rain. The roar of the wind and the white noise of the rain masked his own sounds, allowed him to close on Darren without alerting him.

He did what Darren had done to him, going in low, shoulder-charging, keeping up the momentum. The impact was hard, and he felt Darren leave the ground, and for a brief instant Elliott felt like he could keep this up for ever, carrying Darren aloft, taking him well away from Heidi, tossing him over the edge of the cliff . . .

And then they were both stopped by the Audi. They slammed into it. Both cried out, both fell to the ground, both got to their feet again simultaneously.

Darren lashed out with a backhand that caught Elliott on his eyebrow, splitting it open.

'What's the matter, Ellie?' Darren said. 'Did I hurt your little friend?'

A punch to the temple.

'Poor little Ellie. You're not very good at this, are you?'

A blow to the gut.

'You're such a girl, Ellie. Why are you such a fucking loser?'

A kick to the groin.

As Elliott prayed for it to end, memories replayed in his mind.

He remembered the shoplifter, how he kept using the name Ellie and calling him a girl, just as Darren was doing now.

He remembered Rowan Cosby at school, pinching Elliott's sandwiches and bullying him and punching him on the football field . . . and calling him Ellie.

But above all . . . *above all* . . .

He remembered his father. The words of his that were more painful than any punch or kick.

He's no son of mine.

Elliott had longed for a chance to prove his father wrong and never got one. And deep down, he knew that even if an opportunity had arisen, he would not have taken advantage of it. He had known he would always be a failure in his father's eyes, and it had eaten into his soul every minute of his life.

And now he was simply doing it all over again. Letting his

father down. Letting himself down. Letting Heidi down.

He would die a failure.

A slap across the ear. Darren smiling. Toying with him now.

No.

He might die here, but it wouldn't be as a failure.

Let Heidi know that at least I tried. Let my dad know it too.

And so he struck out.

He didn't know where it came from, this punch, but it had power and it had accuracy and it had many, many years of being a victim pent up inside it.

And it stopped the bully.

Darren's head snapped to the side as the fist connected, and it was like a switch had been turned off inside him. He stood perfectly still, seemingly processing this new experience. Contrition welled up inside Elliott. He had to fight the impulse to apologise, to plead for forgiveness for daring to retaliate.

But then Darren slowly turned his head to face him again, and what it now seemed to Elliott was that he had somehow reprogrammed this monster, introduced a malfunction that had made death the only objective.

So Elliott struck again. He hit Darren squarely on the nose, and Elliott felt bone and cartilage give way, and he knew he'd broken it, and he was amazed at how good it felt to do that to someone, how powerful it made him, and now Darren was clutching at his face and his eyes suddenly contained a glimmer of uncertainty, and Elliott knew he had to follow up, and so he did, with another punch, into the mouth this time, and again he felt things collapse and break under his knuckles, and he

felt surprise and elation that an opponent could be more frag-
ile than he was, and he stepped up the barrage, and now it was
Darren's turn to stagger away from the onslaught, and Elliott
really started to believe he could win, actually dared to believe
he was capable of fighting back and not being a victim and
instead being the man he'd always wished to be and a hero to
Heidi and a son to his father . . .

And then he felt the new pain. The different pain. The more
profound pain.

He stopped fighting and he looked into Darren's eyes and
saw renewed triumph, and then he looked down and saw the
source of that conviction, saw Darren's hand still clutching
the hilt of the knife that had been thrust deep into Elliott's
abdomen.

Elliott stared with disbelief at the sight, and then took a
step back from Darren, who released his hold on the knife, and
then he continued walking backwards, not knowing where he
was going or what he planned to do about this, because this
was serious, as serious as it gets, really, and he didn't know
what he was supposed to do in a situation as serious as this
even though he thought he'd become a hero.

The wind howled and whistled around his ears, and
the rain rattled against his skull, and all other sound was
drowned out, and he looked at Darren, who now seemed
to be laughing at him, and then he looked down at Heidi,
who seemed to be screaming something, but all he could
hear was the wind and the rain and the pulsing in his head,
and nothing else mattered anymore because he was going to
die anyway, his life force was already leaking out of his body,

and probably a lot more of it was gushing out of his veins and arteries inside his body, and that kind of thing kills you, doesn't it, especially when you're in the middle of nowhere in the company of a beautiful woman who would help if only she could and a man who definitely isn't going to offer any help unless it hastens the death.

He stopped moving backwards and he stared down at the handle still protruding from his body, and it seemed so strange to see it there, so odd, because foreign objects aren't supposed to be embedded in you like that. And waves of pain gripped his abdominal muscles as though they were trying to expel the knife, and he looked again at Heidi and realised that he had just considered her beautiful, and he knew now that it was an accurate description, she was indeed beautiful, incredibly so, and he wished that he'd done more about it while he was alive, because, let's face it, he thought, I'm practically dead now.

He dropped to his knees, still clutching the knife, and he felt the rain and the blood washing over his hand, and he felt the pain, and the noises grew louder in his head, and he hoped this wouldn't take too long, he didn't want to suffer for too long, but maybe Darren could be of some help, because wasn't this him coming over, wasn't he getting closer and closer?

Elliott keeled over onto his side and stared at the approaching figure of Darren, who clearly had his own problems, judging by the way he walked and by the way he clutched his head.

'You fucked up, Ellie,' Darren said.

'My name . . . is Elliott.'

Darren grinned. 'Yeah, okay. I'll give you that. You put up a decent fight. You almost beat me. But the thing you need to know is that love always wins in the end. Always. That was your mistake. And so now you have to die.'

Elliott said nothing. Words were no longer important.

'Did you know,' Darren continued, 'that if you get stabbed with a knife or whatever, you're not supposed to pull it out? Helps to plug the blood vessels or something.' He paused. 'I think I'm going to pull it out.'

He took a step closer, started to reach down, then seemed to change his mind.

'I think your friend should watch this.'

Elliott opened his mouth to object, but nothing coherent came out. He didn't want Heidi to see him die.

But what could he do about it? The pain was getting worse, the world was getting noisier and darker. His mind was disintegrating.

He was vaguely aware of Darren starting to move away, heading towards Heidi, intending to drag her across to witness his death before suffering her own.

The noises grew suddenly louder, became a roar. Elliott found himself not knowing what was real and what were figments of his panicking brain, but it seemed to him that the scene in front of him was suddenly filled with light, that Darren was bathed in it and transfixed by it.

And then there was a bang, and the light was gone, and Darren was gone, and all that was left was the wind and the rain.

Unable to make sense of anything, Elliott lay his head back on the tarmac and stared up at the sky and wondered how long it would be before he would be looking down on himself.

He hoped that Heidi was okay, and that she wouldn't be too upset at his passing. He hoped that she would always remember him.

A face filled his vision. It seemed so real. She had long blonde hair and she was beautiful and she was crying, and he wondered why this particular angel had come to him now.

'I'm sorry, Elliott,' she was saying. 'I'm so sorry.'

And then he closed his eyes and went to sleep.

48

Detective Inspector Preminger was unmoved by the tears. He would turn fifty next year and in his long career he had seen it all before, countless times. Didn't matter whether it was an acne-ridden scally or a good-looking posh bird like this one: his only aim here was to dig beneath the surface.

He glanced at DC Gupta sitting next to him. She too betrayed no signs of sympathy, and was champing at the bit to go on the attack.

He looked across the table again, waiting while Rebecca Covington took yet another tissue from the box he had pushed across to her. At this rate, he would have to send out for more before the interview was over. Her head was bowed. Next to her, Andrew Curzon, her eager young solicitor, was busy typing at a rate of knots on his laptop. Preminger suspected he was one of those who was determined to be difficult just because he could, even though Rebecca had already indicated she would cooperate fully.

'Do you think we'll be able to go ahead with the questions

now, Rebecca?' he asked.

She sniffed and nodded. 'I'll try. It's very upsetting. I've been through a lot, you know.'

'I understand that. We just need to clear a few things up, okay?'

'Yes.'

'Good. First of all, can I confirm that you understand why you've been arrested?'

Rebecca raised her head. 'I know what you *think* I've done. You're wrong, though. I didn't murder anyone.'

'We'll come back to that, shall we? Let's start at the beginning. Tell us about Darren Stringer.'

'What do you want to know?'

'Well, how did you meet?'

'In a bar.'

'Which one?'

'A place called Flash Harry's, in Fowerby.'

'When was this?'

'About seven or eight months ago.'

'Was that a bar you frequented?'

'Not really, no.'

'But you happened to be there on this particular night, when Darren was also there?'

He saw the hackles rise on both Rebecca and Curzon, but Rebecca was the first to answer. 'Why do you make it sound so unusual? People go to bars all the time. I'm sure you've been to a bar or two in your time.'

Preminger almost smiled at the weak jibe. 'Were you with someone there?'

'Not at first, no.'

'Didn't go there with a friend?'

'Believe it or not, women are allowed to go into bars by themselves now.'

This time he did crack a smile, although he sensed that DC Gupta was even more keen to land a few verbal blows in return.

'But why this particular bar?' he asked.

'Why does anyone go to a bar? I wanted a drink, it was nearby . . .'

'It wasn't to meet someone?'

She raised her perfectly shaped eyebrows. 'I'm not a call girl, if that's what you're asking.'

'No, it's not what I'm asking. I want to know whether you went to that bar because you knew that Darren Stringer would be there.'

'How would I have known that? I'd never met the guy before.'

'You hadn't discussed him with anyone else, prior to visiting the bar? He hadn't been mentioned to you by a friend?'

'What friend? Inspector, I don't know what you're talking about.'

At this point, Curzon decided he needed to remind everyone of his presence. Preminger had already noticed how the solicitor liked to issue a tutting sound just before objecting to anything put by the detectives.

'I think my client has already made it perfectly clear that she had no idea that the man in question would be present in the bar.'

The man in question, Preminger thought. Like he was just an irrelevance in this total shitshow.

'All right, then. So you're in the bar. Darren is there too. Was he alone?'

'No, he was with a group of work colleagues.'

'A celebration of some kind? Or just a night out with the lads?'

'Celebrating. Well, he seemed to be buying all the drinks.'

'Really? Why was that?'

'He'd had some good luck.'

'What kind of good luck?'

And now we come to it, Preminger thought. The root of all evil . . .

'He'd . . . he'd won the lottery.'

Preminger noticed the hesitancy. Rebecca hadn't wanted this brought into the open.

'I see. A lot of money, was it?'

'A fair amount. Enough to chuck in his job and take his workmates on a night out.'

'And how did you know all this at the time?'

'Well . . . I got talking to him. At the bar.'

'I see. Before or after you knew about his lottery winnings?'

Another tut from Curzon. 'Oh, come now, Inspector . . .'

'It's a simple enough question.'

'Simple, yes. Innocent, no. I've never heard a more loaded question.'

Then you haven't met me before, Preminger thought. I'm only just getting started.

'It's all right,' Rebecca said. 'I don't mind answering. It was *after*. Darren came to the bar, next to where I was sitting. I asked him what the party was about, and ... that's when he told me.'

'You knew nothing about it before that moment? You overheard nothing from anyone at Darren's table before he came to the bar?'

Rebecca injected a note of irritation into her answer. 'I'm not in the habit of eavesdropping on other people's conversations. I like to mind my own business.'

'All right, so you got chatting. Then what?'

'He invited me to join his group for a drink.'

'And did you?'

'No. I didn't know anyone at the table, so I politely turned him down.'

'But you ended up going out with him anyway?'

'Yes. He asked me if I'd like to go for a drink with him on a different night. I agreed. The rest is history.'

And what a history, Preminger thought. A whole book could be written on what had happened since that night.

He sat back in his chair and glanced at DC Gupta, the signal for her to get stuck in. She wasted no time in going for the throat.

'Did you know that, on Friday night, Darren kidnapped a close friend of Elliott Whiston's? A woman named Heidi Liu.'

Rebecca seemed taken aback at the sudden switch to more recent events. All part of the plan, Preminger thought.

'I ... I became aware of it last night.'

'Only last night?'

Preminger saw the doubt in Rebecca's eyes. She stayed silent.

'We'll come back to that,' Gupta promised. 'For now, you may be interested to know that we've already interviewed Heidi. She got to know Darren pretty well while he was holding her hostage. Had a big chat with him about you. According to Heidi, Darren's version of events is that it was *you* who asked *him* to go on a date.'

To her credit, Rebecca's recovery was swift this time.

'That doesn't surprise me,' she said.

'How so?'

'It fits with his personality. He was desperate to believe that I wanted him.'

'So you're saying he was lying?'

'Yes. Absolutely.'

'Okay. Tell us about your relationship with Darren Stringer. Was he good to you?'

'Yes, I'd say so.'

'Did he buy you things?'

'Yes, now and again.'

'Only now and again? What he told Heidi Liu was that he paid for everything. Your house, your car. He took you on luxury holidays. He—'

'Okay, he paid for stuff. Why shouldn't he? He had plenty of money. But that's not why I liked him.'

'So why did you like him?'

'He was funny. He was attentive. He would have done anything for me. Men like that aren't easy to find.'

'You never thought he was a little ... strange? He never seemed a bit obsessive about you?'

'Eventually, yes. But not at first. He could be pretty full-on, but I didn't think anything of it.'

'Did you ever ask him about his previous girlfriends?'

'No. Everyone has a past. It didn't interest me.'

'So he didn't tell you about Sophie Green?'

Rebecca blinked rapidly. This was clearly a surprise to her.

'No. Who's she?'

'Sophie Green is a woman that Darren went out with a few years ago. We know this because she took out a restraining order against him after he refused to accept the end of their relationship.'

'That's . . . that's news to me.'

Preminger believed her. He wondered how different Rebecca's decisions might have been if she had known about Darren's instability from the start. How many lives might have been saved . . .

'So what brought your own relationship with Darren to an end?' Gupta asked. 'I mean, you only went out with him for about six months.'

'Yes, well, that's when he began to show his true colours. He became too controlling. He wanted to know where I was at every minute of every day. He was starting to suffocate me.'

'I see. But again, nothing to do with money?'

'Absolutely not.'

Back to lying, Preminger thought. He smiled inwardly, knowing what Gupta was going to chuck at her next.

'The reason I ask,' Gupta said, 'is that, according to Heidi, you asked Darren to buy you a diamond necklace you had your eye on, and then got very upset when he said he couldn't afford it.'

'I didn't get very upset. I was disappointed, that's all. That incident had nothing to do with us breaking up.'

'Really? Because it wasn't just an isolated incident, was it? Darren had run out of money. He'd spent most of his lottery winnings on you, and that made him suddenly less interesting.'

'No! I've already told you. I left Darren because he was getting weird.'

'Did you tell him this?'

'What, that he was a weirdo? Of course not. I just stopped seeing him.'

'Except that you didn't just stop seeing him, did you? You disappeared completely from his life, without a word of explanation. Don't you think that was a bit . . . abrupt?'

Rebecca simply shrugged. She was on the ropes and wanted a timeout. Preminger wasn't about to give it to her.

'All right,' he said. 'So you moved on from Darren, found yourself a new place to live, a new boyfriend. Didn't take you long to get over your previous one, did it?'

'What can I say? I like companionship. I'm sure you're no different, Inspector.'

'This man, Matt Blaine. How did you get to know him?'

'I'd visited the town before, to see friends. We went out, and one night we ended up in his club. Matt made it clear he was interested, and when it all went wrong with Darren, I thought, Why not?'

'Uh-huh. Would you be surprised to hear that Mr Blaine had been on our radar for some time? A bit of a lad, wasn't he?'

'He's in a tough business. He didn't get where he is by letting people walk all over him, if that's what you're referring to.'

Preminger nodded. 'He did quite well for himself, didn't he? He had the nightclub, a big house. He must have been loaded. Probably even more money than Darren had before he spent it all on you.'

Rebecca glared. 'Why do you keep bringing this back to money? It's nothing to do with money.'

'No? You have your own income, then?'

She blinked again. 'What?'

'I'm asking you whether you have a job.'

'Not at the moment, no.'

'Have you ever had a job?'

'Yes, of course. I'm a beauty therapist.'

'And when did you last have a client?'

'I . . . It's been a while. I'd have to check my diary.'

'It's so long ago that you can't remember?'

She sat up ramrod straight in her chair. 'Look, times are difficult, okay? I fell out with my parents years ago. I know what it's like to go it alone, struggling to make ends meet. I came up north to start a new life. It hasn't been easy.'

'It's never easy, Rebecca. What I want to know is how you've managed, especially without parental support.'

'I've managed. That's all you need to know. It has nothing to do with—'

'Did Richard Fordham help you manage?'

Boom, thought Preminger. Another hand grenade to deal with.

Rebecca struggled to find a suitable reply. 'What?' she asked.

'Richard Fordham. Owner of Fordham Dairy Enterprises.

A few years ago now, but I'm sure you couldn't have forgotten. You must have been only twenty at the time. He was sixty-four.'

Rebecca's mouth opened and closed, but no words were found.

'Really, Inspector,' Curzon said. 'Aren't you clutching at straws here? I fail to see the relevance—'

Preminger kept his gaze fixed on Rebecca. 'Fordham's wife was arrested when she made a scene at a restaurant. She confronted Fordham and the woman he was having an affair with, assaulting them both. According to our records, you were that woman.'

Rebecca had turned distinctly pale. 'I . . . we didn't want to press charges.'

'And that's fine. The point I'm making here is that you seem to have quite a history of dating men who are wealthy enough to look after you financially. And these are just the ones we know about.'

Curzon jumped in again. 'This is getting absurd, Inspector. We're not in court. Why are you doing your best to assassinate my client's character?'

Preminger finally turned his eyes towards the solicitor. 'That's not my intention. What I ask you to bear in mind is that we've got multiple dead bodies on our hands, all with direct associations to your client. Establishing the facts of her relationships with those people is therefore of paramount importance, wouldn't you agree?'

He didn't have to wait for Curzon to back down, because Rebecca did it for him.

'All right!' she said. 'I admit it. I've taken advantage of a few gullible idiots. I'm not proud of myself, but neither is it a crime.'

Preminger stared at her, wondering if she held any trace of remorse.

'You're right,' he said. 'It's not a crime.'

49

Preminger looked again to DC Gupta to bring things back to the present.

'If we could turn now to your involvement with Elliott Whiston,' she said. 'Last Monday evening he came to your aid, didn't he?'

Rebecca lowered her head again. 'Yes. I wish I'd never asked him.'

'But you did, and he helped you, even though it got him into all kinds of trouble. Things got so bad between him and Darren that he approached us, the police. But when our officer rang you to confirm the story, you said you'd never heard of Darren and that Elliott was your stalker. Why did you lie to us?'

'I . . . I don't know. I didn't want the police to get involved.'

'Heidi told us that he came after you, too, and that you hit him with a bottle. Why did you do that?'

'He became . . . aggressive.'

'I see. So if you didn't know it before, you knew then that he could be violent. Still no thoughts of contacting the police?'

'No.'

'Why not? Why didn't you just give us a ring and tell us what he'd done? We could have prevented all this.'

'I . . . I don't know. I wasn't thinking straight. I'd already denied knowing him, hadn't I? It seemed easiest to stick with that. I just wanted to get away from it all. That's why I went to stay at Matt's place.'

'Hmm. Shall I tell you what I think? I think you didn't call the police because you didn't want Matt Blaine to find out what you were up to. You were on to a good thing with him, and you didn't want us ruining it. You thought—'

'That's not true.'

'You thought you'd given Darren the slip and you were happy to let Elliott deal with the consequences.'

'NO! I'm not like that. I . . .'

She started crying again, but Gupta wasn't about to let a few tears get in her way.

'It got worse for Elliott Whiston after that, didn't it? Darren kidnapped Heidi Liu. Tied her up in a garage. Attacked her. Cut off her hair. And when Elliott came begging to you – the only person who could help – what did you do?'

'I—'

'Nothing. You did nothing, Rebecca. You knew that a young woman had been kidnapped, and you chose not to help. Why was that?'

'I didn't think it would get as bad as it did. I thought Darren was all talk.'

'He'd already attacked you! If you really thought he was

harmless, you would have done what Elliott asked. You would have gone to Darren and given him what he wanted. But you were worried that he would hurt you, and it was more important to save your own skin and keep your past secret from Matt Blaine than it was to save an innocent woman.'

Rebecca broke down, sobbing into a fistful of tissues. While Preminger and Gupta waited for her to compose herself, Curzon made another contribution.

'For the record, I'd like to make it clear that none of the things you're accusing my client of are illegal.'

Irritated, Preminger rounded on him. 'Illegal they might not have been, but several people might still be alive if your client had acted a little sooner.' He turned to Rebecca again. 'Did you know that Matt Blaine was going to Elliott's house?'

'No, of course not. I would have stopped him. At the very least, I would have warned Elliott.'

'So you do have a conscience, then?'

Curzon piped up again. 'Inspector, please.'

Preminger ignored him. 'How did you hear about Matt's death?'

'Elliott called me. He told me what had happened.'

'And what was your reaction?'

'I . . . I . . .'

'You left town, didn't you? You ran away.'

'I wasn't running away. I knew you'd want to talk to me about Matt at some point. But I was scared. I needed to be with someone who loves me.'

'Why wait for us to come to you? You've just heard that your boyfriend has been murdered, and it doesn't even cross your mind to call the police? Can you see now why it might look to us that you were simply using him?'

She paused for a while. 'Yes,' she admitted. 'I can see how it might look that way.'

'And can you also see why we're suggesting that you had absolutely no interest in helping either Elliott Whiston or Heidi Liu?'

'But I did! I went to Cromley Point.'

'Yes, let's talk about that, shall we?'

'Fine. Elliott told me he was meeting Darren last night. He asked me about places that Darren and I used to visit. I mentioned Cromley Point. I assumed that—'

'Yes, that's how you knew where they'd be, but what I want to know is why you went there at all.'

'Because ... because I realised I couldn't keep running. I knew that I had to try to help Elliott.'

'That was very noble of you. But you didn't go there straight away, did you? You went somewhere else first.'

'Like I said, I needed someone to talk to. There's only one person I know in the world who would be willing to listen.'

Gupta spoke up once more. 'Tell us what happened, Rebecca.'

Rebecca was crying again. 'You know what happened. I reported it.'

'Tell us again.'

'I ... I went to my nan's house, in Wetherley. When I got there, there was no sign of her. She wouldn't normally be out that late, so I started to worry. I searched the whole house. The last place I checked was the utility room. I was leaning against